NO ORDINARY LOVE

ANGELA WEAVER

Genesis Press, Inc.

Indigo Love Spectrum

An imprint of Genesis Press, Inc.
Publishing Company

Genesis Press, Inc.
P.O. Box 101
Columbus, MS 39703

ISBN-13: 978-1-58571-346-2
ISBN-10: 1-58571-346-5
Manufactured in the United States of America

First Edition 2006
Second Edition 2009

Visit us at www.genesis-press.com or call at 1-888-Indigo-1

DEDICATION

This book is dedicated to my best friend, Courtney.

PROLOGUE

Be careful what you wish for...

Cold filtered air circulated around the African-American man sitting hunched over the flat screen monitor.

You might just get it... Brian Scott tried to shut out the ghost of his mother's voice as he stared at the numerical lines racing across the screen. As he sat alone in the server room, the sound of his fingers tapping against the keyboard echoed over the backdrop of network servers, super computers, and telecom lines in the temperature-controlled room. Isolated from the outside world, the main vault lay hidden a quarter mile underneath the earth. Secured by concrete, steel, and level five security codes, it was the most protected area in the company.

He sat in the middle of the room, his Armani suit and Italian loafers covered by a one-piece protective garment and shoe covers. Brian's brown skin was a stark contrast to the whiteness of the mask partially covering his face.

His latex-covered fingers impatiently tapped against the desk while he watched the completion percentage slowly advance towards one hundred.

Beads of sweat gathered on his brow as the blue status line inched across the screen.

"Damn," he muttered, glancing at the platinum timepiece on his wrist.

A few seconds later when the computer completed copying the program, Brian slipped the disk into his pocket and made sure to erase all the records of his activity. Taking a deep breath, he stood, strode over to the doorway, and then swiped his card to exit the room. The door slid back, revealing a small antechamber with another sealed steel door.

Brian waited until the opening behind him had closed before taking off the protective clothing and tossing it into the disposal chute. After picking up his briefcase, he slid the ID card through the security reader, punched in the alphanumeric code and waited as the door began to cycle through its unlocking procedures. Stepping out of the vault, he waved at a passing group of technicians.

"Is everything okay, Mr. Scott?"

He kept his expression relaxed as he turned to face Karl. The balding Chief Manager of the Server Operations Unit looked up at him with an expression of half worry and half arrogance. Recruited from M.I.T., Karl's expertise in the realm of mathematics, computer science and engineering made him an expert in microchips and computer programming. His life revolved around numbers and statistics, performance and his machines.

"Everything's great, Karl." He patted him on his shoulder. "I just wanted to have a look at your new setup. I'm impressed with the number of E-10k servers you've got in there. The computing power alone is incredible." Brian stroked the man's ego.

"I'm working with the other data centers around the world to create a link that could help us increase not only the processing speed but also allow for faster tracking, retrieval and storage. Once that connection is made we'll have one of the most powerful super-computer networks in the world," Karl bragged.

"Of course, you're doing excellent work. I'll be sure to mention it in the board meeting this afternoon."

Just as the manager began to open his mouth, the chirp of Brian's handheld computer cut him off.

"Excuse me, I guess time just got away from me. I've got to get to that meeting."

He smiled at Karl and waved at the other scientists as he walked down the wide hall.

Entering the transport area, he stepped into the underground elevator waiting to take him back to the head office. In the semi-darkness of the elevator's interior, he stared at the rapidly changing digital readout. The enormity of his actions was beginning to sink in. *My God I might actually pull this off.* He smiled automatically at the executive assistant when he got off the elevator and found her waiting to escort him into the boardroom. He had finally made it into the big leagues. Yet the smile which curved his lips had

strings of bitter irony. He had fought long and hard
for the release of this new technology and now he was
about to throw it all away. Brian had never felt so free.
After taking a chair in the empty boardroom, he
pulled out his computer and began to input the location keys. Hoping the backup would never be needed,
he added an extra, more personal note to the message.
If all went as expected, Alex would never read it.

Taking care to extend the antenna, Brian hit the
power button on his cell phone. Hitting the send key,
he watched as the computer signaled its connection to
the Internet and the completion of the upload of data
to his personal web server. Just as the connection
ended, the double doors to the boardroom opened
and as members of the board and executives from
across the firm entered the room.

He straightened his tie, then carefully shut his
briefcase and placed it on the floor before turning to
greet the CFO.

"Brian, I can't wait to hear what you have to say
about our new initiative. I've been hearing rumors,
you know."

The game was starting, Brian thought, relaxing his
stiff muscles. "Well, I'm here to give you the facts, sir."
Brian smiled as he began to execute the first move.

"Good, my boy."

The CFO, too busy thinking of the potential rise
in stock price as soon as the press got wind of the
meeting, didn't notice the tightening of Brian's grip on
the armrest after he patted him on the shoulder. Brian

smiled again; it was a smile that never reached his eyes. He moved to the front of the room and stood by the window. As the meeting participants mixed their drinks, he stared out at the city below.

Even when the sound of their voices began to fade to a murmur, Brian continued looking out the window. He loved San Francisco with a passion; he'd grown up here and had planned to raise his own family somewhere on The Hill. Yet, now, after all this time, he would have to leave. Letting the tension build in the nervous silence, he turned. The sun had burned off the fog over the bay and bright sunshine bathed the room. He looked into the eyes of the board members, making sure he had their complete attention.

"Gentleman, let me begin by thanking you for your patience and trust. I realize that this has been a tense time for our company and the entire technology industry. Things are in a state of flux right now and the competition is snapping at our heels. The Internet has taken us to new heights in terms of revenue source and decreased expense, but we know that all good things must come to an end."

Brian enjoyed watching the CFO's cocky grin freeze on his face, the corners of his mouth tighten as he gripped the Monte Blanc pen in his left hand.

"The technology industry is under assault on both fronts. On the software side, Microsoft is fighting possible antitrust legislation in Europe. On the hardware side, semiconductor manufacturers have been placed on a watch list as a national security concern. The online age is upon us, and even in its infancy, there are abundant security fears. You have all seen how quickly corporations flee once a web host's security is compromised.

"Hackers no longer need to break into a company's Internet site to cripple it. All they have to do is bombard the servers with useless data, fake emails, and shadow traffic to bring the site to its knees. What does that mean to corporations?" He paused, holding up one finger. "Fact: If the consumer cannot transact his business when he or she wants to, they'll go somewhere else.

"If a customer places a transaction and it doesn't complete, then we are liable. The risks of cyber computing are escalating. As technology increases, so does the threat of a security breach via external or internal channels. Once a machine is linked with others, no matter where that data resides, the entire system is vulnerable."

Brian paused to take a sip of ice water from the glass in front of him before glancing at his audience. He had them in the palm of his hand. "In tomorrow morning's *Wall Street Journal*, you will learn that the CIA's computer system has recently been the target of a moderately successful infiltration. The CIA has access to the most powerful electronic defense systems, influence, and resources, yet it was hacked. What does that say to our clients who trust us to keep criminals away from their internal information or secure transactions? How do we instill trust in our clients? What do we say?"

Brian hit the moment in full stride. Taking two steps away from the window, he placed his hands on the back of a chair. He let the tension build to its highest peak before putting them out of their misery. Giving a practiced smile he continued, "We tell them that we have an active artificial intelligence security system, created to not only defend against intrusion but to seek and destroy the software of the intruder."

He waved his hand in a fluid motion while lowering his voice. "I was given the task of finding a way to make our company internally and externally secure. I felt the need not only to accomplish my task, but also to take it to another level unmatched by our competition. Not only will we be able to offer our corporate and government clients a safe web transaction hosting and information database service but we will also issue a guarantee. We will promise that if anyone comes after their information, we will go after them and wipe them out." Brian picked up a sheet of white paper and balled it up in his hands.

"This new technology will not only seek the machine that is trying to hack into the system, but it will also destroy their system with a very powerful strain of the Melissa virus. There is no place on the web or in the world the intruder can hide. The program will use the intruder's own code to track back and destroy him. The virus is programmed to emulate and return to the source of the attack, where it will infect the microprocessor, wipe out the hard drive, and cripple the machine. All the while, it will be recording the system registration information for our records. Not only will we be protecting our corporate clients, but we'll be in the enviable position of being able to aid the government in updating its threat assessment technology."

Applause filled the boardroom. Brain raised his hands, indicating that he had yet to finish. "This is a war and we will win. The tests for the program were completed last week and were a hundred percent successful. Gentlemen, we will not beat the industry. We will recreate it in our own image."

Brain took his seat and leaned back in the leather chair. He suppressed the urge to laugh as he watched an executive stand and address the room. "Members of the Board, I think I speak for all of us when I say that Brian has done an excellent job."

Brian smiled. *If only you knew.*

ONE

The sound of high-pitched voices and rubber screeching against linoleum floors pulled Alex Thompson from her thoughts. Turning over the graded quiz papers, she put down her pen with a soft sigh and ran her fingers through her hair. From the sound of locker doors slamming shut and the excited voices of children, Alex guessed that the school cafeteria must have served ice cream at lunch. She glanced at the clock on the far wall and smiled.

Just then a gentle breeze wafted through the classroom, carrying with it the scent of freshly cut grass. She looked over the sun-filled space and the corners of her mouth inched further upwards. If this was to be her penance, then God was truly merciful. She not only held a job she loved as an elementary school teacher, but she'd also recently received an award from the National Association of Black School Educators. Alex stood and moved towards the door, only to retreat as wave after wave of fresh-faced hyperactive kids raced into the room.

She leaned against the wall and tried to recall a time when she'd felt so young and carefree. Her thoughts briefly drew her backwards to the time she'd spent growing up on a naval base in Japan.

Returning her thoughts to the present, Alex watched as the last student walked slowly though the doorway and took his seat. The room was crammed with books, paintings, and pictures. She had worked hard to fill the classroom with interesting books and objects that would inspire curiosity and excitement.

Alex closed the door and did a quick mental roll call of the small group before calling them to attention. "Good afternoon, class."

"Good afternoon, Ms. Thompson!" they shouted.

"It's going to be a long one," she muttered under her breath.

It was her last class of the day and by far the most unruly. She tried to be stern with the kids but usually failed. Her students smiled so sweetly and tried so hard, all the while attempting to wiggle out of doing their homework. They were a miniature bunch of con artists this class.

"Please take out your books; we're going to spend today reading out loud." Her announcement was met with a series of groans.

Alex watched as Gregory raised his hand. "Ms. Thompson, I forgot to bring my book," he said.

She shook her head to dispel the smile that threatened to overturn her frown of disapproval. Gregory, her self-appointed class clown, had large, puppy dog eyes, curly dark hair, and round pink cheeks that gave him a deceptive look of innocence. She smiled and picked up a photocopy of the reading assignment and put it on his desk. He did this every time. They both knew that he hated reading out loud.

"Well, Gregory, since you didn't bring your book, you get to start. Please read the first paragraph to the class."

Alex walked to the edge of her desk and leaned back, keeping an eye on the kids. She watched as they bent their heads to follow along with the story.

Alex had picked out a book that she had known the kids would like. *The Boy Who Drew Cats* was one of the many old Japanese fairy tales she'd been told as a child. She listened to Gregory as he read the first paragraph.

"Very good. Rebecca, you're next."

She had each child read until they came to the end of the third chapter. "Now close your books. Who can tell me about Kenji?" Alex watched as their hands shot up into the air and their eyes glistened with interest.

"Mary." She pointed a neatly manicured fingertip at the student.

"Teacher's pet," someone grumbled.

Alex straightened and the room went quiet. "Who said that?"

She looked across the classroom as all their little faces turned away from her and looked towards everyone else. Alex knew the guilty party by the faint blush on the boy's cheeks. Feeling generous, she let him go with a general warning to the room.

"Kids, you all know that I don't play favorites. It hurts my feelings to hear comments like that. You're all my little monsters and I care for you all the same," she said. "Everyone will have their turn, I promise."

Her words had the desired affect. "I'm sorry, Ms. Thompson. I didn't mean to hurt your feelings."

Alex hid a smile as she turned towards the boy. "That's okay, Eric. I know you didn't mean to hurt my feelings."

She gave him a smile and a pat on the head before returning to her position at the front of the room. Just as Alex opened her mouth to ask a question, the school bell rang, signaling the end of school. Having been trained since the first day of class, her little group kept their seats.

She sighed, "We'll continue tomorrow. Your homework is to read the next chapter." She watched them gather their notepads and scurry towards the door.

Alex looked on as the kids ran out of the room, paying the most attention to the lone child slowly gathering his things and placing them neatly inside his backpack. Thinking back to her earlier words about not having favorites amongst her students, she knew that she had told a half-truth.

She approached the child and crouched down so that she was eye level with him. He was slim in a delicate way, with gently slanted dark brown eyes, prominent cheekbones, and straight black hair.

"Chou, how are you doing?"

He nodded his head and looked at her with solemn eyes. "I'm fine, Ms. Thompson. How are you today?"

She rarely saw him smile. She and the other teachers had discussed Chou while eating lunch one day. Like other nine year olds, he loved to read and unlike others in his age group, he had a remarkable memory.

He was one of the brightest students she had ever taught but he was also the quietest. He never spoke up in class and only reluctantly joined in the group projects or discussions. He even kept himself apart from the other kids in his class. She had watched as he sat by himself under the oak tree during recess.

Alex couldn't help being drawn to this child. It was his eyes, she decided. He had an old soul. She knew his mother had died shortly after his parents had moved to America from Hong Kong. Chou was the only one of Alex's students to know such a loss and her heart ached for him because she could relate. She too had grown up motherless in a foreign country. William Thompson and Margaret Harris had met at Tuskegee University and married shortly after her father joined the navy. Her mother had followed him across two continents and only her sudden death from pneumonia could have kept her from his side.

"How am I? I'm not sure." She shrugged her shoulders. "I think Nurse Parker is a little mad at me."

Having caught his interest, she watched as he leaned his head to the side in puzzlement. Alex glanced towards the door to make sure they couldn't be overheard. "I ate the last Girl Scout cookie."

All the children knew that Nurse Parker had a sweet tooth. Alex watched as Chou's eyes widened and his lips curved into a smile.

"You can take her, Ms. Thompson. You're way bigger."

She chuckled and shook her head. "Thanks for the vote of confidence."

"Welcome. See you tomorrow, Ms. Thompson."

She followed him to the door and stood in the long hallway as he walked towards the main entrance. As he went to leave the building, he turned and Alex waved. Chou returned the gesture before slipping out the door. She walked back into her empty classroom, gathered her materials, packed up her briefcase, and headed for her car.

She opened the trunk, dumped everything inside, and moved to close it.

"Damn," she cursed as she realized that she'd left the duffle bag containing her karate uniform at home. She took a quick peek at her watch and calculated the length of time it would take for her to drive home, then go out to the dojo. No matter how fast she drove, it was inevitable that she would be late.

Making a mental note to call her karate teacher, she slammed the trunk, and then got behind the wheel of her Jetta. Alex cranked the car and rolled back the sunroof, letting the warm sunshine in. It was another perfect day in San Francisco. Pressing the play button for the CD player she let the smooth sounds of jazz pour through the car as she pulled out of the parking lot and turned toward home.

TWO

Alex drove home with the music loud and the windows down. Her thoughts of the best route to the dojo from her two-story house disappeared at the sight of a familiar black jeep sitting in the driveway. To a military brat any place with a roof, four walls, and a door was home. But truly, this place, more than any other house she'd lived in, felt like home to Alex. She pulled up to the curb and got out of the car.

"I really don't have time for this," she muttered as she slammed the car door. Alex ran up the stairs and turned the knob, knowing that it would be unlocked. She shook her head.

"Didn't I tell you to get a new lock?" came a slightly accented voice from the far right.

Alex dropped her bag and turned to stare at the intruder. "Did you scare Karen when you picked the lock?"

"No one was home," he explained. "Your roommate left a note. She'll be spending the night at her aunt's house."

Alex glared at the man, but he seemed unaffected. She sighed and dropped onto the couch, looking at him. Rafé's salt and pepper hair, cut short on the side and long in the back, accentuated his sculpted cheekbones. His lean, muscled frame and dark Latin looks had been an ongoing joke between him and her father. Alex bent to stroke her pet cat, Shadow, as he rubbed against her leg.

"So what brings you here, Rafé?"

"Just wanted to bring you a birthday gift."

Alex frowned. "My birthday isn't until next month."

"I don't know when I'll be back in the States and I want you to have it before I leave."

The moment Rafé mentioned the word gift, she looked at him closely. Normal people received money, clothes, jewelry, or gift certificates. She was the only person she knew who received custom made knives and military history books as presents.

Alex cautiously reached out to open the box Rafé had put beside her. She drew in a quiet breath and whistled when she saw the gun nestled within the soft silk cloth.

"Why?"

"Why what?"

"Why the gun and why now?"

He answered her with a nonchalant shrug.

"Why the semi-automatic?" she persisted. "This is San Francisco, not Bogotá."

Rafé's usually cold flat eyes always thawed when she looked into them. She supposed it was the memories of her father that accounted for his affection.

"Niña," he sighed. "Your father saved my life more than once. With his dying breath, he placed you into my keeping. I promised to take care of you. I have to go on a mission and I won't be here to watch over you. So, I want you to have all the things necessary to protect yourself when the time comes."

Alex picked up the gun and tested its weight in the palm of her hand. Her father's disapproval of her joining the Special Forces had been a cause of disagreement between them, but the military had taught her well. Her grip was strong and arm steady. All of the lies and falsified documents that had preceded her return to civilian life could never erase her Special Forces training. She had given five years of her life and half of her soul to the military.

There had been nights that she had spent with her fingers curled around the barrel of a 9mm Beretta as she slept in a vest carrying 15-round magazines. When operations went sour, it was just DELTA force and the enemy in the high intensity shootouts. She frowned, remembering the numerous times that they had made it out of impossible situations only because the enemy had run out of bullets.

She looked down at the gun. The semi-automatic pistol was a dull black with a hard rubber grip and a small left side safety. Alex ran her finger-tips over the etched letters: *Ruger*.

"You've gone on extended covert missions before. What's so different this time?"

He ignored her question. "I've informed Tobias of my absence. He's going to check up on you from time to time."

Alex waved her hand dismissively. "You and I both know that I don't need you or any other member of the team. Ex-team," she corrected herself, "to tuck me in at night. So what aren't you telling me?" The temptation to slip back into the shadows of the military was always there. Although she loved her life as a teacher, Alex still missed the camaraderie of the military.

"Niña, you are my *gurraro pequeno*, little warrior. I just want to make sure that you stay safe."

Rafé was as efficient a killing machine as they come. Military trained in undercover operations, search and rescue and reconnaissance, he was one of the best. Though he was analytical, he couldn't overcome his paternalistic nature. He would trust her to keep him alive in a fight, depend on her to back him up in a mission, but he would worry and that was what lay behind the gift.

"Okay...okay. I give up." She threw her hands up and laughed. "I'm going to make coffee."

Alex took the coffee beans out of the freezer and placed a quarter cup into the grinder. As the sound of the machine filled the kitchen, the scent of coffee beans spread. She placed the ground coffee into the machine and hit the button to start the brewing cycle. After pulling down two mugs from the cabinet, she took milk out of the refrigerator and waited for the machine to finish brewing.

"So what hell hole are you being sent to this time? Or are you getting a cushy undercover job?" She leaned against the countertop and watched the man take a seat at the table.

Rafé shook his head. "Don't know. They will tell me nothing until I arrive for the briefing."

"Not to mention the fact that even if you knew, you couldn't tell me," she commented offhandedly after pouring two cups of coffee.

"You know the rules." Rafé took the cup of black coffee from her hand.

Alex smiled. "So, when do you leave?"

"Tomorrow morning," he answered after drinking some of the dark brew.

Her adopted uncle fixed a searching stare on her. "I need to have a clear head for this mission. Promise me that if you have any troubles you'll contact Tobias."

Alex took a sip of her coffee and then placed the cup on the countertop. She hated lying but she knew Tobias well enough not to want him keeping a close eye on her. She had met him a couple of times when Rafé had asked her to help out with a limited intelligence gathering mission south of the border.

Tobias was a highly skilled assassin. He was the one the military sent for when mistakes were made and someone needed to permanently disappear. When Tobias's sister was beaten and robbed, the family called Tobias. Her attackers never made it to trial.

Mentally crossing her fingers, Alex met his intense stare and lied, "I promise."

His eyes, usually expressive, held a pensive look. "Are you happy?"

Alex blinked twice. "Happy? I don't know. I'm content."

"No regrets about leaving the team?"

"None," she confidently replied. It had taken months for her to adjust to civilian life. But now that she had a job she loved, friends, and karate to keep her busy, she had lost her longing for the dangerous and unpredictable life of a DELTA operative. "I'm grateful that I had the chance to spend time with my father."

"What about the young man?"

"Brian?" She played along with Rafé's seemingly innocent question. She'd bet every penny in her account that he not only knew Brian's name but also his entire life history and credit rating.

"Has he proposed yet?"

"What makes you think our relationship is that serious?"

"Unless the Tiffany solitaire engagement ring purchased last month was for another woman, he proposed to you."

"I told him no."

"Because of your past?"

She shook her head as Rafé came to stand beside her. "I don't love him in the way a husband and wife should love one another. Now, are you satisfied or is there something else you'd like to know?"

He raised a bushy eyebrow and a slight smile curved his lips upward. "That will be all for now." He placed his empty cup in the sink. "I need to pack. You will install a new lock on both doors?"

"Yes, sir," Alex nodded. "First thing in the morning." He was halfway to the front door before she could catch him. "Rafé?"

"Yes, niña?" He stopped on the first step but didn't turn.

"Take care."

"I will." And she had but to blink before he disappeared.

Shaking her head, Alex locked the door before heading upstairs. She opened the closet door and pulled out a small stepladder. Pushing aside empty shoe boxes, she slid back the false panel. Taking her time, she wrapped the gun in the blue material and placed it alongside her other collection of weapons, souvenirs from her time in the military.

The little alcove held a mini arsenal: mace, stun gun, knives, and various other implements of violence she had collected from her time in the military and from her former DELTA teammates. Sliding the panel back into place, she returned the shoe boxes to their original positions. Sparing a quick glance at the watch on her wrist, she hurried into the bedroom, picked up her duffle bag, and departed for the karate studio.

Twenty minutes later, Alex parked her car next to a dark-colored station wagon and turned off the engine. She leaned back, rested her head against the headrest, and drew in a deep breath. Just as she closed her eyes, she heard the door of the dojo open and the excited voices of children. She opened her eyes and watched as little children in karate uniforms rushed towards the parked cars and waiting parents, then got out and went inside.

The dojo was an open space with windows facing west. Alex sighed as the room's peaceful ambiance washed over her. She waited for a minute in the silence before shouting the customary Japanese greeting, which announced her presence. This place was all she'd had to keep the darkness away after her father's death.

"*Tadaima.*"

Alex had begun to slip off her shoes when she heard Sensei's response. "*Okinasai.*"

She was halfway across the room before she saw Taga Sensei. He was a master of the art of stealth.

Taller than the average Japanese male, her teacher was five eleven, thin, and muscled. Seemingly ageless, he had the agility and strength of a twenty year old yet the knowledge and patience to teach karate to both adults and children.

She turned and walked into the dressing room. Stripping off her slacks and blouse, she took her time putting on her karate uniform. Alex looked into the mirror while pulling her hair back into a ponytail and stopped.

She stared at the darkness of her skin next to the whiteness of the karate uniform. How her African-American features appeared displaced by the Asian costume. But it was her large crescent-shaped eyes that stopped her cold. Alex recognized the expression in them as like Chou's: solemn and sad. A memory flashed through her mind: "Daddy, why did Momma have to leave?" She had drawn her legs up to her chest as she eyed her father in his white naval uniform.

"The angels need her, sweetheart," he'd replied straightening his perfectly starched collar.

She remembered seeing her own sad face in the mirror. "I need her too."

Shaking her head to clear away the images, she re-checked her belt, and then entered the training room.

"We will use the swords today, Alex-*chan*," Taga announced.

Without looking towards her teacher, she donned the protective clothing required for kendo. When she finished putting on the body gear, she turned to take the face mask from Sensei's mitten covered hand. Metal bars protected her face, and the woven silk bottom portion of the headdress comfortably covered her shoulders.

After securing her helmet, Alex reached into the rear of the cabinet and brought out two *shinai*. She held tight to one of the bamboo and leather swords and gave the other to Taga Sensei. Holding the sword, Alex performed a standing bow.

"*Onegai shimasu*," she said softly, asking the teacher to grant her the favor of a lesson.

"*Hajime.*"

Sensei's loud shout was her only warning. Like lightning, Sensei hit out with his wooden sword, putting her instantly on the defensive. Her arms felt the burn of blocking his hits. Alex inched backward, giving ground in order to regroup. But just as quickly as she moved back, Sensei moved forward.

In hand-to-hand combat, she was one of the best, but the sword was heavy and unnatural in her hands. Taga Sensei was the master of this art and he wasn't shy about letting her know it. She gazed into his coolly confident dark eyes and memories of being taunted by little Japanese boys as she tripped trying to mimic their fluid kicks rose up in the back of her mind and anger quickly followed.

Yet keeping her cool saved the match as Alex forced her opponent to move closer and to use more energy as she conserved hers. It was impossible to get through his blocks, but she intended to hold her own long enough to force a stalemate. Just when her arms could take no more abuse, Sensei pulled back and lowered his stick. Alex waited with sword up, trying to catch her breath before the second round.

One of the first lessons she'd learned was to never drop her guard. Breathing heavily, she lowered her sword as Sensei reached up with his left hand to remove his mask. She did the same and together they bowed to one another, signaling an end to the fight. Alex felt the sweat-dampened wood slip through her numb fingers and began to laugh.

"So this was triumph?" she croaked under her breath. *Never again.* Every muscle in her body was on fire. She glanced at Sensei as he reached to collect her stick and mask. After picking them up, he just strutted over to the equipment wall, set them down, and then entered the dojo's small kitchen. Alex bent slowly, afraid that any movement whatsoever would make the pain worse.

"Tea, Alex-*chan*?"

She heard his mocking tone from the kitchen. She took a deep breath and stood up straight. Only Sensei could casually ask if she wanted tea after administering such a hard beating.

Alex shook her head in wonderment. No wonder the samurai died out, she thought. All those poor students probably rebelled.

THREE

The next day at school, Alex kept her expression blank as she gazed at the row after row of angry faces. How had she gotten lucky enough to get most of the high-strung, opinionated, advanced students in one class? And it would happen to be her last period group.

"I don't like Buddhists. They're mean."

"Yeah, they kicked him out because he drew cats."

"Isn't it against the law to make kids do chores?"

"Mommy said she'd never make me leave home for not cleaning my room."

"Ms. Thompson, I don't want to go to Japan anymore."

Alex tried not to smile at that last comment. "Class, the story you read was an old Japanese legend about a boy who drew cats instead of being disciplined and doing his chores. Tara, please tell the class what the word 'legend' means."

Tara was a small girl with dark red hair, wire framed glasses, and freckles. Her mother worked at the local library and Tara was an avid reader. "It's an old story or a grown-up fairy tale."

Alex nodded her head. "That's correct. It's a story. No need to get upset."

She watched the rebellion and anger disappear from their faces and wondered how it was that this class had missed the fact that their homework was fiction. "Now, Kevin, why was Kenji expelled from the monastery?"

"Because the monks were mean."

"And…"

"Well, Kenji liked to draw cats a lot. The…" He paused.

"Monks," she supplied.

"Yeah, the monks didn't like it because Kenji forgot to do his chores."

"Good answer." Alex straightened and smiled at the boy. "David, where did Kenji go after leaving the monastery?"

"He went to the Golden Rat's house."

"House?"

David bent over his book and turned the pages furiously until coming to the correct answer, "Temple."

"Perfect." Alex turned and moved towards the whiteboard. She opened her blue marker and drew another temple with a little boy standing outside. "Who's our main character, Maria?"

"Kenji."

"Lisa, where did Kenji live?"

"He lived in a monastery."

"Chou, what was the setting of this story?" The question was hard but she knew he would answer correctly.

"Ancient Japan," came the confident reply.

"Excellent."

Alex continued to draw on the board, missing the beginning of a commotion. She turned just in time to see Brandon holding his nose and Chou standing beside his desk. Just then the bell rang. The kids stayed seated and fortunately all their eyes were directed at the door and not their classmates.

"Class, remember to answer the questions on page sixty-five. Brandon and Chou, by my desk."

Alex directed her attention to Chou first. "What happened?"

The boy just looked at a point over her shoulder and remained silent. Her gaze swung to the other little boy.

"Brandon?"

He didn't open his mouth. Taking an exasperated breath, Alex stared at Brandon, willing him to answer with her eyes. He broke in less than twenty seconds.

"I called him a mean little Jap and pulled his hair. Then he hit me."

"Why did you call Chou names?"

"Because...I don't know." All his bravery fled and Brandon began to cry. His face was white with terror and his nose began to run. "Please don't tell my mom, Ms. Thompson," he begged.

Alex grabbed some tissue and held it up to the little boy's face. He had good reason to be afraid. Brandon's mother was very no-nonsense when it came to school. Alex crouched down and looked him in the eyes.

"Brandon. Stop crying," she warned. He began to cry harder.

"Brandon, I won't tell your mother." Alex caught the triumphant gleam in his eyes.

"But you have to do two things. One, I want you to give a heartfelt verbal and written apology to Chou. Second, you'll write a three page report on Chinese history and read it to the class next Friday." His face fell instantly.

"Now go before you miss your bus."

Alex turned her attention to Chou as he stood ready to accept punishment. She reached out and guided his chin so that she could look into his face. "You hit him?"

He nodded slowly. Alex straightened. She couldn't punish one and not the other. "You know it's wrong to hit people?" She saw a spark of defiance in his expression.

"He called me a Jap. I'm Chinese," he announced proudly.

"Actually to be completely correct, both of you are wrong. You're American," she corrected.

Alex swept Chou's hair out of his eyes and made a show of examining his face for an imaginary injury.

"I don't see any bruises. Brandon spoke his words out of ignorance. You responded out of anger. Both of you were wrong. However, Chou, for your actions you could get suspended from school."

"Will I be suspended, Ms. Thompson?" He stared straight ahead at the whiteboard.

"No, I want you in my classroom at 7:00 A.M. sharp tomorrow. You're going to help me clean." She turned and moved towards her desk. It was an order and dismissal. Recognizing it, Chou nodded and left the room.

Alex made a mental note to request a conference with Chou's father. She picked up her purse and brief-case and was headed toward the door when her cell phone rang.

She looked at the unfamiliar number on the readout and hesitated a moment before hitting the send key. "Hello?"

"Thompson-sensei, it's McNeal. Sorry to bother you, but I could use some help in a police matter."

It took her a moment to match a face to the voice on the phone.

Alex entered the hallway and headed toward the exit. "What can I do for you, McNeal?"

"We need to take a statement from a Japanese woman and our local interpreter and his backup are both out of the country."

"All right. I'll be there as soon as I can."

Alex's head was throbbing slightly as she drove towards the police station. She parked her car in the adjacent parking lot and made her way to the precinct entrance. Trailing behind a group of officers escorting two young men inside, she went to the desk and waited until the duty officer was free.

"I'm here to see Officer McNeal," she half shouted over the noise.

"Are you Ms. Thompson?" She met his scrutiny and held eye contact. The desk officer's brown hair receded and the tightness of his uniform gave testament to the error of fast food and doughnut shop drive-bys.

"Yes, I am." Alex was careful to keep her expression blank. "Is there a problem?"

"Nope, just thought you'd be bigger. Wait over there."

Bigger? What did he mean by that? Had her former students described her as an Amazon? she mused.

She raised her eyes in time to see Officer McNeal come down the stairs. He looks like a cop, she thought. McNeal was one of Taga's intermediate students. Alex took a step away from the wall as he approached.

"*Sensei*." He nodded with a friend's grin. "Thank you for coming."

"Mr. McNeal, please call me Alex. We're not in class." She touched his shoulder and smiled.

"Only if you'll call me Matt. I want to check my karate stance when you say my last name. Sensei—

Alex, if you'll come with me. The young woman's in the interview room."

She followed him down a series of corridors until they arrived at a windowed doorway. She examined the young girl, noticing first that she'd hidden her face behind a wall of dark hair. But Alex could see from the way she wiped her eyes with the tissue that she was crying.

"Ms. Ogata hasn't said a word since we brought her in from the hospital."

Alex turned towards him and her stomach clenched as she quietly asked, "Was she raped?"

"No, but she was pretty beaten up. Cut lip, black eye, sprained wrist, and some nasty bruises."

"You tried talking to her?"

"Yeah, but she just got hysterical and started speaking in Japanese when we attempted to take a statement."

"Do you have the person who did this in custody?"

"Yes."

"Good."

She followed Matt into the room. Taking the chair next to the young girl, she reached over and touched Ms. Ogata's hand. The young girl looked up, startled, as though unaware of their entrance into the room. Both of her eyes were red from crying and the one on the right side of her swollen face was beginning to darken.

"*Ogata-san*. My name is Alex Thompson. Please let me help you," she spoke softly in Japanese. Alex watched as the girl nodded her head slightly. "Who did this to you?"

"I waved bye-bye to my classmate. I didn't do anything." Her story poured out haltingly through sobs and cries. Her boyfriend had gone into a rage after seeing her wave good-bye to a male classmate.

"When I closed the door to my apartment, he hit me. He threw me down onto the floor. He told me that it was my fault, that I should not have made him jealous. He kicked me."

As Alex translated every word into English, the only sounds in the room were the victim's harsh breathing and the scratching of a pencil.

"Can you ask if he's displayed this behavior before?" asked McNeal.

"*Ogata-san*, I know that this is painful for you, but I must ask you more questions. Can you go on?"

"Yes."

"Has he hit you before?"

Alex had her answer when the Japanese woman lowered her head. "He hit me once before. We went to a party and I danced with one of his friends. He called me a whore and slapped me. Ryuichi apologized and I forgave him."

"What is the name of the man who beat you?" Alex asked.

Her lips quivered, "Ryuichi Ataro."

"Thank you for your courage. Remember, you are not to blame. None of this is your fault. He has a problem; he is sick and needs help. However, there is nothing to excuse his actions. No one has the right to hurt you."

Matt stood and took a step away from the table. "Alex, please tell Ms. Ogata that we'll take her home and that she has the option of placing a restraining order on Mr. Ataro."

She turned and translated but added her own advice. "There are those who would help you. Please take the help."

Alex watched the frightened young woman bow her head slowly. She was beginning the long and hard process of gathering the shreds of her dignity. Allowing the woman a modicum of privacy, Alex stood and left the room. Outside in the hallway, she stopped and leaned against the cold concrete wall. She looked up to see Officer McNeal.

"I want to see him," Alex stated.

"I don't think that would be a good idea."

"McNeal. Sorry, Matt. I came at your request and I helped you take a statement. I spoke for that scared young woman in there. I gave you her words. I want that son-of-a-bitch to hear them." He nodded and led her into the interrogation room at the opposite end of the corridor.

The Japanese businessman sat in the black straight-backed chair in front of a rectangular table, playing with his pen, flipping it back and forth as though nothing were amiss. Alex entered the room and sat opposite Mr. Ataro while Matt stood in the doorway. Placing her hands on the table, she waited as he flicked his eyes from her to Matt. The room smelled of antiseptic and stale air. Alex continued to stare as he gave her a mocking smile.

Ryuichi Ataro was in his late twenties and had black, perfectly-styled hair, dark eyes, and features that could have once landed him a lead role in a Japanese animation film. Reining in her anger, Alex spoke. Her words in Japanese sounded harsh in the little room. "Have you no honor? No shame?"

It was her use of Japanese that brought the man's head up. Alex kept going. "You would beat a defense-less woman. Are you not a man? Are you so weak?" Alex watched him pale.

"What do you know of such things, *gaijin*?" he responded.

Alex refused to let him turn things around even though she wanted to let him know that here he was the *gaijin*, foreigner. "You might want to take another look around, Ataro. The only foreigner here is you. And what I do know is that you are a disgrace to your family. You are the one who has brought shame upon himself and his ancestors. And, it will be you who pays for this crime on the next turn of Buddha's wheel." She stood up to leave.

Before she reached the door Ogata's bruised face flashed through her mind. "If you even think of hurting that girl again, I won't rest until I hunt you down. Then we will face one another, alone. No cops, no witnesses," Alex promised. She held his stare, letting the cold threat of violence show in her eyes.

Alex could see that her last words had gotten to the man. Mr. Ataro's hands shook and his face turned pink with rage.

"You think because you know my language that I will fear you? You are just a girl, playing at being Japanese. Neither you nor your cop friends scare me."

"This," he waved towards two way wall mirror, "means nothing to me." His voice hinted of violence and cruelty.

Alex looked him in the eyes and smiled while her eyes remained hard. "Who said anything about hurting you? There are those who don't believe in the American criminal system and it's a big country. No one would care if a woman beater were to disappear."

She turned and exited from the interrogation room. An image of Tobias's face flashed in her mind and a feeling of peace washed over her. Alex knew she could have Ataro killed. The ex-SEAL wouldn't hesitate to cross the line she had drawn for herself after their mission in Somalia.

"What did you say to him?" McNeal asked.

Alex glanced back at the door to the interrogation room before answering. "Let's just say I impressed upon him the consequences should he bother Ms. Ogata again."

Matt nodded. "The guys back at the station couldn't believe that you took down half of my squad."

It hadn't been something Alex had wanted to do but it had been necessary. A teacher had to establish order and respect. There had been those who had not taken well to her substituting for Taga Sensei. They came around after she'd laid them out on the floor a couple of times.

"Well, the officer at the desk did mention that he thought I'd be bigger," she chuckled.

Matt looked embarrassed. "Sorry about that. Guess it's a little hard to imagine that you incapacitated half of my squad."

They walked out of the air-conditioned police station into the soft glow of sunset. Alex observed Matt out of the corner of her eyes. He was tall, with dark brown hair, green eyes, and a football player's physique.

Without the uniform, he would look to most people like an All-American boy. Yet Alex would have known in an instant that he wasn't a civilian. She would have guessed that he was either military or a cop by his walk and the way he constantly scanned the area, looking for trouble.

His eyes belonged to a man who had seen it all and expected the worst. She had seen such eyes before: in the face of her father, in the faces of her DELTA team, and in the face of the woman she saw every morning in the mirror. As much as she tried to forget it, the past never seemed to leave her alone.

"Have you eaten?" His question startled her from her thoughts.

"No," she shook her head. "I came here from work."

He opened his mouth to speak again, but his radio went off. "McNeal, you're needed at the station."

"Acknowledged," he said into the walkie-talkie.

He turned towards her. "Can I give you a rain check on dinner?"

"Another time then." She smiled.

"Thanks for helping out."

"You're welcome."

Alex crossed the street and opened her car door, jumped in, and drove off without looking back.

FOUR

The next day, after bidding the kids good-bye, Alex made a mental note to ask about Chou's absence. She hoped that the little boy had not caught the stomach virus that was making the rounds through the school. Picking up her bag, she left her classroom and stopped to chat with Mrs. Nicholas, the sixth grade math teacher.

The woman's face had a natural pinched look. "I noticed you came in early this morning. Are the little ones keeping you on your toes?"

Alex smarted a little from the tone of condescension that dripped from Mrs. Nicholas's mouth. "I was expecting Chou. He was supposed to be helping me with a project, but he was absent. I hope he's okay."

Mrs. Nicholas's eyes widened. "He looked fine in my third period class."

"Really? Thanks for the info. See you tomorrow."

Alex turned and marched into the school's office. She stood at the computer for a couple of minutes before completing her search and copying an address on a small scrap of paper.

Forty minutes later, Alex turned into the tree-lined driveway and stopped to look down at the paper in her hand. "This is it."

She drove forward to the house. As soon as Alex got out of the car, she caught the scent of flowers and salty sea air. The home was lovely. Wide bay windows and a dark sloping roof seemed to blend with the overhanging trees.

Shaking her head, Alex shut the car door and walked up the stone-lined path to the front door. She could hear the chime echoing from the inside as she pressed the doorbell. She put on a smile as the door opened and an older, petite Asian woman eyed her with suspicion.

Alex bent down slightly, trying not to overshadow the woman. "Good evening. Could I speak with Chou, please?"

The older woman motioned for her to enter the house, then pointed to her feet. Without hesitating, Alex slipped off her sandals, stepped into a pair of red house slippers, and followed her hostess into an adjacent room.

"Please wait here."

Alex nodded and then turned to study the room. The inside was as lovely as the outside. The floor was made of dark polished wood and the walls were decorated with delicate Chinese picture scrolls. To the left of the foyer was what looked like a formal living room. To her right was a staircase. The sound of voices brought Alex out of her reverie. She turned and saw Chou pale slightly as his eyes met hers.

The man who followed behind the little boy startled Alex. Used to being the same height or taller than most Asian men, Alex had not expected to find herself having to slightly tilt her head up to look at him. She recognized the boy's resemblance to the man.

She'd never met Chou's father although she'd had plenty of conversations with his secretary. The man had a habit of canceling teacher conferences. Alex knew she had Mr. Liu's full attention by the intensity of his stare.

He was wearing black slacks and a white shirt with gold cufflinks. His face could have easily been chiseled from a smooth block of shaded marble. In the space of several breaths, she scanned his face and stored the image in the back of her mind. He had a strong jaw line, nicely cut black hair, and eyes much darker than her own, brown ones. They were hooded and assessing, not open and full of laughter. She guessed his age to be about her own making him seem too young to be a father and a widower.

She addressed Chou first by standing in front of him and bending her knees to force eye contact. "I missed you today."

His lip quivered and his gaze once again dropped to the floor.

Alex stood up and turned her attention to Chou's father. "Mr. Liu. Forgive me for not introducing myself earlier. My name is Alex Thompson and I'm Chou's literature teacher."

She saw his confusion and added, "English teacher."

"It's a pleasure to meet you, Ms. Thompson." His eyes never left her as he inclined his head. "But may I ask why you have chosen to visit my son?"

Alex inclined her head towards the little boy. "I'll let Chou answer that question."

Chou hesitated, then said, "I didn't go to class."

"Why did you not go to class?" His father's question, though softly spoken, demanded a swift response.

By the time Chou finished retelling the events that led up to his absence, she had seen more than enough. Emotions had flitted across Mr. Liu's face, from anger to denial before settling on guilt and resignation.

"I know that you and Brandon are good kids," Alex said. "You're one of my best students and I only want you to succeed and to be honest. I'm disappointed in you for not keeping your word. I chose not to have you suspended and I wasn't going to make you scrub floors."

Alex saw the first glimmer of tears in the boy's eyes.

"I'm sorry." Chou's voice was little more than a whisper. "Does this mean you won't be my teacher anymore?"

She playfully swatted his hair. "Of course not. You can't get rid of me that easily. Plus, you've got to help me organize the classroom."

Alex stood and held out her hand. "Friends?"

Chou's hand shot out to give her a high five. She laughed. "Good, glad we got that settled."

"Ms. Thompson?"

Alex started at the sound of Mr. Liu's voice, having completely forgotten about the other person in the room. Her surprise was sharper in that she noticed things about him that she shouldn't have. He was a very handsome man. She noted the way he was dressed in a shirt and tie, the way his skin tone stood out against the whiteness of the shirt.

"Ms. Thompson," he repeated.

Alex blinked twice, and then brought her attention back to the matters at hand. "Yes?"

"Would you like to stay for dinner?"

Alex shook her head in surprise. "I…" She was trying to politely decline when she felt a tap on her arm.

"Please," Chou asked. Alex saw the anxiety in his eyes and her heart melted. She had the skills to take down men five times her size, but she couldn't turn down a boy's polite request.

"I'd love to."

Alex followed Chou and his father down a carpeted hallway and turned into the dining room. The table was set with blue and white Chinese porcelain.

"Excuse me, could you show me to the bathroom? I'd like to wash my hands."

When Alex returned, Chou and his father had just finished setting the food down on the table.

"Please have a seat."

Alex settled into the chair next to Chou and waited for someone to begin the meal. The meal was family style with numerous platters in the middle of the table. When Mr. Liu removed the lids from the covered dishes, the scent of roasted chicken, vegetables, and rice wafted through the air. Trying to lighten the mood, Alex turned to Chou and whispered, "Do you usually eat in the dining room?"

He shook his head, replying, "Only when we have company."

"If I mess up, promise not to laugh," she joked, earning her a smile.

"Please help yourself," said Mr. Liu.

She looked up to see Chou's father staring at both of them. When his eyes peered directly into hers, Alex got the impression of steel beneath his dark gaze just before it was replaced with polite curiosity.

"Thank you."

Alex reached over and placed some of the chicken and steamed vegetables on her plate. Picking up her chopsticks, she began to eat. It wasn't until after the second bite that she looked up from her plate, suddenly aware that she was being watched. "Is something wrong?" she asked, confused.

"No. It's just unusual for me to see someone use chopsticks so well. You're quite proficient."

She pushed aside her annoyance. "Thank you."

"I want to apologize for my son's behavior. I'm partially to blame. I haven't been spending as much time with Chou as I should. You have my gratitude for bringing this to my attention."

The rest of the meal seemed to go smoothly. Chou appeared to blossom under the attention from his father. Alex, for her part, observed the interaction between father and son. She occasionally filled in the silence with humorous stories and lavish praise directed towards her student, keeping the conversation focused on light topics. It wasn't until later as Chou's father walked her to her car that she gave voice to her concerns.

"Mr. Liu."

"It's Xian." He stopped next to her.

She turned and smiled at him. "Call me Alex."

He inclined his head. "Now that we are on a first name basis, what is it that you really want to speak to me about?"

Alex arched her eyebrows before leaning against the side of her car. "I may be out of bounds with what I am about to say but I need to get this out into the open."

"Whatever it is, I'm sure I can handle it." The corners of Xian's lips curved into a tight smile.

The richness of this his voice made her want to lean closer toward him. At first glance, Xian wasn't an overly sexual man, but something about him made her linger close to catch the faint sandalwood of his scent. Overly conscious of how aware she was of him, Alex began. "I didn't want to say this in front of Chou but I'm worried about him."

"Worried? Why? My son's grades have always been excellent. Mrs. Lee hasn't mentioned anything being amiss." He sounded offended.

She stood up straighter. "I'm not worried about Chou's grades. It's just that I feel as though he's deliberately withdrawn from class. He doesn't interact with his peers. I'm not the only teacher who has noticed his behavior."

She watched his eyes narrow. Under the halo of the outside floodlights, his eyes looked almost black. "Tell me, Alex. Do you take such a personal interest in all your students?"

"Yes and no," she responded frankly. "I lost my mother when I was eleven."

A moment passed with nothing but the cool ocean air weaving between them and the sound of the night insects.

Xian nodded briefly. "I'm sorry for your loss, but I can take care of my son."

"And I can look after my students," Alex responded smoothly. His expression shifted from arrogance to surprise and she bit her lips to keep from laughing. It seemed that Xian Liu wasn't used to opposition.

"Is that a challenge I hear?" he questioned.

"No." Alex shook her head as the corners of her mouth curled upwards. "Just making a statement."

She watched as Xian took a step back, but if she wanted, she could reach out and touch him with her fingers. Her heart skipped when he smiled.

"My son is a very lucky boy to have you as a teacher."

Alex nodded and moved to open the driver's door. "Good night, Xian."

His name flowed too smoothly off her tongue and her pulse beat too quickly to dismiss the encounter. She frowned as she slid into the seat and closed the door. Attraction had its place, but not in her life, not after Brian. Hoping that her roommate Karen would be home, Alex keyed the ignition, put the car into gear, and drove away.

Xian stood in the doorway watching as the tail-lights of Alex's car disappeared into the night. He closed the door quietly and hesitated at the foot of the stairs. Placing his hand on the banister, he slowly went up the steps towards his son's room.

For a moment, he leaned in the doorway watching Chou as he bent over his desk writing. Then Xian straightened and stepped through the doorway, but stopped again. He hesitated, feeling the same emotions he had felt when his wife died. Looking down at his hands, he saw that they were sweaty.

He was powerful enough to lead his own company to unprecedented global success, but now he was completely out of his realm. Xian gazed down at the top of Chou's head and words seemed to stick in his throat. *Shay-Lin*. A picture of his pregnant wife flashed into his mind.

This was to be our job, he thought. It had never occurred to him that he would be raising their son alone.

Inwardly, Xian sighed and tapped lightly on Chou's shoulder before taking a seat on the bed. "Can we talk for a minute?"

He watched as Chou slowly put down his pencil and closed the notebook. When his son looked up, Xian could see nothing but sorrow. "Chou, I'm disappointed in myself. I didn't know that you were having trouble at school. It has been a difficult adjustment for you and I should have been there to help."

Chou's gaze held his with an unusually mature shrewdness. "That's okay, Dad. I know you're busy. You gotta work a lot."

Xian was ashamed. "That's no excuse. You should always be my number one priority," he emphasized. "I guess I'm getting old and forgetful, but starting today, I'm going to be the father I should have been."

He held out his arms and gathered his son close. Chou's arms slid around his neck. Xian couldn't remember a better feeling. His arms tightened around Chou for a moment before letting him go and placing him on his lap. "Now tell me what's troubling you."

He felt the boy's shivers. When Chou spoke, his words tore Xian's heart to pieces.

"Why did she have to die?" Chou's voice was ragged.

Unable to answer, he hugged his son tighter and stroked his hair. He took a deep breath, hoping to speak through the tears that clogged his throat.

"I can't answer that question. I know if I could, I would take her place. I cannot give you a reason but I can tell you that we all have our time in this world before leaving to join the next. Your mother's life was short but she gave me a gift so that no matter what happens I'll never be without her."

He looked down into his son's tear-streaked face and his heart turned over. "That gift is you. I love you more than my own life and your mother loved you even more. She will always be with us in spirit."

Xian relaxed against the headboard, tilted his head back, and stared at the ceiling. Chou had moved from tears to sleep. Xian focused on Alex Thompson, maybe because her arrival at his home had precipitated the events that brought him to his son's room.

Alex was unlike any teacher he'd ever met. He closed his eyes and pictured her standing in his foyer. She looked to be in her late twenties or early thirties. The khaki-colored pants and white cotton shirt couldn't disguise that she was fit and nicely rounded. Her dark hair was pulled back, fully displaying her features. She had an unblemished brown complexion and beautiful eyes. Her round jaw and lush lips were vulnerable and made him think of her in ways that gave new meaning to the standard parent-teacher relationship.

Xian shook his head and gently moved his sleeping son onto the bed. After covering Chou with a light coverlet, he stared down at his son for a moment. The facts were in: he had been a lousy father. And having explicit sexual thoughts about Alex Thompson wasn't going to improve the situation. Pushing her image to the back of his mind, Xian turned out the light and left the room.

FIVE

Alex sighed when her cell phone rang later that night. She could count on two hands the number of people who had access to her personal cell phone number. And at that moment, while still smarting from her encounter with Xian Liu, she wasn't in the mood to speak with any one them. Only after she'd checked the number of the incoming call did Alex answer. "Hello."

"Lee," a deep familiar voice responded.

Alex sat down on the edge of the bed and cradled the cell phone with both hands. "Brian."

"So how are you, Lee? Still going to the dojo every other day?"

He had given her that nickname after watching her spar with a fellow student. Brian had found it amusing to compare her to the legendary martial arts champion, Bruce Lee.

"Of course." She smiled. "How are you?"

"I'm lost on weekends without you."

"You don't have to be. Just because I gave back the ring doesn't mean I gave back our friendship. We can still go for hikes in the hills." Alex cradled the flip phone between her shoulder and ear. With both hands free, she began preparing for bed.

"Yeah? Well, that's not possible anymore."

"Why?" Alex questioned while removing her watch.

"Lee, I'm leaving."

Her hands stilled. A range of emotions passed through her, the most powerful being regret.

"I'll be relocating to Latin America," he continued.

"Congratulations," she finally replied. "Is it a promotion?"

"In a way," he answered.

Alex could sense tension in the evasive response. If it were a promotion, he deserved it. He'd worked so hard to achieve success and had spent many late nights surrounded by computers. He was a computer genius, a technology whiz with the temperament of an Italian painter. Some days when they had been together, he had been on top of the world and other days he'd wrapped his anger and frustration around him like a cloak.

She shook her head, pulling back from the memories, and then asked the question that had risen to her mind immediately after Brian had announced he planned to relocate out of the country.

"Are you leaving town because of me?"

"No, I just think it's time I grew up. I love my family and I'm going to miss my mom like crazy but I think distance would be a good thing."

"She still mad at you?"

"Yeah, she thinks I should have fought harder to change your mind."

Alex shook her head. "I tried to talk to her."

Brian's voice took on a weary tone. "I know, but she blames me anyway."

"You tell her you're leaving?"

"I'll send a postcard from Brazil."

"This is going to hurt your family."

She loved the Scott clan. They were a big, warm, affectionate family that had welcomed her like a long lost child. After her father's death, she had been starved for the warmth and kindness Brian's parents had given her. But the desire for family hadn't been enough.

"Not as bad as it hurt me to lose the the woman I love," he replied.

She added simply, "You love me but you aren't in love with me. You proposed that night because of your mother and your work."

Before he could protest, Alex cut in. "Let's be honest. I know your mother, Brian. She loves you and wants what's best for you. She got it into her head that I was the one for you. Nanna pressured you. Then there's your company. No matter how good you are, the executives value stability. Getting married would be a great boost to your career. I'm not accusing you of anything, but it's the truth, whether you like it or not."

In her mind, Alex went back to the night Brian had proposed. To be honest, she had been tempted to accept the engagement ring. The thought of her life as Mrs. Brian Scott, living in a five-bedroom house, driving a Mercedes, and being a stay-at-home wife hadn't been the attraction. No, for Alex it had been the opportunity to have parents again, to be someone's daughter. That was what she'd wanted.

"You're right, Lee. I'm just sorry I took your rejection so hard. I ruined our friendship and made a complete fool of myself. Alex, I'll miss you."

"I'll miss you, too."

Several heartbeats passed before he spoke again. "You could come with me."

She shook her head. "No, I can't."

He was such a strange mixture: strong, giving, caring, and yet possessing a selfish, stubborn streak. She'd never told him about her missions. Instead, she had let him believe that her role in the military was less than what it truly had been. Somehow, she'd known he would try to wrap her up in a cocoon and take away her strength. Alex had seen it while they were dating, but at that moment in her life, she'd needed to feel protected.

"Had to ask." He halfway laughed. And for the first time Alex detected something else in his tone. Something she couldn't place and it made her uneasy. "Brian, are you sure you're alright?"

"I'll be fine. Don't worry about me, Lee. Just be happy. Good-bye."

The hair on Alex's arms prickled as she flipped the phone closed. Maybe it was his voice, the sound of finality, but something about the conversation kept her awake that night.

Two days later at a political fundraising event, Xian lifted his half-empty glass as Gregory Michaels, CEO of the newest Internet startup, walked by. Cocky S.O.B. he thought. They'd met at the last technology symposium. The brash young man had boasted of his assured success. Xian smiled and shook his head. The company was doomed. Their IPO had been a disappointment. If the software company didn't capture market share soon, it would be a prime target for a takeover bid.

He surveyed the opulent ballroom taking another swallow of soda water before setting the glass down on a passing waiter's tray. Alcohol and business never mixed and Xian needed to be alert. He caught sight of his date, Sung Yee, as she worked the room.

Xian smiled warily as he noticed the eyes of the other men in the room watching her every move. Her midnight hair, which was parted in the middle, fanned her face, making her appear more exotic.

Sung Yee loved the attention her looks brought her. In Hong Kong, she would have been one of many beautiful women. Here in San Francisco amongst the moneyed crowd, her exotic air made her stand out as she flitted from one powerful man to the next. She glided towards him with a pout playing on her red-tinged lips.

He slipped into Mandarin when she came to a stop by his side. "Enjoying yourself?"

Looking down into her almond shaped eyes, he wondered why he had never before seen their lack of warmth.

Sung Yee took a sip of white wine and smiled. "You don't seem to be." Raising an eyebrow, she continued in unaccented English, "What's bothering you, Xian? Jealous?"

"No. Just tired."

That was part lie and truth. He was tired of this. The games, the parties, the travel, the client events. Xian wanted nothing more than to be with his son. An image of Chou's teacher rose in his mind. Alex. Such a strong name for a beautiful lady. Looking down at Sung Yee, he found himself comparing the two women and no matter how he looked at it, the woman in front of him came up wanting. Chou's teacher had impressed him with the way she handled his son, and she'd also piqued both his mental and physical interest.

Every time he thought of her, his body responded. Yet hard on the heels of the idea of romantically pursuing Alex came the obvious reasons of why he shouldn't. He wondered how this crowd would have reacted if he'd brought an African-American woman on his arm as his date.

He shook his head at the direction his mind had pursued. Here he was imagining all of these things when he doubted that she had even noticed him or was even interested in him outside of her relationship with his son.

"Xian, are you listening to me?" Sung Yee's high-pitched voice interrupted his thoughts.

"What is it, Sung Yee?" He allowed a hint of displeasure to color his voice.

"I was asking if you would come with me to dinner on Saturday. My parents want to meet you."

"I have other obligations."

She waved her elegantly-manicured fingertips. "You can bring the boy."

He clenched his teeth. "My son's name is Chou."

They had been seeing one another off and on for the past three months and she still couldn't remember his son's name. Again a comparison sprang to mind. During the dinner two nights before, Alex had made Chou laugh and smile. That Chou admired his teacher was obvious.

Beautiful, desirable, and great in bed, Sung Yee would make an excellent wife. She was the newest rising star at one of the West Coast's top advertising companies and they moved in the same social circles. She would be an asset to him, but she would never be the mother his son needed.

"I'm leaving," he said to Sung Yee.

"The evening just started. I need to be here to represent the firm," she scolded, tossing her hair over her left shoulder.

Xian reached out and fingered her soft tresses. Then he dropped his hand, placed it in his pocket, and pulled out his valet check.

"Good night, Sung Yee." He stopped as her hand grasped his arm.

"If you leave me here alone, it's over between us," she hissed.

He watched as her face flushed with anger, making her look even lovelier than before.

"Give my regards to your father," he said coolly before striding away.

It was around ten-thirty P.M. when Xian arrived home. He pulled the car into the garage and pushed the button to let the garage door back down. He got out, opened the side door, and stepped into the kitchen, then made his way in semi-darkness to the front of the house and went upstairs.

Xian stopped at the second bedroom and stood in the doorway looking at his sleeping son. A lump formed in his throat. He stepped quietly into the room and placed a kiss on Chou's head.

"He fell asleep at about nine, Mr. Liu."

Xian turned to see the housekeeper Mrs. Lee standing beside him.

"Thank you for watching over him," he whispered.

"You are very welcome. Chou is a good boy. He is no trouble. Not like my spoiled grandchildren." She smiled, her soft eyes crinkling slightly. "I'll go home now. Have a nice weekend."

He nodded. "You do the same."

SIX

Sunday morning the ringing of the phone broke into Alex's sleep. Alex always rose before dawn, except on Sunday mornings. Since her father's death, she'd stopped going to church and preferred to spend time alone, meditating. She rolled over and just as she reached for the receiver, the ringing stopped. She turned over and closed her eyes.

"Alex, wake up." Karen's voice penetrated the fog of sleep as she gently shook Alex's shoulder.

"What?"

"Alex. It's Brian." Her roommate's voice trembled.

"Tell him I'm not helping him pack," Alex muttered before opening her eyes. It had been over a week since she had talked with him.

"Alex...Brian's dead."

Shocked disbelief brought Alex upright. Brian? She felt tears rise to her eyes as she remembered their last dinner together. Alex took a breath before reaching for the cordless phone Karen held in her hand.

"Hello?"

"Alex, they killed my boy." Grief poured through the phone.

"Pop. What happened?"

"I'll tell you when you get here. Nanna needs you, Alex."

"What's she doing, Pop? Talk to me." She lowered her voice, trying to sound calm. She got out of bed and began to pull on clothes while holding the phone. Brian's mother Nanna was a strong woman, but Alex knew that this news would crush any person. Her roommate stood against the wall watching.

"She knew, Alex. She woke up last night and couldn't go back to sleep. She hasn't stopped crying since the police knocked on the door."

"Pop, when are Marcus and Tony due in?"

"Four-thirty this afternoon."

Alex glanced at the clock on her nightstand. Six and a half hours. She had to calm Nanna down before the boys arrived.

"I'll be there soon." Alex hit the off button and tossed the phone on the bed. Fastening her bra, she then pulled on her shirt.

"Are you okay?" her roommate asked.

Alex moved towards the bathroom. "I'm fine, K." Alex's voice was steady. She washed her face, finger combed her sleep tousled hair, and then grabbed a prescription bottle of sleeping pills out of the medicine cabinet. Karen stood behind her in the doorway.

"Are you sure that you should be driving?"

"Karen, I know you're concerned but I'm okay. I've done this before. I can handle it." She spoke truthfully. The pain wouldn't come for a while.

Alex moved towards her bedroom. "I've really gotta go."

"Call me later, okay? Call my cell phone," Karen said.

Alex stood still as Karen gave her a hug. All her emotions seemed walled off, separated from her. "Okay."

Picking up her keys and purse from the night-stand, she ran down the stairs and jumped into the car.

She didn't arrive at the Scotts until almost an hour later. Traffic. Cars full of people heading to the beach. The middle class neighborhood of the Scotts was devoid of kids in the street. Its emptiness on a Sunday morning seemed unnatural. Alex parked her car in the driveway and looked into the rearview mirror. Two lone television crews waited in silent vigil. Taking a deep breath, she walked up to the two-story, Spanish style house.

The door opened before Alex had a chance to knock. Pop looked awful. The tall black man seemed to have aged ten years overnight. Alex noticed the shadows under his bloodshot eyes, the gray pallor of his skin.

"Pop, what happened?" she asked, following him into the living room. She'd asked herself that same question over and over since picking up the phone an hour earlier.

"They killed him. Oh, they say the shooting was an accident. The officer told me Brian was caught in the line of fire. That don't mean nothing."

Brian's father walked to the window and looked across the street. "Vultures. They won't leave us alone," he murmured, referring to the waiting reporters.

"Where's Nanna?" she questioned. Alex walked with him into the family room and then upstairs. She heard the sound of weeping even before arriving at Brian's old bedroom. Nanna sat at Brian's desk, holding her head. She looked pale and fragile sitting hunched over the small desk.

"Nanna?" she called out softly.

"Alex, have you come to see Brian?" the woman responded in a singsong manner. Without responding, Alex turned and went back out into the hallway.

"Has she slept?" she asked Brian's father.

"No."

"Eaten anything?"

"She won't leave his room."

"Pop, get me a glass of water."

When he came back, she took the glass and entered Brian's old bedroom.

Taking a seat beside her on the bed, Alex softly called out, "Nanna?"

"Hmm." She continued to sit there staring at the wall.

It broke Alex's heart to see the beautiful woman to whom laughter came so naturally so stricken with grief. "Nanna, why don't you take a drink?" Alex enticed, extending the glass of water.

"No, thank you, baby. I ain't thirsty."

"Nanna, can you take these pills for me, please?" Alex cajoled.

She looked up and her watery brown eyes focused on Alex's face. "Brian's not coming home anymore," she moaned.

Alex opened her hand. "I know. But I need you to take these pills, Nanna."

"I want my baby boy."

Alex's heart sputtered at the grief in the woman's voice. Yet she pushed it aside and dropped the pills into Nanna's palms. Nothing could heal a wound caused by death, but sleep, however temporary, would help. Alex cleared her throat and said firmly, "Nanna, take these pills."

She placed the glass into Nanna's trembling hand and kept eye contact as she placed the two sleeping pills in her mouth and drank. Alex placed the empty glass on the desk and pulled Nanna into her arms. Brian's mother laid her head against Alex's shoulder and the wetness of her tears seeped through Alex's shirt.

Twenty minutes later, Nanna's tears diminished and her sobs subsided as the sleeping pills began to take effect. Alex stood up and motioned to Pop, who stood hovering in the doorway. Together they settled her into the master bedroom.

"So sleepy. Gotta wait for Brian to come home," Nanna whispered.

"I'll wait for him," Alex promised, bending down to brush a kiss on the woman's brow. "Go to sleep."

Alex saw the tears glisten in Pop's eyes as he tucked his wife into bed. She turned and stepped out into the hallway, unable to watch such an intimate moment. When he tiptoed out of the room, Alex closed the door. Doing what she did best, Alex took control of the situation. "Pop have you eaten anything?"

"I don't remember."

"Why don't we go into the kitchen and I'll fix you something."

Alex dug through the refrigerator and threw together a couple of sandwiches and placed the plate and a glass of water in front of Pop. She could hear the sound of birds through the window and it reminded her of Brian's whistle. She pushed her own plate away and put words to the questions that had been in her mind.

"Pop, what happened?"

"The car Brian was in was pulled over for speeding. It turned out that the car had been reported stolen. The officer and his partner called for backup and approached." He paused for a moment, his eyes drifting to the right. "A witness said that Brian exited from the backseat with his hands up. Then all hell broke loose. The woman said that the men in the front seat fired first. Brian was hit. The unidentified men fled the scene. Both the officer and Brian were dead when the backup arrived."

Pop slammed his hand down on the table. "The news picked it up off the police radio. They're saying that my son was mixed up with drugs, but Brian couldn't stand the stuff. You know that."

"I know." She walled off the part of her that wanted to grieve. It would do no one any good if she lost control; grief had two sides and Alex preferred feeling the anger instead of the tears.

"Do the police know who shot Brian?"

"They told me they had to do some kind of test."

Ballistics, she thought. "Did they give you any information about the identities of the men Brian was riding with?"

"The witness could only say that they were two white males."

"Did they find the car?"

"They found it burning near the docks."

Suddenly Pop's grief transformed to anger as he raised his clenched fists and shouted. "Why my son? How many black men are they gonna kill?"

The minute Pop said that, Alex took a deep breath. She had to get him calmed down before the boys arrived. Brian was…had been everyone's favorite and his older brothers if left unchecked could make a bad situation worse.

"Pop, your son wasn't the only one to die. Whoever those men were in the car killed a policeman. They may have killed Brian too."

"Why?" he asked. That one word seemed to have been torn from a place deep within his soul.

"I don't know." She shook her head. "But you've got to get some control. Not for me but for Nanna and for Anthony and Marcus. They've lost their little brother. There's no telling what they might do, Pop."

He nodded his head and stared down at the table.

"Have you started the funeral arrangements?" she asked gently.

"Willy will take care of everything."

She stood up from the table. "I'll go to the airport. Why don't you get some sleep?"

He shook his head. "I can't sleep."

"Pop, you're exhausted. Go lie down, please. Just do this one thing for me."

He pushed the chair back from the table and stood. Alex picked up the spare key from the mantel and locked the door as she left.

The hotel room was generic, sterile, impersonal, smelling of cigarette smoke, antiseptic, and blood. Jarick had watched stone-faced as his associate of five years labored to take his last breath. Less than two hours after the gunshot pierced his chest, blood filled Ivanov's lungs. And between one breath and the next, the Russian went from life to death.

Although casualties were always a possibility for men in his line of work, this time, Jarick's mistake had cost Ivanov his life. The consequences of the man's death weighed on him yet he could do nothing.

"I am my brother's keeper," Banovic announced with his fingers together as if in prayer.

But Jarick knew for a fact that his boss was a devout atheist. A chill spread down his spine at his boss's murmured words. Stevan Banovic stood close to the door, staring down at the corpse on the concrete floor as he murmured in Russian. All the planning and calculated enticements, only to have failed at this crucial juncture, Jarick thought.

"Did you get it?" Banovic questioned, finally asking the question Jarick had been dreading. Logic told him that his chance of survival after revealing that he'd failed in his mission was dismal.

"Scott wouldn't talk," Jarick replied. He met Banovic's icy glare and watched the man's lips disappear into a thin line. His boss seemed to stare through him with a look suggesting that Jarick might soon join Ivanov in death.

"You searched him?"

Jarick nodded. "He didn't have the disk with him."

"You blundered, Jarick." Banovic's voice was colorless.

Jarick took a deep breath and managed a seemingly nonchalant shrug. "He changed his mind. We were not prepared."

"Prepared?" Banovic mocked. "You would not have been pulled over if you had not panicked."

"He threatened to go to the authorities," Jarick tried to explain.

"For what? He had no evidence against us. The police pulled you over for speeding, you fool."

Banovic took a step forward and grabbed Jarick by the throat. His fingers locked like a vise and started to tighten. "You killed a policeman. You know that in America you never kill the police or children. There'll be a manhunt."

"They were taking Scott," Jarick managed to gasp and the fingers loosened slightly.

"Does that matter to me now? Scott's dead and we don't have what we came for."

Just as black dots floated in front of Jarick's eyes, Banovic let go. Jarick took two deep breaths and rushed out the words, "Cutter left a message. Scott contacted the FBI and gave them your name. He planned to take the money and flee the country."

Within the space of a breath the rage drained out of Banovic's predatory eyes. "We must move quickly. The deaths were a mistake. Dispose of Ivanko's body and make sure it is not discovered. Search Scott's apartment. I want you to get into his finances and find out everything you can about his last movements."

Banovic paused. "Five years, Jarick. I've waited five years to take my vengeance. Do not fail me again."

Jarick nodded violently, feeling a bead of sweat trickle down his back. "I will bring you the disk."

Banovic turned to leave and stopped at the door. "I will be waiting."

Barely suppressing a shudder, Jarick eyed Ivanov's lifeless face with something close to envy. He feared his boss. If Jarick failed again, Banovic would drag out his death for day for days, weeks.

He leaned over and began wrapping the stiff body in the hotel sheets. First, he would take care of his old comrade and then he would find the disk. It was the only thing keeping him alive.

SEVEN

Xian looked out his window towards the bridge, watching a helicopter weave its way between skyscrapers before heading out over the bay. His office was on the sixty-second story of the Bay Tower, affording him a priceless view of the San Francisco skyline.

Running his fingers through his hair, he turned around and leaned back. Xian glanced briefly at the mounted flat screen on the wall where stock market, financial industry information, and news headlines from around the world scrolled.

The office was like its counterpart across the entranceway: a room designed to display power and command respect from visitors and employees alike. With leather chairs and sleek chrome, it was the modern office set for the technology age.

Inexplicably his thoughts turned to Shay-Lin. He closed his eyes and pictured her face. His brow wrinkled when her image, which used to come so readily to his mind blurred. He opened his eyes and reached into his desk drawer for their wedding picture.

The woman in the photo, young and dressed in a gold embroidered red Chinese matrimonial robe, was smiling brightly. Xian's fingertips traced the cold glass, trying to remember the warmth of his dead wife's skin, the sound of her voice.

"You should be here, Shay-Lin. This was our dream. You wanted to leave Hong Kong and start a new life here in America. You should not have been the one to leave our son behind," he murmured.

The intercom interrupted his thought. "Sir, you have Mr. Calloway on the line."

"Take a message, Nancy. I'm out for the rest of the day."

He laid the picture gently back into the drawer and closed it. The photograph that in the past had always given him some measure of solace had failed to work its magic. Right then he needed something to touch, to feel. What he needed, Xian concluded, was his son.

He rose to his feet, picked up his briefcase, swung his suit jacket over his shoulder, and left the office. After reaching the exit to the outdoor parking garage, the warm breeze and open sidewalks illuminated by the afternoon sun cheered him. Xian could never go back to Hong Kong as his parents wished. He wouldn't betray his wife's dying wish by raising Chou amongst the congested sprawl of high rises, office buildings, department stores, and crowded streets.

Thirty minutes later, Xian parked his car next to the school, let down the window, and turned off the motor. Leaning back in the BMW's leather seat, he loosened his tie and glanced into the rearview mirror just in time to see a station wagon pull up behind him. He turned his attention back to the front. The school reminded him of something, more like someone. A corner of his lip inched upwards. He had not forgotten Alex Thompson. Xian shifted in his seat as the remembrance of her eyes stirred the embers of sexual desire.

At exactly three P.M., the school bell rang and moments later he watched as students began to trickle out of the elementary school building, threading between cars and waiting buses. Xian saw his son amble down the stairs looking for the familiar green Volvo Mrs. Lee drove. He beeped his horn and waved, watching closely as puzzlement and surprise slipped across Chou's face. After Chou got into the backseat of the car and fastened his seatbelt, he pulled off.

"How was school?" he asked.

"Okay," Chou answered, somewhat slowly. "Where's Mrs. Lee? Is she sick?"

"No." Xian glanced into the rearview mirror. "I just wanted to spend some time with you."

Xian drove in silence, unsure of his destination. Chou's next question caused him to narrowly miss running a red light.

"Did you have a funeral for Mom?"

"Of course, why do you ask?"

"The substitute teacher for Ms. Thompson said that she wasn't going to be in class because she had to go to a funeral."

Chou's question settled the destination. When the light turned green, Xian turned left and headed towards the southern edge of the city. He glanced at his son; Chou sat rigid in the seat, staring straight ahead. When his son finally glanced his way, Xian was not surprised by sight of his son's frown. He seemed so much older than his ten years.

"Do you miss her?" Chou's tone seemed to change the question into more of a challenge than an inquiry.

Xian paused before answering, "Every day."

"I don't remember her," Chou replied.

Xian pulled into the temple parking lot and shut off the engine. He placed his hands on the steering wheel and sighed. *How do I handle this?*

Instead of dwelling on the question, he opened the car door and got out, immediately going over to open Chou's door. When he held out his hand to his son, he noticed that it shook. The moment Chou reached and grabbed it, Xian's heart skipped a beat.

Together they walked over to the side entrance of the temple. He pushed against the heavy wooden door and it swung back to reveal a walled garden. Shay-Lin had loved to garden and he'd anonymously donated the funds necessary to have the addition built at the temple.

Xian held on to Chou's hand and led him down the stone path towards a gurgling pond. Choosing a bench that faced east, away from the sun, they took a seat. For a moment, they both sat silently gazing at the water lilies and lotus blossoms that graced the small pond.

Chou was the first to speak. "Why did she die?"

"I can't answer that." Xian faltered for a moment unable to find the right words. "We all leave this life, Son. Some people leave earlier than others. I don't know why your mother was taken from us. But if there is one thing that you should know it's that your mother loved us."

Xian kept his face turned toward the pond. His voice was a mere whisper. "You were her heart. She didn't want to leave us, Chou. She wanted to live and see you grow into a young man, go to school, and marry. She wanted to be surrounded by family and grandchildren."

It was as though the blinders had been taken off his eyes. For the first time Xian understood that Chou's greatest fear was that time would erase his mother's memory. His next words were for them both. "She has never left us. She will always be with us because she loved you too much to simply let go. She's in your heart, in your laugh, your reflection. She is with you always. You are so much like my Shay-Lin."

Sitting with Chou under the setting sun and surrounded by the quietness of the garden, Xian resurrected the ghosts and memories of his former life and laid them bare before his son.

In her black dress and sunglasses, Alex stood under a cloudless blue sky with her eyes focused on Brian's closed coffin. Nature in her strict impartiality had chosen to blanket California with perfect weather. Nature's gift went unnoticed, though, by those crowded into the small cemetery. Grief lay cold and heavy on the hearts of those gathered to say their good-byes to a child dying before his parents.

She shifted her attention to the black-robed preacher as he stood to speak his final words. Alex hated funerals. She had watched as her mother's ashes were given to the East China Sea. Surrounded by her brothers in arms, she'd wept invisible tears as her father was buried at Arlington. She felt again the strength of Khan's fingers as they squeezed her hand. Her former DELTA teammate was someone who had always been there when she needed him.

On this occasion, the funeral home had set up a large canopy for the coffin and flowers and Brian's family sat close to the coffin. Alex had been pressured by Nanna and Pop to sit with them, but her protests won out. She stood as far back as possible, but still she heard the sobs of Brian's mother and aunts under the deep voice of the preacher. As she looked at the dark brown coffin surrounded by yellow carnations and chrysanthemums, the preacher's voice rose over the chirping of the birds. "Grieve not my friends, for Brian is resting in a better place."

When the last words were spoken and flowers were placed on top of the mahogany coffin, she saw Nanna fall to her knees and sob with loud ragged breaths. Alex tightened her grip on her purse; there was nothing she could do. Nothing she could say to ease the mother's pain. Because death had taken the most important people in Alex's life, leaving behind memories and regret, Alex knew the Scott family's loss. It would never go away. They would have to learn to live with it. Wake in the morning and move on.

Alex walked slowly down the grassy slope towards her car.

"Alex, wait up," Anthony, Brian's oldest, brother shouted.

"We need to talk. Can I get a ride back to the house with you?"

She had been trying to avoid this conversation since picking up the two brothers at the airport two days earlier.

Turning she squinted into the bright sunlight. Tony was dressed in a dark suit, silver necktie, and Italian leather shoes. He had worn his sunglasses throughout the funeral. Now he took them off to rub his eyes and Alex was shocked to see his face up close. His normally light brown eyes were red and hollow.

"Of course."

He followed her to the Jetta, opened the door to the passenger side, and folded his tall body into the car. Then cranking the car, Alex let all the windows down. Once she got on the highway, Alex took a second to glance over at her passenger. Tony had leaned back in the seat and his eyes were closed. He was just as she remembered him. Tall, dark, handsome and threatening.

Their first meeting had not gone well. An influential record producer on the East Coast, Tony had flown in for an album release party. He'd been under the false assumption that she was some groupie. After Brian pulled his older brother out of the swimming pool Alex had thrown him into, they had come to a very clear understanding.

Tony was the first to break the silence in the car. "What went wrong? One minute I get a call from my little brother and he's talking about buying a house and getting married. The next minute, he's talking about making it big and leaving the country. Now he's dead."

Alex concentrated on driving. "I don't know, Tony."

"What happened between the two of you?"

"That's personal and you know it."

"You're right but I need some answers."

"Well, I don't have any to give," she snapped. Anger crept out of the tight rein she'd kept on her emotions.

"Damn. This shit will never end. Cops trying to kill every black man in the States. I expect this back in Jersey, but this is getting old."

"A cop died too this time. You're not the only one who lost a brother," Alex pointed out.

"Yeah, next you gonna tell me he was in the wrong place at the wrong time."

Alex aimed a sideways glance at Tony in time to see the muscle twitch in his jaw.

"Bullshit. They saw a black man and they shot him. That cop got shot because he was stupid. He didn't think that his own kind would take him out."

She shook her head as her fingers tightened on the leather-encased steering wheel. "Tony, you're going after the wrong people. What if it wasn't the cops who shot Brian?"

"What?"

The idea had come to her last night. "Brian was in the car with two unidentified white males. Who were they? Why was Brian in the car with them and what was so important that they would shoot at police officers?"

Alex pulled the car in front of the Scotts' home and turned off the engine. They were the first to arrive. She sat back and breathed in the fresh air.

"I don't know much, but I know this. My little brother shouldn't be lying in the grave and his killers won't go unpunished."

A chill of foreboding crossed her skin. This was bad. She placed a firm hand on his shoulder. "Tony, the last thing your mother needs is to worry about you doing something stupid. Let me handle this."

He shook off her hand. "Alex, no offense but this is family."

"Don't give me that. Brian was my friend and we might have been married if things had played out differently. If anyone has the right to the truth, it's me. Your family needs you to keep a cool head, so just let me start asking questions."

A breeze played in her hair as Alex watched the convoy of cars and people arrive at the house.

"Promise me you'll find out who did this," Tony asked.

"I give you my word." In the military, death rarely came as a surprise. Civilians never glimpsed the random violence of war, but the families of dead soldiers suffered with haunting questions about how their loved ones died. Alex would spare Brian's family that burden.

They both got out of the car and joined the line of family and friends in the house.

After spending hours helping in the kitchen, Alex finally escaped to Brian's bedroom. Picking up the phone, she searched through the phone book and dialed the number for the West End police station.

"Police department."

"Officer McNeal, please."

"Hold on."

Her eyes wandered over the immaculate bedroom, studying the pictures of various basketball players decorating the walls. A wave of sadness washed over her at the thought of Brian lying in the cold ground.

"McNeal here."

"Matt, it's Alex Thompson."

"*Sensei*, what can I do for you?"

"I need your help." Alex could hear raised voices in the background.

"Okay, what can I do for you?"

Alex held the phone tighter. "Five days ago there was a shootout. A police officer and a civilian were discovered dead at the scene. The civilian's name was Brian Scott and I need to know what really happened. Can you get me a copy of the file?"

He whistled. "That's some favor."

"I know." She paused. "I wouldn't ask if it wasn't important."

"I can't make any promises," he said slowly.

"I wasn't expecting any."

"What's your home address?" he asked.

"It's 41 Morningside Lane." She looked down at the old Macintosh computer that sat on the corner of the desk. It had been one of Brian's greatest treasures.

"Will you be there later tonight?"

"I'll be there."

"I'll see what I can do."

"McNeal."

"Yeah?"

"Thank you."

Alex hung up the phone and turned to see Tony standing in the doorway. Without a word, she brushed past him and headed downstairs.

EIGHT

Jarick Raekov lowered his gaze and examined the strategically placed articles on the coffee table. Photographs, identification, cash, keys, a leather wallet, credit cards, currency, and checkbooks were all important items in the lives of most men but not in his. He fought the urge to sweep his hand over the table and knock everything to the floor.

"What do we know about Scott's last movements?" He turned towards his agent before sitting down in one of the hotel suite's leather armchairs.

"One week before scheduled delivery, Scott gave a presentation to the SimTek board announcing the creation of a new firewall security system, went to dinner at his usual restaurant, and visited his parents."

Peder continued, "However, two days before our meeting he paid a visit to his private banker and closed all of his accounts. All monies were wired out to another bank. Anton is attempting to trace the fund transfers."

Jarick looked over to the computer expert. Anton's wire-framed glasses were barely visible over the laptop's flat screen monitor.

"Go on." He turned his hard gaze back to his second-in-command. Peder's impervious expression had taken on a pinched look. The tall, heavily built Ukrainian stood with his back straight and his feet together. Jarick recognized the posture all too well. Once Soviet military, always Soviet military, he thought.

"Scott closed his credit card accounts, purchased luggage, and then airplane tickets to Brazil. All transactions were paid for in cash. We found the receipts, along with the other documents, while conducting a search of his apartment."

"What about the disk?"

Peder shook his head. "Nothing. We searched it from top to bottom. His home computer had been wiped of all data."

Jarick's muscled jaw clenched. Every time he thought of how things had gone wrong, he wanted to pick up a gun and shoot something or someone. He wanted to pretend for one moment that Brian Scott was still alive.

If he had to suffer Banovic's torture, then at least he should have had the satisfaction of killing Scott himself. Even dead, the bastard could cost him his sanity as well as his life.

He reached over and stuck his hand into a bag of items they had taken from Brian's apartment. He picked up one of the U.S. passports, flipped it open, and scanned it. The smiling image of an African-

American woman stared back at him. "Who is this Susan Taylor?"

Anton spoke up for the first time. "Susan Taylor doesn't exist. The passport is a very good fake. The woman's real name is Alexandra Thompson."

Jarick moved to stand next to Peder and looked down at the spread of pictures taken at Scott's funeral. His eyes zeroed in on the African-American woman standing at the edge of the crowd. The woman in the black and white close-up could have been a fashion model. She was tall and slender with sculpted features and straight black hair. "Tell me about her," he ordered.

"She was his fiancée."

Jarick slowly turned to face the new voice and raised a heavy eyebrow. "So you have deemed to speak?"

Vlad took a step closer to him. The brawny Lithuanian had more muscles than brains. He'd heard that Vlad had killed four Chechen rebels with his bare hands. He possessed something that money could not buy: loyalty. The ex-mercenary would not only kill for Banovic, he would die for him and that was the only explanation for his presence on his team. But for all his experience, they were in the current situation because of Ivanov's reckless driving.

"Before I had nothing to say." Vlad gave a small shrug and moved to stand across from them at the table.

"How did you come by the information about the woman?"

"I took her photo to the funeral director." Vlad's lips curled with scorn. "All I had to do was show the man some money and he was quick to tell me what he knew."

Although he wanted to smash a fist into the other man's face, Jarick simply tapped his finger against the table, "Could Scott have spoken with her about the disk?"

Vlad gave a small nod. "It is always a possibility. Men talk from the cradle to the grave. They cry to their mothers when they are boys and lie to their women as they push between their legs. Maybe Scott talked, maybe he didn't, but she was his fiancée so it is not without possibility."

Annoyed by Vlad's attitude, Jarick sharply demanded, "What else have you found out about Ms. Thompson?"

"Only that we may have a larger problem on our hands."

In a rare display of emotion, Jarick swore. The situation seemed to be deteriorating before his eyes.

"Here." Vlad carelessly handed over a thin folder.

Jarick flipped open the file, read through it, and then looked up. The single sheet of paper listed very few details: date of birth, education, family, current address, and occupation.

"Where's the rest?" He tossed the file on the table. There seemed to be a six-year gap between her graduation from college and entering teaching.

"That's it. The last record shows that she was a civilian consultant for the military." Vlad frowned. "Her personnel files are confidential. I've contacted our people on the inside, but I doubt we'll find anything."

Jarick took a deep breath as acid began to move up his throat. He turned away from Vlad and towards the dark-haired Russian programmer typing on the laptop. "Anton, have you tracked down the money yet?"

"I'm working on it." Anton looked up briefly before returning his attention to the computer screen.

Jarick touched the bruised skin on his neck before leaning over and whispering in his comrade's ear, "Work harder."

NINE

Alex's desk was covered with wildflowers and daffodils when she walked into the classroom the next morning. It seemed that each one of her students had gone out of their way to let her know she had been missed. The unexpected delivery of beautiful white orchids surprised her the most.

I am sorry for your loss. Xian Liu.

The bold script made more of an impression than she cared to admit. It would do little good to deny that she dreamed of him. She felt her cheeks go warm at the thought. She rarely remembered her dreams when she woke in the morning. But this time, she could recall in vivid detail the touch of his fingers against her skin, the masculine scent of his cologne, the taste of his kiss. She took a deep, calming breath and banished the thoughts from her mind.

When lunchtime rolled around, Alex found she had little appetite. From her seat at a picnic table, she scanned the playground. The laughter and shouts of the children drifted over on the light breeze.

"Mind if I sit down?"

Alex shielded her eyes from the glare of the early afternoon sunlight before nodding at the man who stood on the opposite side of the wooden table. "Not at all."

"My name's Scott. I'm filling in for Mrs. Myles." After taking a seat on the opposite bench, the stranger held out his hand and she shook it. His grip was strong and steady.

"Is Isabella okay?" she asked.

He smiled and tilted his head to the side. "She's fine. Her father had an accident and she went home to help out."

Scott had a perfect disguise. With brown hair held in place with mousse and brown eyes, he would have blended in anywhere in America. He wore brown khakis and a white button- down shirt. Only a pair of thin wire glasses differentiated him from another other white male.

Alex was startled from her thoughts by his next comment.

"I'm sorry, I didn't get your name."

She met his hazel green eyes with a practiced smile. She hadn't given it. The habit of never giving out information was a carry-over from her old life in the military. "I apologize. Alex Thompson, fourth grade reading teacher."

He leaned in closer and his expression changed from polite curiosity to concern. "I met the young woman who was substituting for you earlier this week. I'm sorry about the death in your family."

"Thank you," she said, putting the remains of her lunch back in the brown paper bag. Judging by the increased activity of the other teachers, lunchtime was near its end.

"If you want to talk about it, I'd be happy to listen." He was staring at her with a charming smile, a smile she distrusted.

"I appreciate the offer," she returned with a polite upturn of her lips. "I'll keep it in mind."

She stood and picked up her bag just as the bell rang signaling the end of the break period. Without saying good-bye, she walked towards the entrance of the brick school building with the sun blazing on her back, joining in with the group of students hurrying inside.

Later, after school ended and her last class walked out the door, Alex paused from erasing the whiteboard and turned towards her only remaining student.

"Chou, can you wait a minute?"

She pulled out a Kleenex and wiped her hands before approaching the young boy.

"Yes, Ms. Thompson?"

"Could you give your father a message for me?"

"Sure."

"Please tell him thank you for the lovely flowers."

Chou smiled and Alex felt an unexpected answering warmth. Her fondness for him had turned into something that she couldn't banish.

"You liked them?"

"Yes, I did."

He paused, glancing back and forth between her and the flowers. "I helped pick them out."

"Then no wonder I like them so much," she chuckled. "You have excellent taste in flowers, young man."

She watched a small blush spread over his face before he looked down. "Now you'd better get a move on. I'll see you tomorrow."

An hour later after a slow drive through rush-hour traffic, Alex pulled off the note tacked to the inner door of the dojo and read Sensei's elegantly drawn Japanese script. *I will return shortly.*

She opened the door and stepped into the empty room. She was late arriving. Alex crossed the room, quickly entering into the dressing room to change. Afterwards, dressed in the cottony soft uniform, she stood in the middle of the room and began her stretching exercise and progressed into a series of kicks, punches, and blocks. As she mechanically continued the practiced movements, she closed her eyes. Memories colored sepia with a decade of time moved through her mind like pictures on a reel.

First Alex saw herself as a young girl standing by the sea. Instead of paying attention to another one of her father's lessons, she stared down at her left hand, fascinated by the red blood that had welled from the cut caused by the seashell. She looked up to see her father's brown eyes.

"It hurts, Father," she said.

"Pain is a part of life, Alex," he answered. "One day you'll grow numb to it."

In the next image she moved through a village strewn with dead bodies. The area reeked of death and rot. Alex carried her gun in front of her, as did the others, but those responsible were gone. The villagers had been killed because they had refused to gather the poppies. Her squad couldn't make war to avenge the dead nor protect the cartel's next victims.

Finally, she saw the face of the young Columbian gunman, his eyes wide with surprise that his bullet had not struck her down. Alex saw herself pull the trigger and watch him die.

The sound of the gong as it struck the eighth time brought her back to herself. Alex was drenched in sweat and breathing heavily.

She opened her eyes to see *Sensei* staring at her. She bowed, "*Iterashai*." Welcome back.

"I am sorry for your loss."

His words almost undid her. History was once again repeating itself. This time it was *Sensei*; last time it had been Khan, her DELTA teammate, who had spoken those exact words. She took a deep breath and pushed the pain aside.

"*Arigato.*" Thank you.

"I have prepared tea. Would you like to join me?" he asked.

"I would like that very much." She followed him into the kitchen. The last time *Sensai* had asked that question, Alex had been in physical pain. This time, however, it was mental. Not all the green tea in the world could erase her memories of death.

The next night, Alex pulled into the driveway of her home at about 9:00 P.M. Having spent the entire Saturday leading self-defense sessions at the local community college, she was so tired that she parked her car in the garage before she took notice of the dark maroon Mustang parked on the street out front. She unlocked the garage door and entered the kitchen. Hearing masculine laughter and not wanting to interrupt her roommate and her guest, she headed for the back stairs. But as soon as her foot hit the first step, she heard Karen call out.

"Alex, come into the living room, you've got company."

"Damn," she muttered. Dropping her purse on the side table, she entered the living room to see Karen sitting next to Officer McNeal on the couch. Karen stood up with her coffee mug.

"Welcome home. Matt was just telling me about the beating you gave his squad."

"I gave her the *Cliff Notes* version," he nodded.

Alex smiled. "Don't believe a word he says."

Karen stood. "Are you okay?" Her eyes filled with concern.

"I'm fine," Alex replied.

"I'm going to get finished packing for my trip. Let me know if want to talk," her roommate instructed softly as she hugged her.

"Thanks, K."

"Nice to meet you, Matt."

"You too, Karen. Good night."

Matt broke the silence. "I got a copy of the file you asked for."

Relief poured over her. "Thank you."

"I've got to warn you. As soon as I finished the download, the file was blocked."

"Why?"

"I did some more digging. It looks like the case has been taken over by the Feds."

Alex was puzzled. "Why would the FBI be getting involved with a local homicide?"

"I don't know, but whatever the reason, everything about the shooting has been hushed up."

She rubbed her temples, trying to get rid of her tiredness.

"Can we look at it in the kitchen? I need some coffee."

"Are you sure you want to look at this tonight? The photos aren't pretty."

Part of her wanted to say no. That same part also wanted to run and hide under the covers. But Alex knew that reality and its coldness would never allow her a warm peace. She urged Matt to follow her into the kitchen. Taking out a cup from the cabinet, she poured a cup of coffee and added cream and sugar.

Matt laid the file on the table and Alex moved to open it. She stared down at the pictures. It wasn't as if the faces of the dead surprised her. She had seen death before. In the military, she'd pulled the trigger, set the explosive, thrown the knife. But this time was different. Seeing Brian's motionless body with his blood trickling into the street shook her. Alex paged through the color printouts, stopping at the autopsy and ballistics report. Ten minutes later as she finished the file, she looked up at Matt, her expression serious.

"Did you read this?"

He nodded his head.

"Tell me this isn't true," she said.

"I'm afraid it is. A stray bullet didn't kill Brian Scott nor did the officers on duty. The coroner concluded from the size and location of the entry wound that it was precise and deliberate. Alex, the bullet wasn't police issue, so the conclusion is that someone in the car with your friend pulled the trigger."

She tapped her finger on the table. "His death wasn't an accident; it was murder."

"And there isn't a damn thing the police can do about it," he added.

"What?" Alex asked.

"What I said earlier is true. The FBI has taken over the case. They yanked some high official's chain. My district chief is pissed. One of our own is dead, and he's been shut out."

She watched his fingers tighten around the coffee cup.

After a moment of silence, Matt asked, "Was your friend involved with anything illegal?"

She shook her head. "No way."

"Are you sure?"

"Yes," she answered firmly.

Alex was reaching to close the folder when a sudden high-pitched beep caused her to jump.

"My pager," Matt explained, then dug down into his pocket. "Can I use your phone?"

"Sure."

He hung up the phone after five minutes. "I've gotta go. This information is confidential. If this gets out I could lose my shield."

"Don't worry, Matt. This stays between you and me."

Alex woke the next morning to the sound of the phone ringing. As she picked up the receiver, she looked at the LED readout on the alarm clock:

5:15 A.M. She put her ear to the phone and could hear the sound of loud voices in the background.

"Hello?"

"Niña."

"Rafé?" Alex sat up, pushing her hair out of her eyes. "What's wrong?" He never called when he was on a mission.

"Nothing. I just called to check on you. Are you well?"

She cradled the phone all the more tightly. "I should be asking you that question but I'm fine."

"Good. I know about your Brian's death. Stay out of it. Do you hear me? Do not get involved."

"Yes, sir," she agreed automatically. The lie slid smoothly from her lips. She did not need Rafé to worry about her while on a mission.

"I will be back soon. We must talk." Alex heard a click and then there was silence.

She hung up the phone and got out of bed to start her morning stretches. Sitting on the carpeted floor, she closed her eyes and tried to find her center. It should have been quiet blankness. Instead, Alex found her mind filled with images of Brian laughing, then his body pooled in blood.

Marry me, Lee. She saw his light brown eyes as he knelt in the warm sand.

Toss the ball, Lee. Alex saw Brian wide open, positioned to take a three-point shot. Tears formed in the back of her throat and she pushed them back. Brian still existed like a ghost in the back of her mind. When order returned to her thoughts and breathing became easier, Alex opened her eyes, looking upon daybreak with a renewed resolve. The time had come for her to exorcise his ghost, find his killer.

TEN

Xian Liu was careful not to reach for his son's hand as they neared the entrance to one of the area's newest Asian eateries. Earlier that morning he'd made the mistake of taking Chou's hand as they walked through the shopping atrium's parking lot. His son's look of embarrassment, together with his repeated attempts to pull away, had been all it took for Xian to get the message.

As they waited for a table to clear, Xian took in the diverse clientele of the affluent Fremont neighborhood. The bright colors and rhythmic music of the restaurant lent a relaxed atmosphere. Normally, Xian wore slacks on weekends, but this morning he'd dressed casually. It was cool for early May, and windy, so he wore jeans with a turtleneck sweater. Having spent Saturday morning combing through the shopping center, both he and Chou were more than ready to eat.

Following the young waitress past the waterfall and pond in the center of the restaurant, Xian watched his son's eyes open in amazement at the sight of the large goldfish. Xian's lips curled at the corners, remembering the first time he'd seen such large koi.

After the waitress brought their drinks and took their orders, Xian sat back and asked, "Since we've had so much fun today, why don't we get up early tomorrow and I'll take you to school? We could have breakfast at the pancake shop."

Chou looked up from his book. "I don't have to go to school tomorrow."

"You don't?"

"Dad," Chou sighed.

Xian had to smile at the tone of his voice. "Yes?" He took a sip of pearl tea. It had been too long since he'd enjoyed the sweet Taiwanese drink served with a fat straw and chewy tapioca beads at the bottom.

"It's Parents Day. We get to stay home and you have to go to school and meet my teachers."

"Oh." Xian nodded. The smile dropped as he looked down, trying to recall if or when he'd heard of that event. Over the last week, he'd made a concerted effort to be more involved in his son's life. The fact that he'd missed something that important only made him more determined to further trim his workload and spend more time at home.

"The note's on the refrigerator," Chou supplied.

Xian shifted in his chair before asking, "Any plans for the day off?"

Chou took a bite of the turnip cake. "Michael Younas is having a pizza party. If it's okay with you, I can have Mrs. Lee take me."

"Are Michael's parents going to be there?"

"Yes. May I go?"

"Only if you have all your homework done and your room clean."

Chou's round face lit up with a smile. "Okay." He put his arms on the table and rested his chin in his hands. "You don't have to meet with all my teachers."

"Well then, which ones do I have to meet with?"

"Just Ms. Thompson."

"And why is that?"

"Because she's the only cool teacher I've got."

Xian raised an eyebrow and struggled to hide a grin. "Really?"

"Yeah." Chou sipped his drink and then said, "She's nice and she's got a black belt in karate."

"Is that why you like her so much?"

"No," Chou replied solemnly. "She makes both of us smile."

Xian caught his son's choice of words and he wanted to ask more but the food arrived and all conversation ceased.

Thinking of Alex, Xian paused before picking up the pair of wooden chopsticks. Somehow, even though it had been days since he'd laid eyes on Chou's reading teacher, he could still picture her nimble fingers wrapped around the chopsticks, her dark eyes fanned by midnight lashes. As his body tightened with the direction of his thoughts, Xian vowed that it would be an appointment he wouldn't miss.

The next day Xian sat in a leather chair in the conference room with his fingers steepled atop the table.

"We should make a bid." Carter Wallace's harsh Brooklyn accent was blatantly at odds with his California tan. "The stock's going to even out by the end of the week."

"The company's knee deep in scandal and heavy on technology risk. We can find something better," Don replied.

Xian sat forward and picked up his pen. Usually Monday mornings began and ended with scheduled teleconference calls and meetings; this hastily called meeting had thrown off his schedule. "Name a better target." His voice was even.

"I need more time," Don stalled.

"You always need more time. That's one commodity that we don't have. Either we move or we'll lose out, just like last time," Carter retorted.

Xian was careful to keep his expression unchanged. His ex-boss had taught him well about the dangers of mixing emotion with business. Irritation ran through him, yet none of it showed on his face. They had been going back and forth on the subject since the start of the eight o'clock meeting.

"You know what? Why don't we talk about last time, Carter?" Don interjected. "If we'd bought your little pet project, we'd have been sucked into the largest patent infringement lawsuit in the country."

Xian suppressed the urge to smile, and then sat back in his seat before speaking. "Give me the selling points, Carter. Why SimTek and why now?"

"Because of this man, his ideas and the infrastructure he built." Carter reached into his black portfolio, drew out two sheets of paper, and handed one to Xian and one to Don.

It took Xian only a moment to scan through the press release. "What am I missing? If this is true, SimTek's stock should be selling through the roof instead of sitting on the floor."

"The man behind the creation of the attack and defense system, Brian Scott, died a few weeks ago."

"And what connection does this have to the company's stock performance?"

"Apparently Mr. Scott not only resigned before his death but he also took the program with him. The CEO is under fire to step down and the analysts are out for blood."

Xian chewed on the idea. It was probably a waste of cash if the company's goodwill couldn't be redeemed. He had fought too long and too hard to gain the industry analysts' confidence to let it slip away on a lost cause. His eyes hardened as he stared at the glossy photo of the confident-looking executive.

"Well?" Carter prompted.

"Not enough," he responded impatiently.

"What about this? The research and development team and the hardware alone are reason enough to buy them. SimTek has one of the most powerful systems in the world. The brainpower by itself could turn us a profit if we spun off the division."

"Where did you get all this information?" Don asked.

"I checked out the annual report and hired someone to get a list of the employees," Carter replied. "Almost eighty-five percent of the technology staff is MIT or Cal Tech. Well worth their weight in gold."

"What's to guarantee they won't leave the company?" Xian questioned.

"Contracts, stock options, heavy compensation packages, and pride. I've got their psyche profiles. These scientists built those systems and they've got a lot of autonomy. It would take those brain trusts years and millions to build another setup."

Maybe… Xian's eyes narrowed. It would be a risk. "Carter, you start the ball rolling. Don, you take lead on structuring the deal. I want Bentsen's signoff and a copy of the file on my desk in two hours."

"That's not enough time," Carter interjected.

"Pull any resources you may need," he called out over his shoulder. "I've got another meeting that I do not intend to miss," he said while striding though the double glass doors.

"Beth is a very good reader and if all goes well, I'll be recommending that she be placed in an advanced reading group next year." Alex stood and beamed at the young couple seated at the round conference table. Many school teachers conducted the conferences from behind their large desks while parents were seated in their child's miniature elementary school desk. Alex had learned early on that by sitting at her desk, she'd not only unintentionally distance herself from the parents but also make some of them anxious or fearful about meeting with her, a key authority figure in their child's life.

A polite request to the school janitor had provided a quick solution. Using a conference table and chairs for both herself and parents helped put parents at ease. And she was sure that this pregnant mother was more than relieved to discover that she wouldn't have to squeeze into a small desk.

Alex smiled as the husband assisted his wife to her feet. This was one of the easiest teacher's conferences she'd had today.

"Thank you. Thank you very much. Beth will be so excited." Mrs. Stewart smiled proudly.

Alex felt the pinch of envy. The other woman's skin glowed; her green eyes sparkled. Even her hair seemed to radiate health. She smiled back. "You will have to work with her to help her keep up," she warned gently.

"No problem." Mr. Stewart held out his hand and Alex shook it. "Thanks again, Ms. Thompson."

She had to stifle the urge to correct the man. She invited all of her students' parents to call her Alex, but for some reason it never happened. The ingrained habit of calling teachers by their last names, she guessed. Then again, it had taken her three months after she'd been discharged from the military to address her father as something other than Colonel Thompson.

After Alex escorted the young couple to the door, she walked over and looked out the window. A small sigh of relief escaped her lips. She'd dodged bullets in dark alleys, traversed swamps in the dead of night. At one point the danger and fear of warfare was all that felt normal to her. But this... She exhaled sharply. She'd never get over the nervousness of meeting her students' parents.

Many times the twenty minutes to one hour conference went smoothly. However, today had been more trying than most. The sight of Cs and Bs marching across their child's card caused the smiles of parents to turn into looks of dismay and bewilderment. And then a bit of anger. From that point there would be a tug of war between Alex and the parents. She would try to bring the focus of the conversation back to the child as the parents blamed each other about the quality of their child's schoolwork or the fact that one of them hadn't spent enough time double checking homework.

She could feel a knot of tension low in the back of her neck. Reaching up, she pulled her hair over her shoulder and began to massage her neck, then stretched her arms towards the ceiling. Moments later, the hair on the back of her neck rose and she had the prickly feeling of being watched. When she turned towards the door, the sight of her visitor set off a round of butterflies in her stomach.

With his coat swung over his shoulder and brief-case in the other hand, Xian Liu bore no resemblance to the man she'd met two weeks past. Her trained eyes took in everything from the brown leather shoes, the well-cut pants, to the loosened cobalt tie. She noted the perfect cut of his hair, the expensive Rolex on his left wrist, and the beginnings of a three o'clock shadow.

"Sorry, I'm late."

Before stepping forward, Alex smoothed back her hair and gave him the warm smile she'd given all of the parents, gesturing for him to enter the room. Then she looked down at her watch; it was only three minutes past the hour.

"Not a problem. I'm glad you could come," she said, remembering her irritation when she'd received a note that he would be unable to attend the fall teacher's conference. It wasn't the fact that he'd been unable to attend; no, it was that she'd waited over a half hour for him to show up.

When he stood three feet from her, she fought the sudden urge to drop her gaze. The scrutiny of his look was a touch unnerving. Instead, she moved towards her desk and delicately fingered one of the still fresh white orchids. "Mr. Liu—"

"I think I remember asking that you call me Xian."

Alex nodded slightly. "Xian, before we start I'd just like to thank you for the flowers."

"You're welcome. Chou and I enjoyed picking them out." He flashed a white smile and she felt the prickle of goose bumps at his low, British-accented English.

"Shall we get started?" Alex stepped over to the round table and took a seat.

Unintentionally, she peeked up at him from underneath her long eyelashes. Something seemed to move in the air between them, cling to her skin and pull her towards the source: Xian. She wanted to believe that it was simple attraction, but it wasn't. Whatever it was that heightened her senses and caused things to grow warm and tight in her body was something that she couldn't name or classify. And the one thing she'd learned was that the unknown could cause a mission to fail or get you killed.

Needing to focus on the present situation, she opened her notebook and reached for a pen.

"Busy day?" he guessed.

"Pretty much," she said lightly before handing him a sample of Chou's most recent homework assignment and his report card. "You're my last parent."

"Really?" He smiled.

"Yes." She glanced at him and then away.

"That's perfect," he replied in a pleased voice.

"Why do you say that?" Alex sat back in her chair as Xian leaned forward over the table.

"Because I was hoping that we could continue this conference at a late lunch. If it's okay with you, how about we secure a table at nearby restaurant and finish this conversation over some good food?"

She opened her mouth to decline but the words didn't come out. The thought of getting out of the classroom and taking in the fresh air and sunshine with Xian was vastly more appealing than the alternative of eating one of the granola bars lying in her desk drawer.

"I imagine that you've been in this room all day?" he guessed rather accurately.

She let out a small laugh. "You would be right."

"The weather is beautiful today."

A teasing smile sprang to her lips as she toyed with her pen. "And how would you know this if you've been in meetings all day long?"

Xian laid his hands flat on the table. "I caught about thirty minutes of sun as I drove over."

"Hmm." She put down the pen, sat back and crossed her arms.

"What do you say, Alex? We talk here in this room listening to the growls of my empty stomach or talk on a restaurant patio over lunch."

Just then her stomach gave an answering growl. She sneaked a side glance at Xian before gathering her notebook and papers. "I need a minute to freshen up. I'll meet you outside."

She watched him nod before picking up his briefcase and jacket. "I'll be there."

She waited until she was sure Xian was down the hallway before opening her drawer and pulling out the disposable cell phone she'd brought from home. Technology cut both ways and while she could communicate with anyone in the world with the small device in her hand, it could also be used to track every move she made. Just as she'd expected, the small envelope appeared after she pressed the power key. Only two of the four battery bars remained, but it was enough to retrieve her voicemail.

The smile that had graced her lips fell away after she finished listening and deleted the message. Instead of making things clearer, Joe had only made them more difficult. The former marine turned private investigator had come up empty. All primary electronic data linked to Brian Scott had been erased, emptied, or closed: bank accounts, credit cards, work history, education, and biographical information. Alex hit the power button, turning the phone off, and made a mental note to charge the phone.

Putting everything in her bag, she shook her head and looked down at her watch. In less than five minutes, she would be joining Xian Liu for lunch. Maybe hunger was making her lightheaded, because common sense kept telling her to stay away. Something she couldn't understand pulled at her, intrigued her about the man with the dark eyes and quiet son.

It had taken Xian only a couple of minutes to reserve a table at the small, popular local eatery, but he knew it would take him much longer to figure out why he had asked Alex to lunch. Xian looked up at the clear sky and then leaned back against the side of his BMW. The weather was without a doubt beautiful, but when he looked over towards the opening doors, the woman who started walking in his direction was even lovelier.

Dressed in a casual peasant blouse and gypsy skirt, she could have been a model on a runway displaying *haute couture*. From behind mirrored sunglasses, he appraised her as she strode confidently toward him.

What had started out as mild curiosity had begun to turn into something more, something that made him want to know more about Alex Thompson.

"Together or separate?" He straightened and prepared to open the passenger side door of his BMW.

"If it's okay with you, I'll follow you to the restaurant."

Xian nodded and got into his car. After the short drive to the restaurant, he escorted her inside and ever the gentleman, pulled out her chair. When the waiter finished pouring water, Xian ordered a bottle of wine. Then a buzzing silence seemed to settle over their table. Anticipation, Xian thought. "So how long have you been a teacher, Alex?"

He watched as she touched the water glass to her lips and took a sip before answering. He noticed that her fingers bore no ring. Actually, she wore no jewelry at all, but the lack of a ring pleased him immensely.

"A little over two years," she replied smoothly.

He looked over his menu quickly and then turned his attention back to his lunch companion. He tried to gauge her age but failed. If he looked only at her face with its long angles and smooth skin stretched taunt over her cheeks, then he would put her fresh out of school. But the confidence of her gaze and the maturity of her aura told him that she was much wiser and older than her appearance.

Xian took a moment to loosen his tie before asking, "Do you enjoy it?"

Her lips inched upwards. "Of course."

"Even when they fail to attend your lesson?"

"Speaking of inattendance…"

He could have cursed as the relaxed atmosphere quickly dissipated.

"Hold that thought," he interrupted and then raised a finger to signal to the waiter that they were ready to place their orders.

After the waiter delivered the red wine and took their orders, Xian moved to pour Alex a drink even as he watched her arch her eyebrows.

"I'm not sure wine is appropriate," she commented.

He finished pouring her a glass of wine and replied smoothly, "All work and no play makes…"

"Me a very good teacher," Alex finished.

"Of course," he readily agreed. "But the sun is shining, the food is cooking and we're not at the office...or at school," he added.

He deliberately picked up her wine glass, held it only inches from her mouth. As he waited, he found himself wanting to kiss her. "Come on, indulge a little, Alex. I won't tell."

"You're a very determined man." She raised her wine glass to take a sip of the Chianti. "I can see where Chou gets a lot of his stubbornness from."

Xian laughed for the first time in a long time and it felt good. He also noted that he liked her voice. "My son likes you a lot...and seeing you as you are now, I understand."

He watched as she went still and then sat back from the table. "Xian, I'm still concerned about Chou. He's shown remarkable progress since we last talked, but I still feel he needs special attention."

He leaned in closer and caught the scent of her perfume. Jasmine, soft and sensual. "I don't understand. What exactly do you mean?"

"Before I came to your house, Chou did not participate in class unless asked. It was as though he had consciously chosen to withdraw."

"This behavior is still happening since our last conversation?"

He watched as her hands came to rest on the table. "Yes. Chou has come a long way in the past few weeks but I still think that he can go further. I hope that between the two of us we can keep this improvement going."

The conversation lapsed into silence as the waiter brought out their orders and arranged the food-laden plates on the table.

Xian took a bite of his pasta before speaking. "Alex, Chou's mother died when he was very young. I have tried to raise my son alone. Our move to a new country and environment has upset him more than I realized. My son suffers from the loss of his mother."

She placed her knife and fork down, and then delicately wiped her lips. "What's done is done. What matters now is that you've recognized the issue and that you concentrate on the solution. Chou is a wonderfully intelligent boy and I have enjoyed having him in my class. If you read some of his essays, you'll see that he loves you a great deal. I just think that he would like to spend more time with you. I only wanted to help the night I came to your house."

Xian smoothly sliced through a large meatball and took a bite. "And I thank you for your kindness. You have helped me see the error of my ways. For that, I am in your debt. I appreciate your concern, but please do not trouble yourself further," he replied coldly.

Even though he recognized the truth, her hint that he had failed his son stung and the only response he could muster was to strike back. And in that second, he would have given half his fortune to take back his words as he watched Alex's eyes darken with hurt.

Again, silence reigned at their table and Xian let it. If there was one thing he disliked, it was making an apology.

He had almost finished the meal when he looked up at the sound of Alex's chair moving. His eyes narrowed as she reached into her bag. "All right. I've prepared a package of information for you, including a copy of Chou's grades and the class syllabus. If you have any questions, please email or call." Her tone was businesslike and abrupt.

She gathered her things, placed money on the table, and then stood up. "Thank you for lunch." Her voice could have frozen a volcano.

Without a backward glance, she strode away, seemingly oblivious to the stares of the other restaurant patrons.

As Xian reached out to pick up the wine glass, he hesitated.

I just think that he would like to spend more time with you.

The melodic sound of her voice echoed in his head.

He thought about his endless pursuit to build East International, the challenge of corporate politics, the seduction of money and power.

I only wanted to help.

Again, he saw the flash of hurt in the teacher's eyes as he'd reminded her of her place. He rubbed his brow; the enormity of his behavior staggered him.

He had just brushed off the woman who had given him back his son. Xian muttered an oath as he dug into his wallet and pulled out a fifty-dollar bill.

Shay-Lin had always reminded him of the gentler ways of the world. It seemed as though he would never learn. Dropping the money on the table, he stood and started walking towards the exit to the parking lot. Perhaps he could still redeem himself and wipe away the damage he had caused.

ELEVEN

The smell of cooking greeted Alex as she stepped through the front door. Dropping her bag by the door, she slipped off her shoes and headed towards the kitchen. Leaning against the doorway, she watched as her roommate opened the oven.

"Hi," Alex called, out taking a deep breath as the smell of cornbread filled the room.

"Welcome home, stranger," Karen said.

"Stranger?" Alex echoed. "You have got to be kidding. This from the woman who hold more frequent flyer memberships than anyone alive?" Alex joked.

She watched as Karen turned around and took off her oven mitt. "How are you holding up?" she asked.

"I'm fine."

"You sure?"

"Yeah."

"I'm worried about you. After you and Brian broke up, you kind of buried yourself in your work or in karate. I know his death hit you pretty hard."

"*His murder*," she wanted to say but held her tongue. "What can I say? I like my kids." She tried to move away from the topic.

"I know you love your job, but girlfriend, you're young and single. Life is too short to mess around."

Alex thought back to Brian's unexpected death. "You're right. But isn't that like the pot calling the kettle black?"

"Nope, I've met someone. I'm just biding my time until he comes to his senses."

Alex closed the fridge after grabbing a soda. "Oh do tell."

Karen shook her head. "It's a little touch and go right now. I promised not to tell anyone until after I've talked with my mom and dad."

She whistled. "This sounds serious, roommate. Have I met the guy?"

"I just met him," Karen answered evasively.

Alex took a drink, allowing the subject to drop and watched as Karen began to hum as she stirred the pot of beans and rice. She smiled a sad smile as she pondered how she could have overlooked the fact that her friend had fallen in love.

"Alex?" Karen asked.

"Hmm."

"I really think that it's time you got out more."

Alex wondered where this conversation was leading. "All right."

"Seriously." Karen waved the wooden spoon. "Just have a little fun. Lord knows you deserve it."

"I agree with you," Alex replied. She needed some sort of distraction. After leaving Xian at the restaurant, she'd driven home wondering how she'd managed to ruin lunch. She shouldn't have left but she couldn't have stayed.

"Great. Then we're on for eight tomorrow night."

"What?" she questioned.

"A bunch of us from the office are getting together for drinks. You should come."

"Oh now I get it. You want to go out and drink and need me to be the designated driver."

"Not true." She paused. "Well, I'll need a ride home."

Maybe, Alex thought. But she had one other thing she had to do first. "How about I meet you at the club? I've got an appointment in the early evening."

"You're not just trying to get out of this, are you?"

Alex scooted back in her chair and didn't have to wait long for the cat to jump into her lap. Gently scratching between Shadow's ears, she looked at her roommate and smiled. "No, just give me the name and address and I'll be there dressed to kill."

That next evening, Alex didn't have to lie, cheat, or steal to get into Brian's apartment building. All she had to do was walk through the door and aim an innocent smile at the concierge as her shoes echoed on the marble floors of the elegantly decorated lobby. The luxury high-rise housed businessmen, foreign dignitaries and wealthy socialites, yet its management ran a security based on appearance. And quite simply,

Alex in a tight silver dress that hugged her generous curves looked the part.

When the elevator stopped at the thirty-second floor, she stepped out into the empty hallway with the small leather case of lock picks in her gloved hand.

Her footsteps were muted by the thick Oriental runners that lay over the taupe carpet. She glanced at the mahogany doors lining the cream-colored walls as she stopped in front of Brian's apartment. She dropped her purse as a precaution.

If anyone came out it would look as though she had dropped her purse and was in the process of gathering her belongings. Taking a quick look back at the elevator bank, Alex unzipped the leather case, took out her lock picks, and set to work. Less than a minute later, she picked up her purse and pushed the door open.

Once she was in the apartment with the door locked behind her, Alex turned on her flashlight, scanned the room, and saw that she was too late. Rugs lay at odd angles, the sofa sat in the middle of the floor, African ornaments layplaced haphazardly on the coffee table, and all the paintings were off center.

Brian had been a perfectionist in work and in his personal life. Whoever had searched the apartment had been less than perfect in disguising their search.

Skirting the furniture, she made her way through the living room and walked down the hallway to the study. A half hour later, she sat on the edge of Brian's bed staring out the balcony doors. She'd searched the apartment from top to bottom and still had no clues that would help her figure out why he'd been killed. All of his files, computer equipment, anything that could have given insight into his life, were gone. Nothing of Brian remained except for the pictures.

Aiming the narrow beam on the bedside table, she reached over and ran her leather-covered fingers over the glass frame which housed a photo of the two of them on the beach. In his left hand was a beach ball and his right arm was wrapped around her waist. They both were laughing into the camera.

Frustrated, she gathered her things and just as she stood up from the bed, she heard the sound of a door opening. Letting out a whispered curse that would have done her ex-DELTA commander proud, Alex killed the flashlight, grabbed her small purse, and then slipped quietly out onto the empty balcony. Taking care to close the glass door, she moved to the side of the wall and pressed her back against the cool concrete.

In the silence of the night, she slowed her breathing and concentrated on the shimmering lights of the San Francisco Bay area. If she turned her head to the left, she could see the Bay Bridge in the distance. Suddenly the bedroom light was turned on and light spilled onto the balcony.

As the search moved to the bedside table closest to the balcony doors, she caught bits and pieces of a one-sided conversation. Although she could see nothing but the bottom of the man's pants legs, she recognized the uniform FBI leather shoes. Her jaw tightened as she sought a plausible explanation for her presence should the visitor decide to step out onto the balcony. It didn't happen.

After waiting outside in the cool night air for over half hour, she cautiously entered the darkened bedroom. The lingering smell of aftershave hung in the room. Crouched on the side of the bed, she listened. Hearing no sounds, she turned on her penlight and aimed it about the room.

The floor was littered with clothes and the contents of the drawers. Yet it was what she didn't see that caught her attention: The framed photos on Brian's bedside tables were gone. Removing her shoes, she took her small dagger out of her purse before moving into the hallway.

Using the narrow beam of the flashlight, Alex threaded her way through the scattered pillows and broken knickknacks to the front door.

After slipping on her shoes and running her fingers through her thick hair, Alex listened at the door before stepping into the hallway and shutting the door firmly behind her. She took off her gloves and stuffed them back into her purse.

A chance stop by the police, a shoot-out leaving two people dead, two unidentified suspects, an FBI investigation, and two separate searches of Brian's apartment. She shook her head. Things just didn't add up.

It was obvious they were looking for something. As she pressed the elevator button, Alex spared one last look at the empty hallway. Whatever Brian was involved in had gotten him killed. Now all she had to do was find out what that something was and why someone had killed for it.

Twenty minutes later, Alex and Karen stood inside Envy, one of the city's trendiest dance clubs. The new owners had renovated an old office building so that there were three floors with a circular stairway connecting each level. The main dance section on the first floor was the size of a basketball court but now it stood half-empty. After making their way up the stairway, Alex and Karen found an empty table in the second floor lounge.

Studio lights pulsed to the music and Alex watched the deejay booth from their table by the railing.

"I'll grab the first round of drinks," Karen said before leaving the table. A few minutes later, her roommate returned with drinks in hand. "What's this?" Alex sniffed the brown beverage.

"Mine's a diet Coke. I got you a Long Island iced tea. The bartender told me it's his personal specialty." She grinned mysteriously.

Alex eyed the full glass before taking a sip. She found the taste fruity and sweet and it warmed her throat on the way down.

"Do you like it?" Karen asked.

"Tastes good."

They sat chatting about the weather until a nice looking black man approached the table and asked Karen for a dance.

"Go," Alex urged.

"Are you sure?"

"Yes, I'll finish my drink and join you downstairs."

"Okay."

"Have fun!" she called out to Karen's departing back.

She returned to sipping the tea, glad to have a moment alone. About three-fourths of the way through the glass, she felt more mellow and relaxed.

"Would you like to dance?" came a slightly accented Latin voice.

Startled, Alex looked up. He was gorgeous. His straight black hair was beginning to lighten with silver. His chiseled face was smooth and colored by a natural tan. He reminded her of Rafé except this man's eyes were open and admiring. She lifted her hand and rose to accompany him downstairs.

He placed his hand on her hip and then leaned in close to her ear.

"My name's Omar."

"I'm Alex."

"Alex, what a beautiful name for a beautiful woman."

"Thank you," she replied graciously. Charm seemed to ooze out of his pores, but she wouldn't fall under its spell. When she felt his fingers massage the nape of her neck, she barely suppressed the urge to pull away. She was relieved when the tempo of the music sped up. Pulling back, she put distance between herself and her dance partner. She caught sight of her roommate dancing with a new admirer as she looked around.

She danced until she began to feel the soft buzz of the alcohol wearing off, leaving her sleepy. After three more songs, she bid her partner good-bye. As she turned to leave the dance floor, a hand clamped down on her shoulder.

"Excuse me," she said, turning. The man was tall and muscular with his white blonde hair cut short and square. Alex looked unto his eyes and tensed. Blue, they were cold as ice, reminding her of her first sergeant in Bosnia.

"I would like to talk with you."

She heard his heavily accented voice over the music. When she tried to pull away, he refused to let go of her arm.

"Take your hand off my arm," she said slowly.

Either he ignored her or didn't hear her. It didn't matter to her. Taking her right hand, Alex grabbed his left pinkie finger and bent backward with all her strength. At the same time, she swung her knee to get in a swift hard jab to the groin area.

Alex moved out of the way as the man dropped to the floor groaning. From her peripheral vision, she could see the bouncers moving in from the outside of the dance floor.

"What happened?"

She turned to see Karen's worried face. "He wouldn't take no for an answer." Her voice was matter-of-fact.

"You want to go home?"

"Yes."

"Alright, let's go," Karen said. Walking towards the exit, Alex took one last look over her shoulder at the bouncers as they carried the moaning man away.

The sight of the unfamiliar car parked in front of the house set off alarm bells in her head.

"Do you recognize that car?" she asked Karen.

"No." Karen paused. "And I don't recognize him either."

Alex tensed as their car came to a stop. A man stood up from the stairs of her front porch and moved towards the street. She breathed a sigh of relief as his face came into view.

"Who is he?" Karen hesitated before unlocking the car doors.

"Brian's brother, Tony," Alex answered.

She stepped out of the car and moved towards the house, keeping her face deliberately blank as she locked eyes with the tall, well-dressed man.

"Tony, what are you doing here?"

"Hoping you'd live up to your promise," he responded. "But I can see that you've got more important things to do than find out why my baby brother was killed."

His eyes raked over her from head to toe.

Alex held his eyes, unaffected by the scorn she saw in their depths. Under the yellow glow of the street lamps, she could see Brian in Tony's face: anger and betrayal.

Karen moved between the two of them. "Back off! She's suffered just like you, damn it. I forced Alex to go out with me tonight."

Alex stared at her roommate in amazement. She'd never heard her raise her voice. Her soft-spoken best friend seemed to have lost her laid-back, rhythmic Caribbean accent.

"Karen, it's okay," she said firmly, then took a breath of cool air. The scent of damp grass blanketed her senses. "Tony's just emotional right now."

It was a plausible excuse, but she knew that it was only half the truth. As she stood facing Tony, she saw the gleam in his eyes. The promise he'd accused her of breaking was only part of his anger; jealousy was the other.

"Why don't we go inside? I could use some coffee," she suggested with a casualness she didn't feel.

Tony had loved Brian more than she'd thought it possible to love a sibling. She knew by the set of his shoulders and the outline of the gun she saw on his back that Tony didn't just want information, he wanted payback. A verse sprang to her mind: *Vengeance is mine so saith the Lord*. She just hoped she could convince Tony of that.

The next afternoon as Alex's last class settled down and silently read the first chapter of their homework assignment, someone tapped on the door. She looked up from her work and saw Assistant Principal Monroe's face through the glass panel.

"Excuse me. I have to step out for a minute. Please continue your reading."

She left the room but kept the door slightly ajar just in case.

Alex noticed Assistant Principal Monroe's wrinkled brow and pinched mouth. The fifty-year-old woman never seemed to smile and treated school more like a military training camp than an elementary school.

"Ms. Thompson, these gentlemen would like to speak with you." Her tone dripped with irritation.

Alex had seen the two suit clad men standing near the lockers immediately upon entering the hallway. Out of the corner of her eye, she'd checked them out. Black leather shoes and dark gray suits. It took her only a half a second to recognize the preferred dress of the FBI.

Keeping her face blank, she turned to greet them. "Hello. What can I do for you?" she smiled.

"Ms. Thompson, I'm agent Phillip Murray and my partner here is Bill Patterson. We're with the FBI." They flashed their badges.

Alex allowed a curious expression to creep over her face.

"Ms. Thompson, do you recognize this man?"

She focused on the picture of Brian on the cover of *Technology Today* magazine.

"It's Brian."

"What was your relationship with Mr. Scott?"

"We were engaged but things didn't work out," she answered.

"Did you stay in touch after the breakup?"

"Yes, we *did*," she responded, emphasizing the past tense.

"How long had you known Mr. Scott?"

"Two years."

"You knew him pretty well then."

"Is there a point to this? If not, I have a class to teach," she answered coolly.

"We just have a couple more questions." The agent looked up from his notes, and then continued. "Did Brian mention anything about an important project he was working on?

"No."

"Anything about special meetings?"

"No."

"Did he confide in you about any new business associates?"

Alex shook her head. "Brian disliked talking about his work."

"Did you notice any changes in Brian's behavior prior to his death?"

"Not really," Alex lied as her mind flashed back to the last conversation she'd had with Brian. Only after the fact had she realized that he was planning to leave the country and to go into hiding. "Look Agent…"

"Murray." He gave her a practiced smile.

"I'm sorry but I can't help you. Brian never liked to talk about his work."

"Were you aware that Mr. Scott was planning on resigning from SimTek?"

"Resigning?" she said blankly. Agent Murray's brow creased and his eyes bore into her face.

"Mr. Scott handed in a letter of resignation the morning of his death."

Alex frowned. Why would Brian resign? He'd just been promoted. "I was not aware of that."

"He was leaving the country."

Having noticed the way the agent studied her face, she schooled her features to show confusion. "What?"

Agent Murphy continued, "The detectives found evidence that he had purchased two tickets to Brazil. We believe one ticket was meant for you. I take it he didn't happen to mention that he was planning for the two of you to leave the country?"

"No," she lied easily. "Can I ask you a question, Agent Ramsey?"

"Yes, you may." He placed the small notebook in the inside pocket of his jacket.

"What happened the night Brian was shot? Why are the FBI and not the police investigating his death?"

"Ms. Thompson, we believe that Mr. Scott may have been the target of an international terrorist group. We also think he was being kidnapped when the police interfered and accidentally shot him."

Her voice rose with disbelief. "Why would anyone want to kidnap Brian?"

"Your fiancé was not only a very high profile business executive but also a computer genius. There are those who valued his skills highly. What we need to know is if he ever mentioned any special meetings, contacts, or events to you."

Alex shook her head again and hid her face from the agents. She knew from the ballistics report that the bullet that had killed Brian had not been police issue.

"If you remember anything you think might be of help, please give me a call. Here's my card."

Alex pocketed the business card and turned to go into the classroom. Out of the corner of her eye, she caught Agent Ramsey's searching stare. A niggling sense of unease followed her back into class. Somehow, she had the feeling she would be seeing the agents again.

Jarick stared out of the tinted car windows of the white Mercedes at the carefree scene. Elementary school students had begun to pour out of the school only moments before.

"Tell me again," he demanded without taking his eyes off a little blonde girl as she rushed to meet her mother.

"She left the school at 3:30 P.M. and returned to her home. At 7:00 P.M., she entered Mr. Scott's apartment building. One hour and thirty minutes later, she left the building and proceeded to meet her roommate at a nightclub called Envy."

"Could she have found the Mirror Code?" he questioned. *The disk.* The mere thought of it increased the acid churning in his stomach. Usually he didn't dream but last night, he'd had a vision of his own death.

Gritting his teeth, he turned towards the other occupant of the car. Peder was clad in all black with a leather coat. Even in the mild climate, the Russian seemed to carry the harsh cold of Siberia with him.

"No, if the disk had been in the apartment, either our team or the FBI would have found it."

"Then why was she in the apartment?" Jarik asked that question more to himself than to his agent. Something about the woman haunted him. Alex Thompson. There was a missing piece somewhere and he had a gut feeling that she was the link to what he needed.

"I do not know. After leaving Scott's apartment, we followed her to that nightclub. Vlad went inside; I watched from the car. After two hours, she returned home."

Jarik's eyes narrowed as his mind raced. "What about Scott's parents?"

Peder shook his head. "We have not been able to perform a search of the house. It has been under twenty-four hour observation by the FBI."

Jarik turned back towards the now vacant entrance of the school building. He was running out of time and options. Banovic would be distracted only for a short time. "Work the girl first and if she doesn't know about the disk, she'll have to help us find it."

TWELVE

The clock on her nightstand read 12:47 A.M. With a sigh of impatience, Alex got out of bed, pulled on her robe, and headed to the kitchen. If she couldn't sleep, then there was no use tossing and turning. From past experience, she knew action was the best relief for insomnia.

After brewing a pot of coffee, she went downstairs into the basement. It was the one room that she'd refused to change after her father's death. An antique Japanese writing table stood between two lace-covered French doors that led out to the back garden. Her parents' wedding picture stood a lonely vigil underneath the small brass reading lamp.

A beige sofa faced two comfortable leather chairs that her father had bought in Germany. He had spent months completing his study. She imagined him building the in-wall bookshelves, running the wiring for the lights, and organizing his book collection. Alex knew every inch of the room and sometimes she imagined that she could smell the sweet tobacco of the colonel's pipe.

Shaking her head, she turned to the right, pulled out the chair and took a seat at the desk. She needed to find out what was going on in Brian's life before his murder. Alex switched on the computer and sat back. Brian didn't gamble, didn't take drugs, or drink alcohol. According to his parents, Brian's behavior hadn't changed in the weeks before his death. And that left her with only one other possibility: work.

She went online and began with the *San Francisco Chronicle*, searching for information on SimTek, between May 10th when she'd last spoken to him and May 25th. Finding little information, she continued digging through the archive. The only mention of SimTek came with the retraction of an earlier press release related to a break-through security program. Alex noted the incident, then logged off the public internet. It took her a moment to enter the proper identification to log onto one of the military's secure connections. Putting her fingers to the keyboard, Alex sent out a priority-encrypted message. It was time to call in some favors. If she could get the blueprints for SimTek tonight, then tomorrow she'd be one step closer to figuring out who or what she was dealing with.

As the sunlight began to creep through the blinds the next morning, she set the blueprints and diagrams aside, sat back, and rubbed her dry eyes.

"Good ole, Roderick," she muttered sarcastically. Logging off the computer, she flexed her shoulders and rolled her head forward and backwards to loosen the tight muscles in her neck. The ex-CIA turned multimillionaire security consultant had done his job all too well. Although it was possible for her to enter Brian's office at night, it would take time and resources, neither of which she could spare.

Alex grabbed her coffee cup, went upstairs, and padded into the kitchen. Ignoring the twinge of pain in her back, she poured a cup of last night's coffee. She needed to get into Brian's office. The only question was how and when. As her mind examined the situation from different angles, her eyes fell on a brochure left on the kitchen table. Putting her cup on the counter, she walked over and flipped it open.

Refresh A Day Spa, one of San Francisco's top personal spas had sent Karen a catalogue of their new all-day aromatherapy and Thai massage treatments. As she looked at the first page, which was completely devoted to all-day relaxation and beauty packages, her mind pulled up an image of Gretchen, Brian's executive assistant. She'd met her twice, the first time at a company dinner party and the next at Brian's birthday celebration.

The stylish older woman would never be able to resist the opportunity for a full day of pampering. With her mind busy formulating a plan of action, Alex automatically poured her coffee in the sink, put the cup in the dishwasher, picked up the spa brochure and headed back downstairs.

As the yellow-orange rays of sunlight began to break through the clouds on Saturday morning, Alex looked into her rearview. With her hair pulled back into a ponytail and thin wire framed eyeglasses, she looked the part of a computer technician. After checking her watch, she reached over to the passenger seat, picked up her computer satchel, pulled the door handle, and got out of the car.

As Alex's footsteps echoed in the empty parking garage, she paid special attention to the movement of the security cameras and remaining cars. It seemed that she wouldn't be the only one working on Saturday.

Promptly at 9:00 A.M., she pressed Gretchen's smart chip badge against the door panel and walked though the silver-frosted glass sliding doors.

"Good morning." Waving her badge in the security guard's direction, she aimed a sleepy smile at the uniformed guard.

"Good morning," the man glanced at her then looked downward at the monitors.

Having memorized the blueprints, she bypassed the first bank of elevators and went to the second set furthest to the right. For a second time, she pressed the smart chip laden card against the sensor panel and entered the elevator bank. She stepped into the express elevator, pressed her badge onto a second panel and then selected the executive floor.

As the lift shot upwards, she loosened her grip on her satchel. The prep work for her mission had taken two days. She'd spent half of one night outside of Gretchen's two-story townhouse waiting for the traffic to die down. Once she was sure that she wouldn't be seen, Alex had used a flashlight to peep through the window of Gretchen's car. She figured that Gretchen, like many others, habitually left her badge in the car so as not to forget it. Sure enough, Gretchen's SimTek badge stuck out from the in-dash compartment. Next, Alex had written down the vehicle registration number and left. The next day, she'd emailed the V.I.N number to Roderick and that afternoon FEDEX had delivered a package to the school containing a key to Gretchen's car.

When Gretchen arrived at the luxury spa, Alex had been waiting. She was in and out of the woman's vehicle in less that a minute. If all went according to plan, Alex would return the badge later that afternoon.

Stepping out of the elevator, Alex scanned the empty floor noting the lack of security cameras. Recalling the schematics from Roderick's blueprints, she turned to the left and headed in the direction of Brian's office. After making two turns, she came to a stop in the doorway. This was the place where he'd spent most of his waking moments. Her eyes went straight to his desk and her heart lurched. Alongside a picture of his family sat her picture. Drawing a deep breath, Alex walked over and pushed back the chair. Placing her satchel on the floor, she pulled out a screwdriver and got to work removing the computer's casing. Taking little time, she disconnected the computer's hard drive and inserted it in a special case before putting it into her satchel.

Once she finished replacing the computer's cover, she left the room and moved to the glass cubicle opposite Brian's old office. Gretchen's desk was in perfect order. She pressed the power button on the computer tower and picked the lock on the under-desk file drawers while the machine started up. She methodically paged through folers of expense account reports, travel itineraries, meeting notes, work orders, and other files. When it came time to log onto the system, Alex turned over the keyboard and located Gretchen's password. Brian always joked that security was the worst at his office even though they were the best at protecting their client's data.

She glanced down at her watch: twenty minutes.

She put her hand on the mouse, located the application she needed, and clicked on the calendar and scheduling software. Gretchen had access to the schedules of everyone on the executive floor, but there was only one Alex wanted. It took her two minutes to pull up the schedule of Brian's last weeks at the company. With little time to waste, Alex copied the files and sent them to her email address. Once the transmission was completed, she erased all the session information from the computer so that no one would know of her intrusion.

She had just shut down Gretchen's computer and monitor when she heard voices. Alex put her computer bag on her shoulder, crouched down, and made her way toward the elevator lobby. Her finger had just pressed the call button when a hand landed on her shoulder.

"Where do you think you're going?

"The 37th floor." She gave a timid smile and took a step back. I got off on the wrong floor.

"What's your name?"

"Alex Thompson," she responded while maintaining eye contact.

"Your badge, please," the man's sharp tone brooked no argument.

She took out the modified badge, showed it the thin, gray-haired man. Taking care to keep her expression calm, Alex looked towards the man's left side and noticed the slight tattletale bulge that came from carrying a sidearm. Then she noticed that they both wore earpieces.

"What were you doing on this floor?"

As she heard the multiple chirps that announced the arrival of other elevators, Alex replied coolly. "I just told you. I got off on the wrong floor."

"And what will you be doing on the 37th floor."

Alex locked eyes with the man and kept her tone as neutral as possible. "Installing a CD-ROM drive."

She glanced to the left to see a group of suit-clad businessmen enter the hallway. "Now if you'll excuse me, I have work to do."

"Wait just a minute." For the second time, the man reached out and placed a restraining hand on her arm. She fought the instinctive urge to turn and twist the hand away. "I need to look in that bag."

Alex handed it over. "Be my guest."

"And if you don't mind, my partner will need to pat you down."

Playing her role as the innocent to the hilt, Alex rolled her eyes to the ceiling. "You're kidding, right?"

"No. This is a secure floor and until our investigation is concluded, access is limited. Just cooperate and we'll get you back to what you were doing."

"Is there a problem, gentlemen?" Alex froze at the sound of the familiar voice. Turning completely around, she locked eyes with Xian Liu as he stepped from the elevator. Her pulse sped up as a flash of recognition crossed his face.

"Agent Reynolds and Braden. We're from the National Security Agency," the man replied confirming what Alex had halfway guessed. She stepped back when he took his hand off her arm to reach inside his jacket and take out a leather-covered badge. "Nothing for you to be concerned about, sir. We just need to ask Ms. Thompson a few questions. We instructed building management to make this floor off-limits."

Xian met her hard stare with an equally measuring look. Her cover was a millisecond away from being blown sky high. "Is the young woman attending the meeting?"

"She says she got off on the wrong floor," Reynolds answered.

"I can vouch for that. The elevator was called to this floor. I think you should let her get back to work."

"And who are you?" The taller of the agents turned towards Xian.

"Xian Liu. I'm attending the executive meetings upstairs," he answered. Xian's dark eyes narrowed and the corners of his lips turned upwards in an icy smile.

The announcement knocked Alex off her balance, but she kept her expression blank as he gestured towards the man wearing a pinstriped suit. "Now, if you've finished harassing the staff, I'm sure Mr. Harris over there will direct you to someone better equipped to answer your questions."

Alex turned her attention to the silent NSA agent who was intent on thoroughly searching her bag. "Could I have my bag, please?"

"What's this?"

For a second, Alex's pulse sped as he pulled out the special case holding the hard drive. "That's the CD-ROM drive that I would be installing now if you hadn't delayed me."

He dropped the case back into her bag and roughly tossed the satchel to her. "It's clean."

"If you'll excuse me," Alex nodded slightly and pressed the call button. Thankfully, the elevator doors immediately opened.

"Can you hold that elevator for a moment, please?" Xian called out.

Alex bit the inside of her lip as her carefully laid plan continued to disintegrate right before her eyes. Her mind searched frantically to piece together a plausible explanation for her presence at SimTek.

Xian gestured towards one of the waiting executives. "Dan, why don't you help these gentlemen and then go ahead and get London, Tokyo, and Hong Kong on the conference call. Start negotiations on the integration figures. I'll be back in twenty minutes."

Xian didn't take his eyes off Alex as he entered the elevator. The hair on the back of her neck prickled from the stares of the NSA agents, but she released the door and pressed the button for the 37th floor.

When the elevator stopped, Xian reached out and pressed the close button, then the button for the lobby. "We need to talk."

"I have work to do." She turned to look at him.

"I don't think your boss is going to be upset. It's Saturday, remember? No one in."

"You're here," she pointed out.

He grinned. "Special circumstances."

Xian decided to wait until they were outside of the building before speaking. "Would it be too much to ask why you are here and why those men are so interested in your presence on that floor?"

"Yes, it would." Alex stepped towards her car, only to back up a step as Xian slid past and stood in front of the driver's side door.

"My silence comes at a price, Alex." For the past two days she'd haunted him. And while the question of what she had been doing on the executive floor had yet to be answered, he had something else on his mind.

Her heart went still, then began to beat hard and slow against her rib cage. She didn't like owing him anything, especially since she was still smarting from their last meeting. "And that would be?"

"Dinner at Metrozzo. I'll pick you up 6:00 P.M."

He watched suspicion darken her eyes. "Why?"

"I owe you an apology for my behavior at lunch the other day."

"Apology accepted." She nodded curtly. "Dinner declined. If you'll excuse me, I have to go."

As she reached past him to open the door, Xian took a step to block her. "Your eyes betray you." He moved closer and she held her ground even when part of her wanted to step away.

"What do you mean?" she asked, knowing what he was hinting at.

"When we met for lunch the other day, I was close to being convinced that you didn't feel the attraction flowing between us."

"And now?" she asked.

"Have dinner with me." Neither of them had moved. Xian fought the urge to lift his hand and caress the inviting curve of her neck.

"Can I take a rain check? I'm scheduled to teach a karate class this evening," Alex lied. She'd gotten what she'd come for and now it was time to pay a visit to the salon and return Gretchen's security badge.

The corners of his lips twitched upwards. "Where do you teach?"

"Taga's karate studio."

"What time?"

"Six to seven," she answered quickly.

Xian shrugged his powerful shoulders. "Sounds good. I'll join you. I need a good workout."

THIRTEEN

Xian hit the floor hard after barely managing to dodge Alex's foot. He pushed up and took two steps back while trying to get his breath.

Damn, she's good, he thought as he felt the stab of pain in his shoulder. He wiped away a bead of sweat on his brow.

"Nice move," he commented, adjusting the belt of the borrowed gi.

"Thank you."

"I'm sure your missing class is sorry to have missed this."

Her eyes twinkled with silent amusement. "There never was a class and you know it."

"You're an excellent liar, but there's one thing that gives you away." He grinned.

"Really?" She shrugged her shoulders.

He expected her to ask what that one thing was, but instead Alex gestured for him to step closer. "I think we digress from our purpose here. Care to try that move again?"

"By all means."

Xian raised his arms and stepped towards her cautiously. It had been a long time since he'd underestimated an opponent so badly. He wouldn't make the same mistake again. They hit out against one another, testing each other's skills. Xian wove in and out of Alex's reach, staying on the defensive.

He fell into the rhythm of her movements. "What the—" Before he could blink, Xian felt his legs being kicked right out from under him and he fell back. He had only enough time to relax, lessening the pain of impact with the mat. He looked up to see Alex standing over him. Smirking.

"Need a hand?" she asked.

He quickly reached up and grabbed her hand, but instead of pulling himself up, he pulled her down. Alex's eyes widened and he watched as she curved her body into a ball, preparing to roll away once she hit the mat. But he was faster. Before she could recover, he moved over and covered her body with his own.

Xian looked down at her face. It was fanned by a halo of hair, which had slipped loose. Her dark eyes framed by long curling lashes sparkled. He caught her scent: floral and lush. Instinctively, he loosened his grip on her wrists, aware of their slenderness, and aware too of the rise and fall of her chest, the tension in her body, the growing warmth in his own.

"I believe that this calls for you to say uncle." He grinned at Alex, noticing that she had not broken eye contact for a second.

"Not in this lifetime," she replied.

He felt her relax and then he was on his back looking blankly at the ceiling as he listened to the sound of Alex's departing footsteps.

Later, after they'd both showered and changed clothes, Alex stepped aside as Xian followed her out into the parking lot.

"Goodnight, Xian." Alex reached into her pocket and pulled out the key she needed to lock the studio door. Half of her wanted to return to the mat and continue the game he'd started only minutes before and the other half wanted to curse. She felt more invigorated than she had in months and it was because of him. She could still feel the silkiness of his hair on her fingertips.

"It's still a bit too early to be saying goodnight, Alex."

"What?" Her brow wrinkled as she clutched her gym bag.

"I promised myself that I would see you home."

"Look, Xian…"

He interjected, "I insist, Alex."

Alex rolled her eyes upwards towards the night sky and shrugged her shoulders. A man with a code of honor in San Francisco. As long as he stayed off the subject of her presence at SimTek that morning, everything would be fine, she thought. "Suit yourself."

Sure enough, she saw the silver BMW in her rearview mirror as she pulled into her driveway. Seconds later, adrenaline shot through her as she looked at her house. The front door was slightly ajar. Knowing that her roommate was in New York, Alex walked cautiously up to the front door and slowly pushed it open with her foot.

The downstairs was trashed. Books were strewn on the floor, pots knocked over, lamps broken, everything in disarray.

Alex was startled by Xian's voice. She turned to see that he was standing beside her in the entry of the house. She blinked when she noticed the furry bundle in his arms.

"He was hiding in the bushes. Is he yours?"

"Yes, his name is Shadow." Alex reached out and the cat jumped into her arms.

She watched as Xian pulled out his cell phone. "I'll call the police and check upstairs."

She nodded and began to pick her way through the mess, mentally noting that though it seemed at first senseless, there was a pattern. The sight of the study conformed that it wasn't an ordinary case of vandalism; someone had been looking for something. They had pulled every one of her father's books from the shelves and taken her computer. It had taken her over a year to feel secure in the house and only seconds to rip away the security of the new life she'd hope to create for herself. Shaking her head, Alex went back upstairs; she was in the kitchen when the police arrived.

"Ms. Thompson?"

"Officer." Alex addressed the man in uniform.

"Can you tell us what happened here?"

"I came home and the front door was open. I walked in and found the place like this."

"Does anyone else besides you live in the residence?"

"Yes, my roommate Karen Moore.

"Is Ms. Moore here?"

"No, she's in New York for business this week."

"Looks like they entered through the side window. Anything missing?"

Alex turned to see the second officer enter the kitchen with a pen and pad. "As far as I can tell just my computer, my roommate's computer, stereo equipment, and some other electronics."

"Ms. Thompson, I suggest you call your friend as well as your insurance agent. You shouldn't stay here until everything's fixed. Officer Cole and I will talk to your neighbors, see if they saw anyone suspicious, and then file a report. We'll check the local pawnshops and if anything comes in, we'll let you know. If you discover any additional missing items, please give me a call at the station."

"Thank you, Officers." Alex nodded her head and rubbed the back of her neck. She could feel a headache coming on.

"Is there another phone number where we can contact you should something come up tonight?"

She rattled off the phone number for her regular cell phone, then paused. "Thank you, but I'll be staying…"

"At my home," Xian stepped in. "Here's the phone number. You might want to try it as well."

She watched as he led the officers out of the kitchen. The numbness had begun to wear off by the time he returned.

"What was that about?" she challenged, glaring daggers at him.

"The officer said that you shouldn't stay the night here and I agree. You'll stay at my house. I have plenty of room and Chou will be happy to see you."

"Xian," she struggled to keep her voice flat.

"Yes?" His voice dropped lower, nearly causing Alex to move closer.

"I appreciate your help, but I'm fine. This isn't your problem and I can handle it myself."

"I'm sure you can, but the people who came here probably don't know that."

She tipped her head to the side. "Two days ago, you invited me to lunch. Now you invite me to your house. Why?"

"You have a very suspicious nature for a school teacher."

"And you happen to be extremely pushy, but you didn't answer my question."

To be honest, Xian didn't know how to answer it fully. He wanted to protect her but more than that, he wanted to be close to her. Alex Thompson was a puzzle which kept drawing him back to place the scattered pieces. "I was mistaken in my judgment earlier."

"About?"

"I should not have been so harsh with you before." He fought with the next sentence. "I regret my words. It is difficult for me to share my son. You have helped me regain his love and trust, and I was ungrateful."

"I've already accepted your apology." Alex was taken aback by his answer.

He took a step forward with a half grin forming on his face. "I would like to make amends."

"You don't owe me anything." She adjusted her grip on Shadow as the feline began to purr. "I'm just doing my job."

He tried a different approach. "Would you worry your parents so badly by insisting on staying here alone?"

"My parents are dead." Her voice was even. The words held no power. Time had robbed them of the sting.

"I'm sorry," he apologized.

"It's okay." She mustered up a smile. "I'll walk you out."

Xian raked his fingers through his hair. "Don't be stubborn. If you won't come with me then I'll stay here."

She responded as he'd known she would. "No. You can't stay here."

His mouth quirked. "I'll hold the cat while you pack."

Recognizing the determined glint in his eyes, Alex shrugged her shoulders, handed Shadow over to Xian's waiting hands, then reached into the kitchen drawer and drew out the hotel number of the Grand Hyatt in New York and dialed.

She dialed the phone. "Hyatt Grand Central. How may I direct your call?"

"Karen Stone's room, please."

The phone rang three times before the answering service came on. "Karen, it's Alex. We've had a problem at the house. Someone broke in while I was at out. Among other things, they took your old computer. I'm sure that the homeowner's insurance will cover it. I'm going to be spending the night with a friend. I'll call you again sometime tonight."

Without a word she went upstairs to her room. She pushed back the door and saw her clothes and underwear strewn about on the floor. Whatever it was that they were looking for, they didn't find it. They'd picked the wrong house this time.

"No military secrets or family heirlooms here," she muttered ruefully. She went to her closet and pulled out the stepladder. Reaching back, she moved the panel and breathed a sigh of relief on discovering that her hidden compartment had not been found.

Alex grabbed one of Rafé's presents and carefully replaced the compartment cover. She opened the box on her bed and picked up the semi-automatic, gingerly inserting the clip and checking the safety before placing it in her bag. She threw some clothes and underwear into the duffle, then went into the bathroom to grab some toiletries.

When she returned downstairs, Xian was sweeping up the broken glass. He had covered the broken window with cardboard from a box in the garage. Finished with the sweeping, he walked over to the kitchen countertop and a waiting Shadow jumped into his arms.

"Traitor," Alex muttered under her breath as she grabbed two cans of cat food.

"Did you say something?" He smiled.

"No."

"Ready to go?"

Alex nodded her head and started towards the front door.

"Wait," he said. She stopped in mid-stride and turned back towards Xian.

"What?"

"Why don't we trade? You take the cat. I take the bag."

Even before he finished speaking, Xian was handing the cat over to Alex. She automatically dropped the duffle and cradled a purring Shadow. Without speaking, she turned and picked her way through the hallway. Once outside, she took her time locking the front door and made a mental note to tell Rafé about the effectiveness of the new locks.

"We'll take my car," Xian announced.

"Why?" she questioned.

"Burglars are less likely to break in if they think that someone is in the house."

Alex let out half a laugh, "A little late for that, don't you think?" Nevertheless, she followed Xian to his car.

The trip to Xian's house was conducted in silence. Alex faced the window, concentrating on the passing scenery as her hand automatically stroked Shadow's fur. The events of the past month rotated like tumblers in a lock as she tried to find the correct combination.

Chou greeted them at the door. Alex stood behind Xian and watched Chou's father bend over to give the boy a big hug.

"Dad, you're home."

Xian turned towards the silent woman behind him. "Son, Alex had an emergency at her house. I've invited her to stay with us for a couple of days."

"One day," Alex corrected. Shadow picked that moment to jump out of her arms. The black cat strolled over to Chou and wrapped his tail around his leg while rubbing against his jeans.

She smiled ruefully, "Chou, meet Shadow."

"Wow. Can I pet him?" His eyes were as big as saucers.

"Sure, he's had a long day. If you give him some cat food he'll love you forever." Alex handed him a can.

"Dad, may I?"

"Of course, Son."

Chou turned and headed towards the kitchen, constantly glancing over his shoulder to make sure the cat followed.

"Let me show you to your room."

"...said the spider to the fly," she quipped.

Xian picked up her bag and she followed him upstairs. She stood in the doorway of the bedroom as Xian entered and placed her bag on the bed.

"If you need anything, let me know."

"Thank you."

He bowed his head slightly and left the room. The guest room was enormous; the curtains were drawn back, revealing a backyard garden. The window seat was covered with decorated pillows. In the left corner, a tall mirror stood next to a dark mahogany dresser.

Alex opened her bag and searched for a pair of jeans and a T-shirt. She picked up her clothes, walked into the adjoining bathroom, and closed the door. After turning on the shower, she stripped off her clothes, jumped into the warm, pulsing stream of water, and just stood there, letting the heat relax her muscles. Opening her eyes moments later, she finished washing and turned off the water.

"Damn," she muttered quietly after drying off and noticing that her bra was nowhere to be found. She wrapped the towel around her body before opening the door. Her bra lay on the floor in the bedroom. As she bent down to pick it up, she heard a light knock on the door. Before she could respond, it opened.

Alex couldn't tell who was more surprised. She straightened and faced the door. Xian had changed into khakis and a polo shirt. He stood in the doorway wearing an apron and slippers.

"I came to tell you that dinner is ready." His voice was strained.

Normally, she didn't embarrass easily but something about Xian's admiring stare made her grip the towel as she forced herself to meet his gaze. What she saw in his eyes made her heart stop and then beat faster.

"Thanks, I'll be down in a minute."

Alex turned and practically sprinted into the bathroom. She closed the door and leaned against it, inhaling deeply. Her face was hot, flushed and her breathing shallow.

What in the world is wrong with me?, she uncurled her fingers from their tight grip on her towel. She wasn't a girl fresh out of school with no control, but for a brief moment she'd felt unsure.

After closing the door to the guest room, Xian returned downstairs to the kitchen. He stood over the sink and gazed out the window, deep in thought. He hadn't meant to stand there like an idiot. He shook his head in bemusement. *When was the last time I felt so alive? The last time my fingers burned to touch a woman's skin?*

"Shay-Lin," he murmured to himself. He had wanted no woman other than his wife. She had been his only source of joy before his son.

It seemed as though it had been an eternity since anyone had made such an impression on him. He had dated some of the most beautiful and powerful woman in the city, and no one intrigued him as much as his son's teacher did. He enjoyed the way she challenged him. Her combination of beauty, mystery, and danger was powerful.

He closed his eyes, remembering the sight of her standing in the towel, her full breasts outlined in soft light, the smell of jasmine. The image would not leave him. He thought of her upstairs getting dressed. He wanted her. Xian frowned. *What the hell am I going to do?*

Dressed in jeans and with her hair hanging loose, Alex followed the sound of laughter to the kitchen. Track lighting ran the length of both sides of the island and a recessed wine rack lay over the fridge. An apron-less Xian was standing by the oven with his hands folded across his chest, laughing. Alex turned to follow the direction of his gaze and saw Chou on the floor with Shadow. The cat was impatiently swatting at the string Chou held over his head.

"Hello," she cheerfully announced. Both of them turned to look at her. Alex avoided Xian's gaze by walking over and bending down next to Chou.

"Be very careful, Chou. Shadow hates to lose." She smiled.

"Chou." His father's voice was firm yet tender. "You can continue to play with Shadow after dinner. Now go wash your hands."

When Chou returned Alex picked up the rice bowl and placed it on the kitchen table next to the vase of fresh flowers. After a few more trips to the kitchen, dinner was ready. They all sat down and began to eat.

She looked at Xian and saw him looking pointedly at her chopsticks. "I've had years of practice," she said.

Eager to enlighten his father, Chou spoke, "Dad, Ms. Thompson grew up in Japan."

Xian's look of surprise brought a smile to Alex's face, but wanting to forestall further questions about her past, she changed the topic. Over dinner, Alex kept up an easy conversation by entertaining Chou with stories of Shadow's exploits.

"You've gotta be joking, Ms. Thompson," the boy laughed.

"Nope," Alex answered as she picked up two glasses and carried them towards the kitchen. "Shadow is a certified attack cat. My Uncle Rafé trained him. If I were ever in danger, he would defend me."

"Ms. Thompson?"

"Yes, Chou?"

"Do you play Nintendo?"

Alex smiled. "Of course, my roommate's niece and nephew come to visit all the time, and we have a lot of fun."

"Want to play Pokémon Stadium with me?"

Alex heard Xian come up behind her. "Chou, have you finished your homework?"

"Yes, Dad."

Three hours later, Alex cradled a sleeping Chou in her arms. His warm presence seemed to wrap peace around her. She gently shifted the child and prepared to wake him.

After finishing up an unexpected business call to a subsidiary in Taiwan, Xian stopped at the door to the den. At the sight of Alex holding his son, something long buried welled up strong and deep, threatening to overwhelm him. He thought her asleep, but he watched her face soften as she looked at Chou. Her expression held such tenderness that the barrier around his emotions seemed to fall away and his heart lurched. She had given him a new purpose and he swore that he'd again never let anything come between him and his son.

"I'll take him," he whispered.

When she looked up into his face, Xian found his gaze wandering to her lips.

"I've got coffee brewing in the kitchen. Have a cup," he whispered.

Alex nodded and stood up. She stretched her aching muscles and then bent to turn off the game system before going into the kitchen. The room was redolent with the scent of coffee beans. She curled one leg under and sat down at the table.

She looked up as Xian joined her at the table.

"He's...how do you say it? Knocked out." Xian grinned.

"He's had a busy day," Alex replied, remembering Chou's description of his trip to the zoo with Mrs. Lee.

Xian stood up and minutes later returned with a tray bearing a carafe of coffee, cups, sugar, and cream. Alex watched Xian's hands as he placed a mug in front of her and poured the steaming coffee. She added cream and sugar to her cup, took a sip, and then smiled. "Jamaican."

Xian looked surprised. "How can you tell?"

"Some people study wine. I'm a coffee connoisseur."

His next words caught her off guard. "It must have been hard for you growing up in Japan."

"How would you know?" Alex snapped before thinking.

Xian didn't hesitate with his reply. "I was not born in Hong Kong. My parents were from a small farm in southern China. We later moved to Hong Kong, where I discovered firsthand that although the island has returned to the People's Republic of China, mainland Chinese immigrants are not welcome."

Alex's tone softened. "Is that why you came here to the States?"

"It was my wife's wish to raise our son in America. She dreamed of trees and grass, a home by the water with a garden and plenty of open sky."

"Do you miss Hong Kong?"

"Do you miss Japan?" he asked rhetorically. "The East is in my blood. My parents still live in Hong Kong and we go twice a year to visit. I can't talk them into moving here. Its ways were once all that was familiar to me. My family is now rich, but Hong Kong has a long memory. There are those that won't let us forget we were once poor."

Xian had been lucky. On a rainy Thursday morning, he'd arranged for his family to be smuggled over Hong Kong's border while he'd stayed behind. He'd paid a heavy price, helping run the local branch of Sun Yee On "New Discipline." The Hong Kong-based organized crime syndicate had turned what had once been a former resort for Communist leaders into the de facto capital of organized crime.

"So you came here to start over?" she questioned.

"Yes, I came to America to begin a new life. What's your story? How did you end up being born in the 'land of the rising sun'?"

"I was a navy brat," she replied offhandedly, brushing back a stray strand of hair. "My father was in the military. My mother died when I was young. Dad didn't want to come back to the States after she died, so a nanny raised me. I lived in Japan until I was seventeen, when we moved to Germany. I left Berlin and returned to the U.S. for college."

"What a remarkable childhood you must have had."

"You could say that." Her lips curled into a half smile and Xian wondered at the undertone of irony in her voice.

"You're living proof as to why one cannot judge a book by its cover."

She arched her eyebrow. "And so are you."

"What made you settle in San Francisco?"

Alex stared into the milky depths of her coffee. "I found out that my father was dying of cancer. I moved here to spend some time with him. I liked the place so I decided to settle down and take up teaching. End of story."

Two years, she thought. Time had only given her two years to be with him before his death. Not enough. Not nearly enough to make up for all the missed moments.

Alex kept silent about the other reasons she'd left the Special Forces. The blood, the death, the unending darkness of an undercover war.

"And your decision to become a teacher?" he questioned.

"I wanted to be around children so I became a teacher."

"Have you always been a teacher?"

"No." She struggled to keep her face bland.

"What did you do before?" Xian's voice was curious.

Alex answered truthfully, "I was in the military."

Xian had anticipated many answers but that wasn't one of them. He stared at the woman sitting across the breakfast table. Examining her closely, he noticed the muscles easily rippled in her arms as she lifted the coffee cup. He should have guessed from the way she handled herself during their martial arts practice session. Each new piece of information revealed a more intriguing woman.

"Did you join to make the world safe for democracy?" he asked jokingly.

Alex sat her cup down gently on the table. "No, nothing that patriotic. I joined to keep from being locked up in a Filipino jail."

"What did you do? Deface a national treasure? Jaywalk?"

She shrugged her shoulders and smiled ruefully. "I took a bet."

"That must have been some bet."

Alex could tell that Xian wouldn't let this go. She sighed. "The summer of my junior year in college I went to the Philippines for a martial arts tournament. I won the women's competition and I was full of myself. The last night one of the male competitors was spoiling for a fight. I was game to earn some quick cash so I was happy to oblige him." She looked Xian in the eye. "He ended up in the hospital re-learning to walk."

"How would that have landed you in jail?"

"He turned out to be the son of a local politician. One of the spectators at the fight just happened to be Army Colonel Eilliam Tagner. I didn't know it then but it was no accident that he was there," she replied, surprised at how easy it was to talk to him.

"Why do you say that?"

"Tag was looking for me. It doesn't take long for word to spread in tournament circles. He knew I could fight and had a gift for languages. I didn't know it at the time, but earlier that year, Tag had approached my father about having me join the army. Of course Dad refused, not for his daughter." Alex paused for a second to swallow the gathering bitterness. Her father staunchly believed in keeping women out of military combat.

"When Tag found me in the Philippines, I was right where he wanted me. I had no choice. I couldn't call my father." Her mistake had cost her time and freedom.

"What happened next?"

She shook her head. "I found myself on an airplane to Fort Bragg. I spent the next five years of my life in the military.

Xian refilled her cup and then his own, all the while watching her closely, wanting to find out more.

"What did you do in the military?"

"A little bit of this and that. Some counterintelligence, field duty." She was deliberately being vague.

"Your father must have been proud," he assumed.

She shook her head, seeing the image of her father's solemn face. "No, I couldn't help being a disappointment to my father. You see, I was the wrong sex."

"What do you mean?" He rubbed his chin while staring intently at Alex.

"He was sure I would be a boy. I don't think he ever got over the fact that his little 'Alexander the Great' turned out to be a girl," she said without bitterness. "And I did get tired of proving I could be better."

Her eyes grew empty. "I'd rather not talk about this anymore." There were still nights she woke with her body covered with sweat and screams echoing in her head.

"You do know that you're Chou's favorite teacher?"

"Your son is one of my best students." She watched as he picked up his cup and took a sip. All the while his eyes never left her face and it made her catch her breath a little. The handsomeness of his face called to her flesh, but the darkness of his eyes touched a place in her soul.

"Have you never thought of getting married and raising a family?" Xian straightened in his seat, wanting to know the answer but also knowing that he wanted a specific outcome.

"No."

"I only ask because I think that you would be a wonderful mother."

"Thanks."

"You're not engaged?" His voice held an amazed tone.

"I've had one proposal."

"You turned him down?"

Alex gently placed the mug on the table. "He died." The pain in her head flared to life.

"I'm sorry."

Xian looked at Alex a second or two, wanting to say more, but he let it go. Instead, he stood and walked around the table. Alex tensed as she felt his hands on her shoulders and exhaled as he began to knead her muscles.

"This will help take away your headache."

"How did you know?"

"You rubbed your temple and the pain was reflected in your eyes." His hands continued to massage her neck. "Just try to relax. Let the pain go."

Alex let her eyelids close. She caught the faint scent of musk and her palms began to sweat. In the silence of the room, she could hear the rhythmic pulse of her heartbeat echoing in her ears.

She felt his kiss on her skin and her pulse began to beat like a hummingbird's wings. His hands began to move from her shoulders. She could feel his fingers caressing the nape of her neck. Alex could not have stopped it even if she wanted to. She let him gently guide her head and she fell into his kiss.

He kissed as if he were an explorer and her mouth was a new world upon which he tread slowly, cautiously. The sound of the clock striking eleven pulled her back to her senses. She abruptly ended the kiss by standing up and taking two steps back.

"That shouldn't have happened," she said in a tone that brooked no argument.

"Are you sure?" he asked. His eyes were dark.

Something about the way he watched her reminded her of a well-fed cat. "Yes," she said softly before turning to start down the hallway. Xian's next words stopped her in her tracks.

"You pull your anger and strength around you like a wall to keep people away, only letting children through the gate."

"Adults around me have a bad tendency to disappear," she whispered.

"We all must leave this life eventually, Alex."

She started at his words and walked away, climbing the polished oak stairs in a daze. Taking care to close the door to her bedroom, she changed into her oversized sleep shirt, and placed her gun underneath the pillow. She settled herself under the cotton sheets and turned her face into the pillow as a single tear slipped down her cheek.

Xian didn't know where his parting words to Alex had come from. Although he wished he could, he found no reasons for what he was feeling. Nor could he find an excuse for his kissing her. Whatever was happening between the two of them, he wanted to explore it.

"Damn." Xian scarcely stopped himself from going after her. He didn't know why he'd said what he'd said, why he'd kissed her. He raked his finger through his hair and gritted his teeth. No, he knew:

the image of Alex standing in the towel still wet from the shower; the sight of his son in her arms; her face serene and her arms curling protectively around his little boy; the undeniable temptation of her lush lips and erotic scent.

He smiled after placing the cups in the dishwasher. She wasn't ready to acknowledge the attraction, but he was. And there wasn't anything she could do about it. Xian reached over and turned out the light, and then walked of the kitchen.

FOURTEEN

"What the...?" Xian woke startled and got out of the bed. Without reaching to put on his robe over his pajamas, he left his bedroom and traced the faint whimpering sounds to the guest room: Alex. He opened the door and saw her tossing and turning on the bed. Crossing the room, he laid his hand on her shoulder with the intention of waking her but before he could blink, he found himself staring up at the ceiling from the floor.

Hurriedly placing her weapon back underneath the pillow, Alex reached for the lamp. "Xian, are you all right?"

"I'm okay." He took her outstretched hand and maneuvered himself to sit on the edge of the bed.

"Nightmare?" he asked.

Alex slowly nodded before edging over to sit at his side.

"Do you have them often?"

"No," she answered truthfully. Time had helped distance her from the memories. She used to wake many nights bathed in a cold sweat but the dreams had faded as she'd become more and more adjusted to her new life as a teacher. Tonight the nightmare had come back strong and intense. Maybe it was the stress of Brian's death, the break-in, or her feelings for Chou and Xian, but the image of the Somali boy's face still lay in her mind.

"Do you want to talk about it?" he softly inquired.

Alex shook her head. "Not really." It hadn't been a nightmare, it had been a memory, and her body shook with the scream that she hadn't been able to voice.

"It might help. For the longest time after my wife died, I couldn't sleep. I would find myself waking up in the middle of the night talking, speaking to Shay-Lin as though she were lying there beside me."

Unexpectedly Alex felt tears well behind her eyes. She had spoken about the boy's death only to Rafé during the mission de-briefing. She had seen the sympathy in his eyes that day, but there had been no time to cry. She'd had to pack and re-join the team.

"I…" She stopped and then continued. "It isn't grief that gives me nightmares, Xian. It's guilt."

"I don't understand."

"You couldn't." Needing to move away, Alex stood and went to the window. She didn't want to see his face when she made her confession. Clenching her fingers, she went back, back to the first time she'd laid eyes on Tag. He'd been watching her from the other side of the metal cage the Philippine police had called a jail cell.

She remembered what he'd said. *"Listen to me good. From the moment you walk out this cell, you belong to the United States Army, Ms. Thompson. There's no going back, no calling your daddy. From here on out every move you take, every breath you take, everything you hear and say is for Delta Force. You are mine to train, mine to teach."*

She blinked her eyes and began. "I was one of our military's elite, Xian. They sent me into situations that no man could have come back from alive. I lied, cheated, stole, killed, tortured, and deceived until I got to the point that I didn't know who I was anymore."

She turned briefly to look at him and continued, "I wanted to prove myself at first and then everything changed. I started to like it. The rush of going on a mission is powerful. I was the only woman to ever be assigned to a counterintelligence team. They called me 'Blade' because of my skill with a knife."

"Go on," Xian urged, not allowing the surprise to show on his face. It was like watching the pulling off of a mask.

"I was sent to Somalia with orders to infiltrate one of the rebel groups. There had been a rumor that they'd gotten hold of a cache of Russian short-range missiles. I was to gather information and neutralize the warlord." She shivered, remembering how she'd played the part of an African nationalist, how easy calculated flirtation had been.

"The plan was for me to get close to the general by pretending to be a journalist interested in writing his story. When he trusted me enough to invite me to his house, I was supposed to give him a poison that would make his death seem like a heart attack. I thought poison was a coward's weapon and I hated to use it, but orders were orders. I was making a sanctioned kill and erasing one more evil from the world."

Alex didn't look up as she felt Xian's presence next to her by the window, but her words became more rushed. "It was my fourth or fifth mission and I was still green. I learned later on that it had been a test, which I passed." Her voice lowered with poignant understatement. "I played it by the book until I heard the sound of the door opening; I turned and instinctively pulled the trigger just as I'd been trained. When I turned the body over, I saw it was one of the general's sons," she choked out.

Xian put aside his original intention of being emotionally detached and gathered Alex's shivering body into his arms and led her over to the bed. Sitting her down, he silently stroked her hair as she wept.

He'd been married but he didn't know a great deal about how to handle a crying woman. All his instincts told him the best thing he could do for Alex would be to listen. And as he held her, he began to get a glimmer as to what had drawn her to teaching.

Finally, Alex drew reluctantly away from him and sat up straight, brushing her hair away from her face. Her calm expression belied her wary eyes. "Go ahead, say it."

He reached out and wiped the last tear from her face. "I think that if I had been in your position, I might have done the same thing. You did what you were trained to do. The lives that you've saved will restore the balance."

"I killed a boy. The battleground is a place for adults, not innocent children."

He shook his head, "You did what you had to do at the time and you've paid a heavy price. Let the past go. You have a duty to the future." He sighed and rubbed his hand roughly across his brow. "We've all done things that we regret."

"What did you do? Get a parking ticket?" she asked sarcastically and immediately regretted it.

"Have you heard of the Hong Kong Triads?"

Alex nodded her head, remembering some of the information she had been given during her time in the military. The rise in power of Asian organized crime had necessitated that DELTA be prepared if ever a hostage situation came up.

"I got my start in business as a member of a smaller group in China. At first, we just smuggled stolen cars into China from Hong Kong. I was young and the thrill of wearing expensive clothes, receiving attention from women, and having money in my pocket outweighed my honor."

Xian turned towards Alex. He needed to see her face as he continued his story. "I've done it all, things that I can't even mention. Before I met my wife, I controlled half of Huizhou's growing black market and prostitution trade.

"I moved my family to Hong Kong so I wouldn't have to see their disappointment and continued my illegal activities. It broke my mother's heart when a neighbor informed her that her son was nothing but a criminal. I invested my money wisely and built up enough money to start my own company. When Shay-Lin became pregnant, everything changed. We left Hong Kong and moved here."

Throughout his confession, Alex had kept eye contact with him. "They wouldn't let you go that easily," she asserted. She remembered how difficult it had been for her to extricate herself from DELTA Force. It had been a three-month ordeal and only her father's intervention had gotten her discharged.

"Again I was lucky." His smile was filled with bitter irony. "Blood money must always be washed clean. That was my price for freedom. For more than a year I was the soap and water, funneling drug money through my subsidiaries. You have a name for it—money laundering."

"I guess we have more in common than I thought," she nodded.

"More than you know." Xian leaned close, caught her face between his palms and pressed a slow, lingering kiss against her lips. Only when it seemed that he had to break off the kiss or take her then and there did he lift his face, inhale deeply, and pull away. "I guess I'm not being a very good host, am I?"

"I woke you up, remember?" Alex pointed out.

"True. But now I should let you sleep."

"Xian," she called out as he neared the door.

"Yes?"

"Thank you for listening."

He held her gaze from across the room and smiled. His heart felt lighter than it had in months. "Anytime."

FIFTEEN

Alex showered the next morning and put on a sundress and sandals. Standing before the full-length mirror, she pulled her hair back and paused, then decided to let her hair hang loose. When she finally slept last night after Xian left it had been a restless sleep as mind and memory worked together to make sense of her past.

It had all begun with the fact that she'd wanted to prove she could be a substitute for the son her high-ranking father had never had. To accomplish that goal, she'd undertaken the study of the martial arts and had earned her place as a master karate student.

She'd wanted to go into the military right after high school but her father wouldn't allow her to enlist in the navy. For three years, she'd appeased her father. Her decision to enter a Philippine martial arts tournament had been a major turning point in her life. What she'd hoped would be an excellent opportunity to gain her father's attention instead had ended up landing her in jail. Colonel Tagner arranged for her freedom and in return she'd become a member of DELTA Force. The months of physical and mental conditioning, hazing, and rigorous training had transformed Alex into one of the military's top soldiers. But psychological testing and mission simulations couldn't have prepared her for the chaos of Somalia, the destruction of Kuwait, or the realities of life as a government sanctioned assassin.

Blinking to clear her mind, Alex picked up her bag, headed downstairs, and hesitantly entered the kitchen.

"Good morning, Ms. Thompson."

"Good morning, Chou."

"Would you like Corn Flakes or Rice Krispies?" Xian asked, pulling out two boxes from the cabinet.

She smiled and took a seat at the table. "I'll have what Chou's having."

Xian brought the bowls over to the table, "Corn Flakes it is then. Would you like tea or coffee?"

Alex felt herself blush with the memory of the night before. "Coffee, please."

She tried to avoid his piercing gaze. She had only taken a few bites of her cereal before Chou stood up.

"I'm done."

"Go brush your teeth and get your school books together."

"Okay, Dad."

Several moments passed after Chou left the kitchen. Xian was the first to speak.

"Did you sleep well last night?"

"Yes. I slept like the proverbial log," she lied.

"Good. If you had not, I would have moved you to the second guest room for tonight."

"Xian, thank you for your hospitality, but I've imposed on you enough. I won't be staying here tonight. I need to begin putting my house in order."

"As you wish."

Alex was surprised at how disappointed she was that he didn't argue with her decision.

"Shall we go?"

She picked up her bag on the way out of the kitchen.

"I'll take that and put it in the car."

"Thanks. I'll drop by and pick up Shadow some-time tonight if that's okay."

"Sounds good."

Chou kept the conversation going all the way to school. Xian pulled up to the curb and Alex watched the school kids pass by.

"Chou, I'll be picking you up from school today."

"Okay, Dad."

"Why don't you run on to class? I need to chat with Ms. Thompson for a moment."

"Okay, Dad. I love you."

"I love you too, Son."

The little boy bounced out of the car and ran to join a group of kids heading into the building. Alex reached into backseat to pick up her bag. Her fingers had just touched the straps when Xian's hand lightly gripped hers.

"I'll take you home this afternoon."

She turned and drew a soft breath. Xian's face was close, too close. To someone outside, it would look like a kiss. If either of them moved, it would be a kiss. Lowering her gaze, Alex relaxed her fingers and pulled away.

"Xian, I don't want to seem ungrateful but you've done more then enough."

"Alex, leave the bag. I picked you up from your home, I will return you."

She looked at his exotic features and his calm dark eyes and fought the urge to lose herself in his gaze.

"What is it you want from me?"

"An 'A' for my son in his English class?" he joked.

She regarded him for a moment. His eyes twinkled with secret promises and long nights that had nothing to do with sleep. She sighed and turned to open the door. "See you later, Xian."

Before she could pull the handle, Xian said, "I do not regret kissing you last night, Alex. In fact, I'd like to do it more often."

She didn't look at him because she knew without a doubt his lips wore a confident grin. She pushed open the car door and walked toward the school's entrance without turning back.

"Hi. Mind if I join you?"

Alex nodded her acceptance, and then went back to grading papers, hoping that the young substitute teacher would take the hint that she wanted to be alone.

"I heard about the break-in at your place. Are you okay?"

Alex tensed. "I'm fine. I wasn't at home when it happened." She gathered her papers neatly in a pile and looked up at the substitute teacher's concerned face.

"Did they take anything?"

"No. The police suspect that they were looking for money or jewelry. Stuff they could easily pawn. When they couldn't find what they wanted, they just messed up the place and left."

Before he could ask another question, the bell rang. Alex stood up quickly and gathered her stuff.

"If you need any help just let me know." He smiled as he stood up.

"Thank you, Mr. Brown."

"Scott."

"Scott. I appreciate your offer."

She gave him a smile and turned. As she walked towards the school, she knew he was staring at her. She had one overriding thought in her mind. She hadn't told anyone about the break-in.

Alex was preoccupied for the rest of the afternoon. When the final bell rang, she was relieved to be getting out even if it meant seeing Xian again.

"Ready to go, Chou?"

"Yep."

"Let's hit the road."

When they exited the building, they saw the silver BMW parked at the curb. Xian was leaning against the side of the car finishing a conversation on his cell phone. Chou flew down the stairs and was greeted with a big hug by his father. Alex felt her heart catch at the sight.

"Okay, all in."

She smiled and got into the front seat and pulled on her seatbelt as Xian closed the door.

Chou spent the next twenty minutes telling his father all about the day's activities. After they arrived at her house, Alex reached for her bag, only to find it missing.

"I placed it in the trunk," Xian explained.

Alex narrowed her eyes. On the surface, his actions appeared minor. But she knew that Xian didn't do things without a reason. "Thanks."

"I'll carry it in for you."

Alex was about to protest when Chou's head peeked out over the backseat.

"Dad, I need to use the bathroom."

"Okay, I'm sure Ms. Thompson will let you use hers."

Caught off guard, Alex moved towards the back of the car.

"I don't think that would be a good idea," she whispered through gritted teeth.

"It's okay. Get out, Chou."

She glared at his grinning face, turned, and marched to the front door. She unlocked the dead-bolt and hesitantly opened the door. Alex's eyes widened at the sight. The inside of her house was orderly and clean. All the books were arranged on their shelves, paintings had been returned to the walls, new plants lined the windowsills, and the carpet bore the marks of fresh cleaning. The house smelled of freesia. Alex turned around slowly.

"Ms. Thompson, may I use your bathroom?"

"The bathroom's just down the hall, second door on your left, Chou," she instructed automatically.

Alex began to make her way through the rest of the house. Every room had been cleaned, the broken window fixed, her clothes neatly folded and put away. She returned to the living room and saw Xian sitting comfortably on the couch.

"You did this," she stated.

"Yes."

"Why? When?"

He shrugged, his dark eyes hooded. "Why? I have no answer except I wanted to help. When? In my business people owe me favors. Besides, if you have enough money or power you can get anything done."

Just as Alex was about to let him have it, the doorbell rang. She was good at judging people, figuring out what made them tick. Their motivation, their hates, their loves, their secrets. Everyone except this man. Alex looked towards the door in confusion. She wasn't expecting anyone.

"That would be for me." Xian smoothly stood up and walked across the room to answer the door.

A young teenager stood outside holding a pizza. "California pizza delivery. One large pepperoni and mushroom pizza and a six pack of Coke. Your total is $20.75, sir."

Xian handed the boy thirty dollars, "Keep the change."

The smell of pizza began to fill the air. An excited Chou came through the door.

"Dad, I smell pizza."

"Yep, let's go into the kitchen."

Alex stood there in shock and then headed in the opposite direction. The damn man was trying to take over her life.

"Ms. Thompson, don't you want pizza?"

Chou's innocent question pulled at her heart. She turned around and smiled, all the while glaring daggers at his smirking father.

"Of course, sweetheart. I was just going to wash up."

"Ms. Thompson?"

"Yes."

"The bathroom's that way."

"Thank you."

She felt her face burn and her hands itched to slap the grin off Xian's face.

Alex picked up the plates off the kitchen table and set them down in the sink.

"Let me help you," Xian volunteered.

She turned quickly to find him standing close. "That's okay. You should go play Nintendo with Chou," she suggested.

His response was a laugh that sent delicate shivers down her spine. "No thanks. I've taken all the beatings I can stand for the day."

"The tough life of a businessman."

"Somebody's has to keep the world moving," he grinned. "I spend a lot of time at the office or on the phone."

"So what do you do for fun?" she asked after pouring two cups of coffee.

Xian rubbed his chin. It had been a long time since he'd thought about anything other than work. "We used to go boating on the weekends. Shay-Lin and Chou loved to fish. She would catch them and throw them back in." He shook his head. "The boat's been in dry dock for months."

"You should get back out. The weather's perfect for it."

"You're right. How about we go this Saturday?"

She ducked the question. "I think that Chou would love to spend time out on the boat with you."

"No, you and me, Alex. Chou has been invited to spend the weekend at his best friend's house."

She raised her eyebrow and sat back in the chair. "Are you asking me on a date?"

He grinned and sat forward, looking into her eyes. "I believe I am."

"I'm tempted to accept." She smiled and took a sip of coffee.

"Then you should give in to that temptation," he suggested, looking at her over the rim of his mug. "Think of the cool breeze, beautiful water, a glass of wine, a nice dinner."

"You make it almost impossible to turn down."

He leaned forward, and placed his hand atop her own. "Then don't."

Alex looked from the sight of their hands to Xian's suddenly serious face and her mouth went dry. "I can't."

"Can't or won't?" he challenged. "Does my skin color affect your answer?"

"Of course not," she fired back. "I've just got some issues to resolve before I let anyone into my life right now."

Xian pushed back his chair and stood up. "As you wish."

She stood quickly and moved around the table to lay her hand on his arm. Xian was good at hiding his emotions but she could read body language better than most people. "Xian, don't take what I said the wrong way. I don't play games."

"Really?"

"Yes," she firmly replied. "I've got a lot of things happening right now. Not to mention getting the students ready for spring break. Trust me when I say that I'd love to spend some time with you on your boat, but I can't right now."

Xian nodded and gently took Alex's hand in his own. He watched her eyes darken when he raised it to his lips and placed a kiss on her palm. "I'm going to hold you to that."

"I know."

An hour later, Alex leaned against the doorway and watched as Xian placed a sleeping Chou into the backseat of the car. She wasn't surprised when he turned and walked back towards the house.

"I'll pick up Shadow tomorrow," she said.

"No need. I will bring him by. Chou will not want to part with his new friend."

"Must be a family trait," Alex joked.

"We Lius tend to be very persistent." He smiled.

"Drive safely."

"You are not sad to see me go?" Xian asked, pretending to be hurt.

"My heart is breaking," she replied. She had to struggle to keep from laughing.

Somehow he always managed to get in the last word. "I would help you put it back together."

She didn't know who was more surprised by this admission. She moved to enter the house but paused to call out, "Xian. Thank you."

That night Alex slept lightly. The sound of a creaking floorboard in the hallway awoke her. She slid her hand under the pillow and clicked off the safety of her gun. Feigning sleep, she cradled the Berretta. Its cold heaviness was reassuring.

The door opened quietly. She cracked her eyes and peered into the darkness. When she caught a glimpse of somebody, she rolled over to the opposite side of the bed, away from the door, and dropped to the floor.

"Don't move," she ordered, aiming her gun at the open doorway.

"You're slipping, Blade. You should have heard me long before now."

Only one man called her by that name. He was the only person who was better at throwing a knife than she was. "Damn it, Tobias. What the hell are you doing here?"

"Visiting an old friend."

Alex snorted, then rose to stand beside the bed. "Couldn't you have called?"

"It's easier for you to lie over the phone."

"Why would I lie?" she challenged.

"The real question is, why haven't you called?"

She watched as he settled into the lone chair next to the window, his large body causing the wicker chair to creak. Only when she could see that his hands were empty did Alex relax her grip on the gun. She clicked on the safety and started to switch on the lamp.

"Don't turn on the light."

She reached up and roughly combed her fingers through sleep tousled hair, pushing it away from her face. "There's no reason for me to contact you, Tobias."

"Correct me if I am wrong, but Rafé told you to call me if *anything* happened."

"My house was broken into. Big deal. First it was Rafé, now you. What more do I need to do to get you people off my back?"

"Find a husband."

"You're *loco*," she bit out. "What does Rosanna have to say about your coming over here in the middle of the night?"

"She wants me to tell you to stop by more often. Her older brother wants to meet you."

Alex sighed and sat back on the bed. "I'm not in the mood for this tonight. Rafé is just being paranoid."

"Really, Blade? Did paranoia kill your ex-fiancé and search your house? Why don't you take a look out the window?"

She stood and went over to the window and pulled back the curtains.

"You see that white van?" he asked.

"Yes, so what?"

"Man, are you slow. You should spend less time babysitting and more time paying attention to what's happening around you. That van has been parked opposite your house for the past three days."

Stung by the reprimand, Alex gritted her teeth and constructed the weakest of excuses. "My neighbors have company."

"Not unless they're relatives of the FBI. Your phone line has been tapped, and your military records accessed from at least three different locations. I'm willing to bet you're being followed. Now the real question is, what does the FBI want with you?"

"I don't know," she replied.

"Try again. What does Brian's murder have to do with you?"

"Seriously, Tobias. I don't know. I've been up to my neck with my own personal stuff." She glared at him, frustrated by the questions he asked, questions that had no answers.

"Look, Blade, I know you want to find out who killed Brian but it may be time to let the FBI handle it."

"I'm just asking a few questions."

"Well, stop. I don't know what you've gotten yourself into but you need to get out fast. I read the police report. Whoever broke into your place was looking for something. Whatever you're involved in, finish it before I have to."

She had suspected as much from the way in which the house had been searched without more items being taken. Hearing Tobias confirm her suspicions, Alex sat up straighter. Adrenaline surged through her bloodstream and heightened her senses. "I'm off the team, Tobias. You don't get to tell me what to do."

"I have my orders, Alex. Rafé left me a fake passport and a ticket to a nice isolated beach down in the islands. I'll knock you out and drop you off and let him pick you up."

He wasn't bluffing. He would intervene. He wanted to respect her independence, but he would lock her up rather than go against Rafé's orders.

"Here." He directed.

She felt something small hit the bed beside her. "What's this?"

"Mobile phone and a letter from Khan."

"I already have a cell."

"Yeah, and you should have used it. This one is equipped with a GPS locator beacon. You hit the red button and I'll be able to track you."

"Tobias…"

"No excuses next time. It's either this or I take you to my house and you can help my seven months' pregnant wife."

He blended into the shadows. "Blade?"

"What?" she bit out.

"One last thing. Whatever mess you're involved in, you have seventy-two hours to get out."

"Why the time limit?"

"You didn't think Rafé would be gone forever, did you?" With that, Tobias disappeared into the dark hallway.

"Damn," she cursed. "This just keeps getting better."

Alex opened the drawer to her nightstand and pulled out a pen flashlight. Holding it in her mouth she picked up the letter. There was no address on the envelope, only an elegantly drawn name: Leila.

Her ex-partner had given her an Arabic name that meant 'night.' She remembered how the Iranian agents had laughed at the appropriateness, given her race. She was sure they hadn't been laughing the night she and Khan tied them up before slipping across the border.

She looked down at her alias drawn in elegant script on the envelope and opened it.

After reading it, Alex refolded the ivory letter. It contained reference to Khan's sister that only she could understand, as well as an indication that her ex-partner was coming back to the States. She rubbed her head and stuck her hand under the pillow, cradling the cool handle of the gun in her left hand. She shivered in the warmth of the room as she remembered the cruel husband of Khan's sister.

There must have been a reckoning between him and Khan. Otherwise, Khan wouldn't have left. She would bet, from the hint in the letter, that Khan had managed to make his brother-in-law disappear. Clinging to that knowledge, Alex closed her eyes and let sleep come gently with her hand wrapped around a gun.

SIXTEEN

Xian closed the front door as soon as Ms. Lee's car left the driveway. The house was unusually quiet. He went into the den expecting to see Chou sitting on the floor playing video games, but found the room empty. Puzzled, he went into the kitchen and set the table for dinner. As he put the last covered dish on the table, Xian stared down at Alex's black cat. It was uncanny how the cat's dark eyes resembled those of its owner.

Xian placed the large dish of rice in the center of the table and then scooped some into the smaller individual bowls. He stood at the bottom of the stairs and called out, "Dinner's ready. Come down to eat."

"I'm not hungry," came the faint reply.

"If you want to spend the weekend at your friend's house, you will come downstairs and eat."

Xian went back into the kitchen and sat down at the table. He picked up his chopsticks and had begun to eat when Chou entered the room. Xian stared hard at his son. Chou was pale and his eyes were downcast. He knew instantly something was wrong and spent the next ten minutes watching his son pick at his food.

"Chou, are you okay?"

"I'm fine."

"Are you sick?"

"No."

"Then why are you not eating?"

"I'm just not hungry, Dad."

Xian put his hands on the table. "Chou, you have to know that you can talk with me about anything that's bothering you."

"I can't."

"Why?" Xian tried to sound as calm as possible even though his anxiety was increasing each passing moment.

"I promised."

Xian stood up, walked around the table, and took a seat next to his son. "Whatever this is that's bothering you, we can talk about it. I'm your father, Chou. It's my job to take care of these things." He smiled.

His son shook his head.

"Who's the secret about?"

"Ms. Thompson."

"Who asked you to keep the secret?"

"Ms. Thompson."

Xian became tenser at each answer. "Chou, I'm sure that Alex, Ms. Thompson meant for you to keep it from the other students, not your father."

"Really?"

"Yes."

"Are you sure?"

"Of course."

"Well, I wanted to talk to Ms. Thompson about convincing you to get me dog, so I followed her out to her car. When I got to the edge of the school, I saw her with two men, and I was about to call out when…" He swallowed, then rushed, "Dad, it was so cool. She didn't even blink when the first guy pulled a gun. She just grabbed it and kicked. I didn't see what she did to the other man, but it must have hurt pretty bad because he was crying, Dad. And she even made them take off their clothes before getting in the car. Just like the movies on TV."

"Chou, why were you still at the school? Where was Mrs. Lee?"

Chou looked down at his feet. "I told her Ms. Thompson would bring me home later."

"Why did you tell her that?" Xian asked.

His son took a deep breath. "I talked to Ms. Thompson about getting a dog and she said that she thought you might be okay with it. I wanted her to bring me home so that she could convince you to let me have a dog."

Xian rubbed his hand across his brow. His son's life had been in danger for the sake of a dog. "Chou, what did the men look like? Were they police officers?"

"No, I don't think so. They had funny accents."

Xian struggled to keep his face neutral as both fear and anger roiled in his stomach. He'd never felt more helpless. The people who had tried to kidnap Alex could have harmed Chou. He was angry with Alex for putting her own and his son's life in danger. But most of his of his anger was directed at his own blindness. Alex's presence at SimTek on the day of the take-over finalization, and the break-in at her house should have set off warning bells.

"Dad, will Ms. Thompson be okay? Those men were evil looking."

Xian stood up and put a hand on Chou's shoulder. The last thing he wanted to do was alarm his son. There was the possibility that the people who had threatened Alex could have seen Chou. The sooner he got his son out of town, the better he'd feel. "Everything will be fine, Chou. I'll look after Ms. Thompson. You worry about what clothes you want to pack for the weekend."

"What about Shadow?"

"Shadow?" His brow wrinkled.

"The cat, Dad."

"Oh, I'll take him home."

"Dad."

"Yes, Chou."

"Can we have a dog?"

"Let me think about that one, okay?" He gave the boy a hug and ruffled his hair. "One more thing, Son."

"Yes Dad?" Chou smiled up at him.

"No more secrets."

"I promise," replied Chou.

"Good. Why don't you go and start eating dinner. I've got a couple of phone calls I need to make." He then turned and walked out of the room, going into the study and closing the door behind him.

Waiting in his car for Alex to arrive, Xian watched as neighbors out walking their dogs hurried into their homes to avoid the coming rain. The beginning of the storm came exactly as Alex pulled into the garage. Xian waited for five minutes before he reached into the backseat and picked up a half-asleep Shadow, then made his way to the front door and pressed the door-bell.

The moment Alex opened the door Xian could tell something was wrong. He held out the cat in front of him and lowered him to the ground. Shadow dashed into the house.

"Thank you for bringing Shadow home. Have a safe trip back, Xian."

As she moved to close the door, Xian deliberately stepped inside. "We need to talk, Alex."

"I'm really not in the mood for company tonight. How about I call you tomorrow?" she suggested.

"Not an option." Xian suppressed a grin of amusement at her look of surprised annoyance.

He watched as she glanced over his shoulder to something outside.

"Fine. Come in."

Alex heard her cell phone ring just as she closed the door. "Come in and have a seat." She picked up her purse from the entryway table and pulled it out as she walked into the livingroom.

Before answering she checked the caller ID. "Hello?"

"Alex, where the hell have you been? I've left at least two messages on your cell phone. Are you okay?" Alex pulled the phone back from her ear, wincing at the loudness of Karen's voice. She looked at the phone screen and sure enough, the voicemail indicator was blinking.

"I'm fine. I wasn't home when they broke in. Your computer and some other things were taken." She could hear the sound of a voice coming from a loud-speaker in the background.

"Where are you?" Alex asked before her roommate could start asking questions.

"I'm at JFK airport."

"Are you coming back?" Alex asked.

"That's why I'm calling. I need go to the islands to visit my parents."

"That's great. Give them a big hug and kiss for me."

"Hold up. I want you to come with me."

"What?"

"I want you to buy a ticket and meet me in the Bahamas. With all the stuff that's been going down, you need a vacation. Besides, it's spring break."

"Thanks for the offer, but I have some things that I need to do here. This isn't a good time for me to jump ship." She looked pointedly at Xian. He'd followed her into the living room but instead of taking a seat on the sofa, he leaned against the doorway.

"Damn, my flight's boarding."

"Then you better hang up the phone and go catch it."

"Don't think that I'm letting this go, Alex."

"Have a nice flight, K."

"I'll call you when I land."

"Take care of yourself."

"As long as you stay out of trouble."

She hung up the phone and turned towards her unwelcome visitor. Alex's breath caught in response to the intense look in Xian's eyes.

"Why did those men try to kidnap you today?"

Xian watched as her face visibly hardened. He growled, "Who were they and why did you make my son promise to keep silent?"

Alex flinched at the edge in his voice. She swept her hands through her hair and pushed it back into place. She lifted her chin and stared at Xian.

"It doesn't concern you." It bothered her the way he sounded concerned and protective. What upset her the most was the fact that a part of her liked it.

"I disagree. You brought me into this, first by giving me back my son and second by asking him to keep a secret from me. Not to mention that you lied about your employment at SimTek."

"What do you mean?"

"I had someone check the records. Alexandra Thompson has never been in the payroll system."

"Maybe they made a mistake," she replied.

"I'm on your side, Alex. You don't have to lie to me." His voice softened almost as if he were speaking to a frightened child.

Alex watched him carefully. She wanted to talk to someone…anyone, but she deliberately ignored the feeling and took a step away from Xian.

Something in her eyes pushed him. He hadn't felt such intense emotions since his wife died. Something about Alex triggered all of his protective instincts and letting go of his restraint, he reached out to take her arms.

The thread of reason Alex had been holding onto snapped when she felt his hand on her shoulder. All the bottled anger bubbled to the surface and Alex responded automatically. She hit Xian. When the red haze cleared, Alex took a step back willing her heart to slow its furious pace.

When Xian was sure Alex was calmer, he stepped closer and pulled her into his arms. He smoothed back her hair and ran his fingers over her neck, massaging away the tightness. Alex laid her head on his shoulder and closed her eyes. Her arms wrapped around him, hesitantly, gently.

"Look at me, Alex." His voice dropped to a low seductive whisper. His dark eyes searched her brown ones. She felt soft, warm, and fragile in his arms.

"I only want to help you."

He'd asked for something simple, to help. But she knew that embedded deep within Xian's desire to help was a request. He wanted her to trust him. Alex bent her head to hide from his intense gaze. Chaotic feelings of attraction were blurring her logic. Alex lifted her face again and stared into Xian's face.

He watched as her almond-shaped eyelids swept up to reveal eyes holding guarded trust and mixed desire. Instinctively, he lowered his head and touched his lips to hers. His kiss wasn't gentle and neither was her response. Alex's hands slid up to the nape of his neck. Xian felt her fingers running through his hair and shivered. His body reacted to her heat, her scent, and her feminine curves.

Alex's heart jumped and her blood began to heat. Letting go of his shoulders, she backed away and reached backwards to lean on a chair to steady herself. She touched her fingers to her swollen lips and looked at Xian. He stood there calmly, his arms crossed and his eyes amused.

It took Alex a moment to realize that the top three buttons of her blouse were undone. With slightly shaking fingers, she re-buttoned her blouse and moved to sit down. Taking a couple of deep breaths, Alex sought to diffuse the explosive situation.

"That wasn't supposed to happen."

"It happened, Alex." He lifted his hand, displaying two fingers. "Twice."

Alex shook her head. "I was going to apologize for hitting you."

"You changed your mind?" Xian raised an eyebrow.

Alex smiled at the teasing note in his voice.

"Tell me what those men wanted," he said.

She met his stare with a steady look. "I appreciate your offer to help, but I can't afford any distractions and I don't need a hero. Besides, you really can't help me with this, Xian…."

She looked at his expression. It had changed little, if at all. Alex sighed. There was no way to get around it. The man was persistent.

"Take a seat. This is going got be a long story."

Instead of taking a seat at a distance, he joined her on the sofa. Alex deliberately ignored the way he sat as close to her as possible. She scooted over but couldn't seem to escape the musky scent of his cologne.

Needing something to do, she began to absent-mindedly twist a lock of her hair as she laid out the events of the past four weeks. At the mention of Brian's death, she closed her eyes and took a deep breath. Pushing on, she told him of the visit from the FBI and the ballistics report, but made sure to leave out her midnight visit from Tobias. Then she ended with the afternoon encounter with her would-be kidnappers.

"Apparently Brian had something called a Mirror Code and they want it pretty bad."

"What did he mean to you?" As soon as he asked the question, Xian realized he didn't want to know the answer.

Alex looked up with startled surprise. "Who?"

"This Brian. What was he to you?" he asked curtly.

"It's not important." She stood and began to move away, but Xian's words stopped her in mid-step.

"Alex, don't pretend there is nothing between us. We only have to be in the room with one another for you to know the truth. I ask again. What was this Brian to you? I will not fight a ghost." The minute he spoke the words, Xian knew they were a lie. Nothing had ever stood in the way of something he wanted.

"He was a friend," she answered.

"Is that what they call that type of affection in this country? Is it customary for a friend to propose marriage to another?"

Alex blushed and turned to face Xian. She was taken off guard by his remembrance of their previous conversation.

"He was my friend; he was my brother, my family. Brian was someone that I trusted and he had my back. I knew that no matter what, he would be there for me. How could I not have feelings for him?"

"You loved him?"

"I loved him, but I wasn't *in* love with him. And it haunts me that he died knowing that." Alex's voice trembled and she bit the inside of her lip. The possibility that her actions could have set him on the wrong path troubled her.

Xian stood and watched, knowing that she was on edge and one push would send her over. He had seen what guilt could do to a person and it was eating at

Alex. He steered the conversation back to the threat at hand.

"These men think you have this Mirror Code?"

Alex stood and began to pace. "They were probably looking for it when they broke into my house," she admitted reluctantly.

"They'll be back," he stated. "You can't stay here."

"I'm not leaving," she answered. "Besides, I'm safer than I've ever been."

Alex grinned at his puzzlement. "Didn't you notice the white van sitting out front?"

"Yes."

"Well, guess who's watching us now? The FBI," she quipped in a singsong manner.

"I don't understand," Xian responded.

"Go ahead and take a look out the window," she suggested.

Xian stood up and pulled back the curtain. Just as Alex had said, a white van sat parked on the street opposite her house.

Alex distractedly looked down at the pile of yesterday's mail lying on the table. She'd been about to sort through the pile when Xian rang the doorbell.

"Xian…" Her voice trailed off as something caught her eye. Alex bent to pick up the large brown envelope. No return address. It sat there with just her name printed in bold black letters. She didn't remember seeing it in the mail.

"What is it?"

She gingerly opened the envelope and pulled out the single sheet of paper. Stapled to the top was an elementary school picture. Chou's small face was circled in red. Beneath the picture was an address and a time. Fear unlike anything that she had ever known curled in her stomach. She couldn't speak as Xian gently pulled the letter from her nerveless fingers.

Xian looked up from the letter to see Alex turn towards the window, her shoulders slumped and head bowed. The lingering anger he had carried since Chou told him of Alex's attempted kidnapping vanished.

Alex felt the weight of Xian's stare on her back but didn't care. She was caught between two pillars of self-blame and rage. She heard him come up behind her and tried to move away, only to be stopped by his hands. Alex closed her eyes and forced her body to relax. She felt Xian's warm fingers on her shoulders and sighed at the touch of his hands. She had to force her mind to focus on the task at hand.

When she spoke her voice was calm and clear. "I won't let them hurt your son."

"I know. *We* won't allow it."

Alex reluctantly pulled away. She turned towards Xian but didn't meet his stare. Guilt clawed at her, its nails digging into her mind and exposing memories best left buried. She blinked and the ghost-like figures of those she couldn't save floated before her eyes. This was not the military. The enemy had never been so close to home.

"I'm sure that the threat is harmless," she lied, trying to put him at ease. "But just in case, you should go back home. I have to go and change."

The meeting place was one that she knew by reputation. Cocktail dress and suits. Alex did what she did best: She assumed control to mitigate risk.

Xian smiled inwardly at her attempt to get rid of him. "It's good that I didn't change out of my suit."

Alex turned, puzzled. "What?"

He deliberately sat down on the couch and checked his watch. "You had better hurry."

"I'm going alone." She glared down at him from the stairway.

He simply crossed his legs and sat back. "Chou was supposed to spend the weekend at a friend's house. I'm going to call Mrs. Lee and tell her to take Chou out of town for the weekend."

"I'm not kidding about this, Xian." Alex exhaled loudly. He wasn't taking her seriously. "Again, I appreciate your offer to help but this is my problem and I'll handle it."

"Wrong, Alex. We aren't playing by your rules anymore. Whoever is after this program threatened my son. We do this together."

Frustration spilled out into her voice. "I can't protect you. I won't take a civilian into a dangerous situation."

"The last time I checked you were a teacher. When did you re-enlist in the army?"

Alex hit him again with the truth they both knew. "I wasn't in the Army. I was in the Special Forces, part of an elite counterintelligence unit, Xian."

Xian deliberately widened his eyes slightly as his lips curled into a smile. "I feel safer about my son's education already."

Alex turned and stomped up the stairs, frustrated, but secretly relieved not to have to face this on her own. Going to the closet, she pulled a lacquered box from the secret compartment and removed the weapons. Then she took her time getting dressed. After donning a black silver patterned dress, she pulled on her panty hose, then strapped the tiny derringer mid-thigh. She carefully wrapped the specially crafted armband to the upper part of her bicep and slipped in the lightweight silver blade.

Alex added the matching jacket and went into the bathroom. She parted her hair in the middle, then pulled back the sides and secured them with black chopsticks so that her tresses hung straight down her back. After applying mascara and eye shadow, Alex lined her lips with brown and filled them in with a light hazel lipstick. She slipped on her shoes and grabbed her purse, then headed downstairs.

When Alex reached the bottom stair, she saw Xian standing next to the front door.

Xian watched as Alex made her way down the stairs. She was an enticing picture. He wanted to cover her slender neck with a strand of cultured pearls, the only thing that he could think of that would enhance her sensual, elegant grace. Alex was the very essence of a beautiful and fragile woman, yet he remembered the ease with which she'd flipped him onto the mat.

"I know where the club is, so just follow me," she said.

She walked towards the door and reached to pick up her car keys from the table. His hand landed on top of hers, startling her.

"We'll go in my car," he replied, his voice holding a slight British clip.

Alex opened her mouth to argue.

Xian placed his hand on her arm. "We're supposed to be on a date, remember? We go together."

Xian frowned as he felt something hard on Alex's arm. "What is this?"

"Armband with a silver dagger."

"No high tech stun gun?" he teased.

Alex was mildly surprised at his knowledge of weaponry. "Too noticeable. My uncle had this made for me."

He raised his eyebrow slightly. "I'd like to meet this uncle of yours someday."

Alex regarded him for an instant before turning back towards the door, "No, you wouldn't."

Xian smiled and took her hand. "Smile, Alex, your adoring FBI watchers await."

He opened the front door and placed a quick kiss on her lips. Alex gritted her teeth to keep from hitting him. Then Xian played the perfect gentlemen,

holding the umbrella over both of them and opening
the car door for her.

They pulled out of the driveway and Alex looked
into the side mirror. Sure enough, the white van
pulled out slowly and began to follow. Unconsciously,
her fingers curled into a ball. From a very early age she
had learned to depend on herself, take control. She
was used to taking care of herself. She had come to
like the sense of strength and confidence it brought.

The feelings Xian brought to the surface scared her
as no other. With Brian, she had felt as if she were in
a safe harbor. Brian had always been calm. He had
accepted her actions and allowed her her space. Xian,
however, felt like a tsunami, tearing through and
blowing her carefully constructed life to hell. She
couldn't understand his insistence on staying, helping,
caring even as she tried to push him away. Alex closed
her eyes and began counting in Japanese, hoping to
distract her wayward thoughts. *Ichí, ní, san, shí, gó,
rokú, shichí, hachí, kyúu, júu.*

Xian stopped at the stoplight and glanced towards
the woman at his side. He felt desire surge through his
body. He had chosen to be alone after Shay-Lin's
death. Yet being with Alex made him feel alive again.
She was a mystery and a challenge. He looked at her
profile in the soft glow of the streetlight.

Her skin was deep brown, like burnished wood.
Her lips were lush, now slightly parted in a pout. Her
long eyelashes fluttered. Alex's hair lay roped against
her neck. He wanted to reach out and finger her hair.

She reminded him of the statuette of an Egyptian princess he had seen on a visit to a museum. Xian resumed driving, trying to concentrate, but was intensely aware of her scent. Alex's perfume seemed to glide across him and he breathed deeply, inhaling the scent of jasmine and sandalwood. He cracked the window to let the fresh air cleanse his thoughts.

Pulling into the restaurant parking lot, he joined a line of waiting cars. Xian reached out and touched Alex's cheek, liking the feel of her smooth skin and excited by the way she unconsciously turned her face into his palm.

"Alex, we're here."

She turned to look out the front window and saw the line of cars ahead. Once they reached the entrance, Alex picked up her purse and accepted the hand of the waiting valet attendant.

Alert to the attention directed towards her, she allowed Xian to place his arm around her waist. They'd moved to the sidewalk leading to the club's entrance when a tall figure blocked her way. She looked up to see the familiar face of the tall Russian she had kicked in the parking lot earlier that day.

The man didn't look happy to see her and she wasn't thrilled to see him either. Alex tensed, seeing the anger in his face as his jaw clenched.

He spoke in a heavily accented voice, "If you would come with me." He signaled that he wanted Alex to accompany him alone and gestured towards the entryway. Alex moved to follow but felt Xian tighten his grip on her arm.

"Alex and I came together and we will leave together." His voice was cool and emotionless.

Alex watched as the Russian slowly pulled back his jacket to flash the gun holstered on his left side.

Xian looked pointedly towards the street. "If you look to your right at that white van, you'll notice that there are two FBI agents sitting inside watching us. Now you can either let us both in or arouse their suspicion. What's it going to be?"

Alex turned towards Xian and looked at him. One half of her was impressed by the maneuver and the other half was furious at his intervention. They were here to explain that there was a mistake being made, not to get killed.

"Please come this way," said the tall man.

The room they entered was small. The sound of loud music trickled up from a carved stairway to the left. Couples sat at round tables talking over candle-light. The stage, which took up the far right wall, was occupied by a quartet of jazz musicians.

An unassuming young man appeared in front of Alex. Slender with blonde curly hair, pale skin, and square jaw, he was dressed in black and his expression was wiped clean of emotion. He led them through the rows of tables to one placed at the far end of the room, away from the stage.

There was a man sitting at the table. Alex noticed that the table was hidden from view because of the remote location and dim lighting. The man stood as they neared and he spoke a few words in Russian. Another man appeared out of the darkness.

She tensed but made no movement to reach for the weapon in her purse as he approached. He waved a wand over both Xian and Alex. She stood still and watched them work. It took her less than a moment to recognize the bug detector. The fact that they were checked for listening devices and not weapons let her know that her nemesis didn't see her as a physical threat. Before moving back into the shadows, he spoke to the man at the table.

"Please be seated, Ms. Thompson."

His accent was hard to place, definitely Eastern European but not completely Russian. He was a big man, tall and heavy. His hands were large and his arms muscled. The man's brown hair was peppered with silver and had been cut short around the sides. It was his eyes that Alex studied. She had seen eyes like his before. They were cold, colorless. She knew with a certainty that as long this man was alive she wouldn't sleep easy. This was a man who wouldn't hesitate to kill.

He never took his eyes off her as he gestured towards Xian. "I did not expect you to bring company."

Xian answered before Alex could speak, "I didn't expect you to threaten my son, Mr...."

"Banovic."

Alex placed her hands on the table. "Now that we've gotten past the introductions, Banovic," she smiled politely, "would you mind telling me exactly what it is you want from me?"

His eyes flicked to Xian and then back to her. He sat back against the chair and placed his hands on the table, his fingers steepled.

"I want the disk, Ms. Thompson."

Alex gave him an innocent look. "Disk?"

"Don't play games with me. I am not a very patient man."

"Well, doesn't this work out well? I'm an elementary school teacher so I have plenty of patience. I can teach you some."

"Ah, yes. You are an elementary school teacher with a Special Operations background, known for getting out of tight situations with low body counts."

Alex paled slightly but schooled her features into a tight smile. "And this matters to you?"

"I believe Brian gave you something which belongs to me. I want it."

"Not only do I not have it but Brian and I had broken up long before his death."

"Really?" He leaned forward. "Then why did he call you before his unfortunate accident?"

Accident? His death had been due to murder. Alex held her tongue. No sense digging a deeper hole for them to crawl out of. "He wanted to tell me that he was leaving the country."

"And you hadn't planned on leaving with him?" He raised an a heavy eyebrow. "

"I didn't know."

"Then why were you at his condo, Ms. Thompson?"

Her estimation of Banovic rose another notch. He had not only accessed her records, but he also knew about the plane tickets and the phone call. She quickly changed the topic. "What's on this disk anyway?"

Banovic smiled. Alex was struck with the memory of venturing to a local village on a class trip. The Okinawan farm had contained a snake house. She had watched as a mongoose stood still, tracking the progress of a habu snake across the short grass. Waiting...enjoying the moment before the kill.

"Why don't you ask your companion, Ms. Thompson? I'm sure getting back the program Mr. Scott designed is a top priority for him, given that his company just staged a successful takeover of SimTek." He smirked.

Alex resisted the urge to look at Xian. Banovic was playing a dangerous game and she couldn't afford to get sidetracked. She'd had enough of this man. Suddenly sick to her stomach, Alex felt as though she would vomit as the taste of something long buried rose in her mouth. All she wanted to do was take out her gun and shoot Banovic. As long as he thought Brian had given her that damned disk, they were all in danger.

"Why do you think Brian gave me the disk?"

"You, Ms. Thompson, were the only one he had contact with before his unfortunate accident. Your background makes you the perfect person to keep it safe for him. You see, he was planning on leaving the country with you, my money, and the program. But your ex-fiancé had an attack of conscience."

Banovic stood. "Ms. Thompson, I don't care if you have my disk or not. You have seventy-two hours to find it or I will destroy everything and everyone you care about, starting with the boy."

In seventy-two hours, she'd either be facing Rafé or getting killed. Alex shook her head. She didn't know which was the lesser of the two evils but she had had enough of this man and his veiled threats. She stood and watched the bodyguards out of the corner of her eyes. Xian stood up beside her, took her hand and squeezed it. She didn't know if it was for reassurance or a warning.

"I look forward to our next meeting. And Ms. Thompson? Do not involve our friends the FBI." His voice hinted at things dark and menacing.

Alex turned to see the second man standing guard. He was of medium height, had short spiked hair, and wore dark clothes. Nothing set him apart, except for what was in his hand. His fingers seemed to caress the handle of the Glock semi-automatic. She held his stare for a moment and felt recognition. His gaze held an unspoken promise. She tightened her grip on her purse.

SEVENTEEN

Alex let Xian lead her away from the table while everything in her screamed to turn around and fight. She thought he had grabbed her hand, thinking that she was afraid for herself or Chou. In reality, she was far from afraid; Alex uncurled her fist and saw a perfect set of crescent moons indented into her palm.

She feared for the people who threatened Chou's life and for what Xian would think of her. Knowing that anger made her careless, she pushed it back. Instinctively, she knew that someone was going to die and another ghost would haunt her dreams. It wasn't until they reached the stairs that Alex looked up and discovered that Xian wasn't heading for the exit but downstairs into the dance club.

Alex pulled her hand from his and stopped on the bottom step. The music seemed to reach out and wrap itself around her. She felt the vibrations against her skin and the beat echoed in her head. The lights pulsated with the rhythm of the music, bathing the crowd in a multicolored glow. Alex moved back against the wall to allow a couple to pass.

"Why didn't you tell me?" she shouted over the noise.

"I intended to. When I had the opportunity."

"You've had plenty of chances." She dodged as Xian tried to touch her arm.

"To be honest, I didn't make the connection between you and Brian Scott until an hour ago. My company bought SimTek because of its overall .technology infrastructure, not because of one experimental security program."

She looked at him warily. She tried to make decisions based on the facts, but in the end it came down to her instincts and they hadn't failed her yet.

"Trust me, Alex." His voice was a loud whisper over the pulsating music.

Alex held his gaze for a moment longer, and then nodded her head. "You heard the man; we have seventy-two hours to find that damned disk. We've got to get out of here," she shouted out over the music.

He held out his hand. She took it without thinking and was pulled onto the dance floor.

"What are you doing?" She had to move closer in order to hear his response.

"Dance with me," he whispered in her ear. "We're being watched."

He turned them around quickly and Alex scanned the room through the haze of smoke. She instantly got a full view of the watchers Xian was referring to. They were in the darkest corner of the room and were wearing uniformly dark navy suits. Alex could have spotted them anywhere but they stood apart in a room filled with the trendy and moneyed young elite of San Francisco.

Alex shifted to fit into Xian's body and laid her head on the curve of his shoulder. She felt him tighten his grip around her waist and she unconsciously relaxed, allowing her body to match his rhythm.

At some invisible sign, the music slowed, and Alex allowed herself to play the part of the adoring girl-friend.

Xian felt the tension leave Alex's body and smiled. In his arms she seemed fragile, precious. Feelings long buried rose to the surface of his heart. Xian lowered his head and inhaled the fragrance of her perfume.

"We should do this again soon," he whispered in her ear, his lips lightly kissing the nape of her neck. He felt the shudder that flowed through her body.

Xian looked up again to check on the watching agents and he tensed. One of the suit-clad men placed a cell phone in his pocket and turned to the other. Xian realized that something had happened and had begun slowly dance away in the opposite direction when he saw the agent point toward them.

"Come on. We've got to get out of here." He took hold of Alex's hand and headed towards the closest door.

"What?" Alex turned and instantly recognized the situation. They moved together through the crowd, keeping ahead of the agents. As soon as they made it to the door, Alex broke into a run. Xian unlocked the car with the remote and they jumped in. "What happened?"

"Don't know but judging by the look on their faces, whatever it is doesn't bode well for either of us." Xian started the car and put it into reverse. Alex braced herself as Xian hit the brakes. Turning to look out the back window of the car she saw that a black Suburban with tinted windows had boxed them in.

"Damn." Before she could turn around, the doors to the car were jerked open and she was pulled out.

"What the hell?" Alex saw a stocky, suit-clad man with a serious expression.

"Ms. Thompson, I'm Agent Blake with the FBI. You will come with us."

Alex grabbed the car door and held on. The man turned, surprised that she wasn't following meekly behind him. Alex looked at Xian. Two agents stood next to his door.

"Why?" she demanded loudly, aware of the gathering spectators.

The agent's face looked as though set in stone. "We have reason to believe that your life is in jeopardy. We're placing you in protective custody, ma'am."

"You've got to be kidding," she bit out impatiently.

"Ms. Thompson, do you recognize this man?" Alex turned towards the new voice. One of the agents from the club stood three feet away. Alex schooled her features, barely managing not to betray her surprise. The agent held a picture of Trevor, Brian's best friend.

"Yes," she replied coolly.

"His name is Trevor Collins. Mr. Collins was found unconscious and beaten in his apartment less than an hour ago. He is now on life support at the hospital. We believe that you will be the next person targeted."

Alex stood still in shock at the new turn of events. She didn't have time to react when the agents grabbed her arm and pushed her into the backseat of the sedan. She stared as the other agents surrounded Xian and felt helpless as the car pulled away.

What else can go wrong? Alex sat down on the bed, frustrated. The hotel suite the agents had chosen to lock her in was generously sized with a view of the city. The FBI had questioned her throughout the drive and continued after arriving at the hotel. She'd managed to produce vague answers to their questions but Alex knew that they would ask again and again until they got the answers they wanted.

Trying to think of anything except Trevor's bruised and beaten body lying on a hospital bed, Alex picked up the remote control and turned on the TV. *All this for a disk*, Alex thought. *Damn it, Brian, where would you hide it?*

Alex stared unseeing at the television screen, until something caught her eye. She turned up the volume as she stared at the latest commercial hawking handheld electronic organizers to the masses. Then she stood and went to the adjoining door to talk with the FBI; she had a hunch but needed access to a computer to verify it. She turned the doorknob and cracked opened the door but stopped when she heard her name.

"Cooper, we've got a problem."

"What?"

"Just got the word from HQ that the spooks are putting pressure on the chief. They want the girl. Think that she can help them get Banovic."

"Damn it. This is exactly what we don't need. Get on the phone and stall. The girl knows more then she's telling. My gut keeps telling me she's the key to this thing and I'm not going to let some satellite jockeys steal my case."

Alex quietly closed the door and began to plan. Within moments, she was in motion. She entered the bathroom and turned on the shower. Returning to the bedroom, she took a deep breath, grabbed her purse, inched back the sliding glass door, and went out onto the balcony. The wind blew through her hair as she gripped the railing and took a look down. Bad move.

The fifteenth-floor balcony stood high above the city streets.

"Just a walk in the park. You've done it before, you can do it again," she murmured.

Alex tossed her shoes and purse onto the other balcony, trying to forget the fact that it had been a while. Saying a silent prayer, Alex hitched up her dress and carefully lifted her leg over the railing. It took a minute for her to find a toehold on the ledge. She concentrated on keeping her center of gravity towards the building and moved slowly towards the divider, which separated her room from the next.

After taking a long and steady breath, she released all the air from her lungs and skirted around the center barrier to the other balcony, letting out an audible sound of relief at the darkness of the hotel room. Taking no chances, she swung over the railing and crouched down.

She placed her ear against the glass, counted to ten and then slid the door back. Thankfully, the room was unoccupied. Grabbing her shoes and purse, she stepped in and crossed to the door. After checking that the hallway was empty, she was out the door in a flash and disappeared inside the stairwell. If any of the hotel staff or guests noticed Alex's brisk walk through the lobby a few moments later, none commented on it. She sailed out the door and smiled at the bellhop before jumping into a waiting cab.

Alex could tell that the cabbie had just finished his evening meal. The interior reeked of curry. She tossed him a fifty-dollar bill through the window in the plastic separator screen.

"Take me to the Cyber Café in Union Square."

She reached into her purse and pulled out Tobias's cell phone to dial Xian's number. Her heart gave an involuntary leap at the sound of his voice on the other end of the static-filled line.

"Alex, where are you?" he asked. "I've been trying your cell phone for the past hour."

"No time to talk, just meet me at the Cyber Café in Union Square. I have an idea about where we can find some information that might get us out of this mess."

Alex was typing away by the time Xian arrived at the café. She had taken up residence on the empty second floor. It was all she could do to stay in her seat and not get up and put her arms around Xian when he walked in.

He moved gracefully and lithely like a man in control. Alex shook her head, hoping to rid herself of emotion, and turned back to the computer screen with its flickering hourglass.

"Alex, what happened to the FBI?"

"I left them."

"What?"

She filled him in while she polished off her café latte and carrot cake muffin. "They aren't concerned with the people who killed Brian. All they want is to keep the CIA from taking over their case."

"They're not going to let you go that easily. You just made fools of them." Xian sounded more amused than worried.

"What are you looking for?" he asked.

"Information on Brian's last movements."

"You're breaking into his email?"

"No. Brian loved his electronic organizer. Trevor and I joked that he was obsessed with the thing. He kept everything on it and in the beginning he was always nervous about losing the stored data. So he bought space on a web server just so he could have a secure backup location to store information. Brian was really meticulous about uploading everyday. It makes sense that he'd keep information relating to the Mirror Code safe."

"Wouldn't Banovic have gotten this already?"

"I don't know. There wouldn't be a way to track the exact point where he uploaded the data. The company operates multiple web sites. Only by inputting a specific address would the info be sent to the right directory."

"You know where it is?" he asked, peering at the screen.

"Brian gave me access to his account. Our class was working on a web page and he let me use some space to store content and images."

Alex's lips lost their smile as she looked at the screen and began to read the last entry in the system. It was made a week before he was killed.

Xian's smile fell as he saw disbelief and sadness flash through Alex eyes.

"What is it?" He moved to look over her shoulder and read.

Dear Alex,

If you are reading this, then everything has gone wrong and my plan has failed. What started out as a challenge ended up with me getting in way over my head. I thought I would show the world what a black man could do and at the same time teach those bastards at SimTek a lesson,

*teach them that this boy is a man. But I made the mistake
of letting Pandora out of the box, Lee. I planned to give
them the disk, take the money, and run. I hoped that you
and I would find a nice little spot down south. But I guess
that didn't happen. These people are serious, Lee. I need
your help to protect my parents. I learned too late that
money couldn't buy happiness or persistence gain your love.
I will never forget you, Lee. Mozart never sounded the
same without you. I only hope that you have the strength
to do what I couldn't.*

Alex reached up to rub her brow. The headache,
which had started at the hotel, pounded like a jack-
hammer inside her skull. The note gave substance to
her mounting suspicions. She couldn't help but wonder
if her rejection had played a part of Brian's decisions.

"Alex," Xian began.

"What?" Alex tried to whisper but her voice
sounded loud in the half-empty room.

"We've got to get out of here."

"Why?"

She turned, following the direction of his gaze, and
saw the two black sedans pull to a halt on the street
below. She turned quickly and hit the power button on
the PC. They were halfway to the exit door when Alex
stopped. "How did they…" She reached into her
pocket and pulled out an innocuous looking hotel key
card and threw it back towards the window. They
managed to sneak out the back door right when the
FBI agents entered the café.

"There she is!"

Alex turned to see two agents coming around the corner of the building. In unison, they ran toward her.

"Stop!"

"Where's your car?" Alex demanded.

"One block down."

Alex glanced behind her. The agents were yelling into their radios.

When they rounded the corner, Alex saw the silver BMW. "Give me the keys."

Alex caught them as she ran to the driver's side of the car. She jumped in, started it, and peeled off, leaving the cursing agents behind. Alex whipped the car through traffic. Anger rode her like the wind and she sped through the street as if she could run from the memories.

"We've lost them," Xian declared.

Alex gave a quick look into the rearview mirror before turning left on the expressway onramp. She said nothing, just stared straight ahead.

"You can slow down now," Xian urged as Alex began passing cars. He reached out and touched her shoulder lightly. She jumped.

"Alex, we don't want to escape the FBI only to get arrested for speeding."

The speedometer eased down and Xian sat back. "So we're back to square one," he exhaled. Her response when it came was unexpected.

"No." She shook her head. "I know where he hid the disk. Brian hated Mozart. He only tolerated it because I liked it."

"Where?" Xian's voice trailed off as he reached for the ringing car phone.

"Don't," Alex yelled but it was too late. Xian had already hit the talk key. Alex drove, not understanding a word but furious with the potential mistake Xian had just made. Car phones could be tracked. Even if the FBI had somehow overlooked it in the beginning, they wouldn't now. Not after her escape. Alex began to plan. First, they would have to ditch the car. The sound of rapid Chinese filled the car.

"Son of a bitch!"

"What is it?"

"The bastards have my son." Xian felt rage run up and down his spine. A low murderous hiss escaped his lips

"When…how?" she asked.

"Somewhere on the outskirts of Oakland. His nanny just stopped for gas and went in to pay. This is my fault. I told her to use cash so that she couldn't be tracked. I didn't think they would have her followed."

Alex pulled off the interstate and drove until she found a gently lit residential area. She turned off the ignition of the car, laid her head back, and closed her eyes. The pounding in her head had come back with a vengeance, along with unimaginable fury. She turned towards the backseat and grabbed her purse. Reaching in, she pulled out her cell phone, praying that she was making the right decision.

"Are you calling the FBI?" Xian asked.

"No. I'm calling in backup. The plan just changed."

"What plan?"

"The one that says we play by their rules. We're going to get Chou back and then we'll take care of those bastards."

"So now what?" Xian questioned. Frustration was eating him alive.

"We wait."

Alex flipped open the phone and hit the red button. They sat in silence, each buried in guilt.

Xian was numb by the time the black Ford Explorer pulled up next to the car fifteen minutes later.

"Xian, we've got to go. We need to ditch the car," Alex revealed.

"Why?"

"They're probably tracking us down right now as we speak. We probably don't have much time left. Once the FBI is able to triangulate the location of the last cell tower you used, they'll be here."

He nodded, understanding the logic behind her words. Xian followed as Alex got out of the car. She got into front of the Explorer and he into the back. Within seconds, they were on their way down the empty streets of suburban San Francisco.

Alex turned towards Miguel. Though partially illuminated by the passing streetlights, his face was unreadable. He had shifted his weight so that his weapon was within plain sight and easily accessible. Miguel was not happy about bringing Xian along.

"Where's Tobias?" she asked in Spanish.

"He needed to take care of something. He'll be waiting back at the house. Where do you want me to drop him?"

Alex gave Miguel a meaningful look. "He comes with us."

Miguel arched an eyebrow and his lips pressed into a grim line before he turned his attention back to driving. Alex suppressed a sigh. One more thing to deal with.

Alex looked unseeingly into the night. Her thoughts centered on Chou. *What have I done?* She stared out at the passing scenery and slowly began to pay attention to the direction in which they were traveling. They were in the valley area she had driven through many times before.

"Where are we going?"

Miguel replied in Spanish, "Rafé's house."

"Why?"

He shrugged. "I was told to bring you there."

It took Alex a second to respond, "Is he there?"

"*Sí.*"

"What's wrong?" came Xian's voice from the back-seat.

Alex quickly responded, "Nothing." She was torn between relief and anger. "It looks like we just got lucky."

The car pulled up into the driveway of a rather ordinary two-story house in the valley. Rafé and Tobias were standing on the small porch. Alex closed her eyes and felt the wetness of tears against her eyelids.

"Alex, who are these people?" Xian asked.

Alex was quiet for a moment, wondering how to explain to him that they were government-trained assassins and the nearest thing she had to family. She settled on an in-between answer. "The cavalry."

They exited the car slowly. Alex reached out, took Xian's hand, and led him up the driveway porch. She watched Rafé's eyes as he looked pointedly at their entwined hands, then shot her a look of disapproval and concern. She let go of Xian's hand, walked past the two men and into the house.

She turned to see Miguel enter the house and shut the door. Walking into the living room, her eyes went to Rafé. He was thinner than the last time she'd seen him. She decided to get the introductions over with. "Rafé, Tobias, Miguel, this is Xian Liu. Xian meet my…family."

Despite the relief of seeing her adopted uncle alive, Alex could feel the tension in the room. This was the first time Alex had let anyone outside the group into their circle. She knew that she had broken an unwritten rule.

"When did you return?" she asked Rafé.

"Why is he here, Niña?" Rafé asked in Spanish. The dry flatness of his voice sent a shiver down her spine. He didn't look at her but focused his attention on Xian. If the situation weren't so serious, she would have laughed. They looked like wildcats poised to spring.

Alex replied in the same language, "It was necessary to bring him."

"Is he the reason you are being hunted?" His voice was cold. Alex knew Rafé well; he was pissed. She looked towards Tobias and Miguel who also wore looks of disapproval.

Alex didn't hesitate. "No. Blame Brian. This is his mess. Xian was trying to help me and got pulled in."

"Why did you bring him with you, Niña?"

"They took my son," Xian answered in fluent Spanish.

The room held utter silence. Alex turned to look at Xian. His voice was emotionless and Alex studied his face in the low light of the room. She could see the tension in his eyes. Alex turned towards Rafé.

"We need all the help we can get," she spoke in English. Rafé nodded and left the room. Alex uncurled her clenched fists and followed behind him.

"He's worried about you," Tobias whispered in her ear.

"As I am about him." And she was worried about Rafé. This man who was her father's protégé had been a constant in her life. She knew that he thought of her as his daughter. She worried that his world, the one she had been a part of for a while, the one filled with the blood, violence, terror, subterfuge, and deceit, would never let him go.

"What's happening, Alex?" Rafé asked.

"Brian happened, Rafé," she sighed. "Before he was killed, he created some kind of computer program that can hack into secure systems. The people who did this kidnapped Xian's son."

Rafé's eyes narrowed. "What else?"

"Both the FBI and a man named Banovic want it," she added.

Rafé nodded. "Tobias, find out all you can about our friend Banovic."

"Niña, do you know where the disk is?"

"Yes," she said flatly. Brian's cryptic note regarding Mozart had been the clue she'd needed. When they'd first begun dating, he would pick her up from school and they would have a picnic in the park while listening to the summer series concerts.

Instead of looking towards Rafé, she stared at Xian who was leaning against the wall with his fingers curled into fists. "He hid it in Golden Gate Park. If I'm right, you'll find the disk near the northeast corner of Spreckels Lake, most likely buried next to a tree-trunk bench next to small statue of a Dutch windmill."

"I'll go collect it."

"Xian, can you go with him?" she asked, catching Rafé's intense look. "Two hands are better than one and we need to get that disk."

Rafé picked up his coat and Alex watched the two leave the house.

EIGHTEEN

When Xian arrived back at the house, he immediately went downstairs to the basement. He'd spent the past hour digging up dirt in the park and all he could think about was Chou. When they'd finally found the small box containing the disk, he'd had an insane urge to crush it underneath the heel of his boot. Shaking off his thoughts, Xian opened the door and saw Tobias and Alex staring at the computer screen at a picture of the man from the restaurant, Banovic. He glanced at Alex and saw the lines of tension around her mouth. Xian didn't turn as he felt Rafé and Miguel come to a stop beside him.

"What is it?" he asked.

"Change of plans," Alex stated flatly.

"What is it, Niña?" Rafé asked, coming up behind Xian.

"We split the team. I go solo to the meeting point. You get the boy."

"What happened?" Xian's voice was sharp with fear for his son. Alex closed her eyes and took a deep breath. She opened her mouth only to be forestalled by Tobias.

"The man who took your son has done this before. Five years ago, a terrorist group kidnapped the family of a wealthy Swiss politician. They demanded a ransom of twenty-five million for their safe return."

Xian looked towards the screen as a memory began to tickle in the back of his mind.

"He paid the money?" he guessed. Xian felt the knot in his stomach twist even tighter.

"Yes, but the wife and daughter were returned in body bags. Interpol, Scotland Yard and the CIA have been trying to link Banovic to the crime for years. So far he's been able to keep his hands clean. The man was a ghost up until five years ago."

Tobias called up a picture of two men exiting from an upscale building. "If it's illegal and moves in or out of Eastern Europe, Banovic either knows about it or is behind it. The man is rumored to have ties with Shamil Basayev, the leading Chechen warlord and a couple of other minor arms dealers on the CIA's most wanted list. Banovic has been under heavy scrutiny for a while, according to his file. No personal connections that can help us. Anyone who could be of use mysteriously disappears. His source of funds is untraceable."

"What about his history? Birth records, family?" Rafé asked.

"No one can figure out where he came from or what he's up to. The man is a ghost. They've pegged his origins to the former U.S.S.R. That's about all we know. He has no family. The CIA doesn't even know his real name. There was a rumor that he died in a small skirmish five years ago."

"Who are the men with him?" Alex pointed to the screen.

"Banovic travels with trained guards. He's got two that he keeps with him at all times. The man to the right is Anton Reshiev. He's probably the one Brian made contact with. The man was a professor of cryptology until the university he taught at went under. The others are ex-Russian military 'for hire.'"

"What will they do to my son?" Xian questioned.

Rafé answered. "As long as he thinks we have what he wants, the boy'll be fine."

Alex watched Xian pale under the florescent lights.

"Did you get the disk?" she asked.

Xian took the CD-ROM out of his pocket and held it up the light. Bile rose in his throat at the thought of his son being held because of one man's greed. "We found it exactly where you said it would be."

"I'll take it." Tobias stood and took the disk from his nerveless fingers.

"What are you going to do with it?" he asked.

"Find out what's so important about this disc and to make sure that we have some leverage in case this thing goes down wrong."

"What do we do now?" Xian asked.

"Wait. They'll contact me soon enough," Alex answered wearily. Frustration leaked into her voice. "What does he want the disk for? Money? Power?"

Alex closed her eyes and opened them to see Rafé standing by her side; she had not heard him move. She continued, "According to his file, he's already rich. The man practically owns several small towns. There has to be something we're missing."

"Niña, you need sleep."

"I can't. Too wired."

"Sleep, Alex. You need to be on all eight cylinders for this."

Alex nodded her head and headed towards the stairs. Some part of her wanted to turn and bury herself in Xian's arms. It was that feeling of weakness that pulled her together. Alex turned towards the hallway and made her way to the guest room. The bedroom was spacious with soft carpet. She walked to the window and pulled the curtains back. Moonlight bathed the room.

She took off her jacket and hung it on the bedpost, along with her knives. Alex kicked off her shoes and buried her toes in the carpet. The image of Chou's smiling face as he played with Shadow rose in her mind. Closing her eyes, she reached out and began stretching.

Xian watched her from the doorway. From where he stood, Alex looked like a ghost or spirit, ethereal. He stared as she moved though a series of kicks and poses. Her hair spread over her shoulders like a dark fan, hiding her face from view. Her balance and grace showed with each twist and arm movement.

Xian shook his head and turned. He meant to leave, to go to the next room and lie down, but instead he found himself stepping inside and quietly closing the door. Xian slipped off his shoes and moved to stand behind Alex. Her scent wafted over him and he was lost. It was insanity. But nothing seemed to matter except this moment, this woman. Slowly, he raised his hands and began to mimic her movements.

Alex felt his presence at her back but she continued to stretch. She slowed and like a reed in the wind, she felt her body sway towards Xian. Through half-closed eyes, she watched as Xian's arms followed hers like a shadow. She turned her head slightly and followed the movement of his hands as they mirrored her own, close but not touching. Goosebumps prickled along her skin as the warmth of Xian's breath brushed her. His touch when it came was electric; Alex lost her balance and stumbled back into his arms. She felt Xian's strong hands lift her slightly. She quickly found her center and stood utterly still.

She could hear her heart beating like a wild thing in her chest. Alex looked towards the window and raised her arms, struggling to remember where she had left off stretching. Again, she felt the warmth of his hand as it brushed her shoulder.

Xian leaned over and trailed kisses down her neck, then slowly pulled down the zipper of her dress. Alex stepped forward and let the dress fall to the floor, leaving her standing in a black slip. She turned and looked at Xian. Staring into his face, she felt as if she were looking into her own soul. In the space of a heartbeat, it was as if the floor underneath her feet slowly gave way and she gradually sank into his embrace. When she raised her eyes, she had not moved but found herself in his arms.

"Alex," Xian began, his voice thick with unspoken words. He had tossed and turned in his bed since first laying eyes on her. She was like a haunting dream, a constant desire unfulfilled.

Alex breathed deeply, understanding the war that waged within him. It mirrored the battle within her tortured heart. She let her hand slide between their bodies and under his shirt. She wanted to touch him, feel him, hold him as though he were her lifeline. Alex felt his fingers gently guide her chin upwards.

"Alex," he murmured again, but the tenor of his voice had changed and dropped to a whisper. She saw the uncertainty in his midnight eyes. She smiled and raised her arms to encircle his neck. Weaving her hands into his hair, she reveled in its silky texture. Reality faded. It was just the two of them, lost in their own world.

Alex let her hand slide down the length of his neck and down his back. She had known this moment would come and she welcomed it. In the midst of the storm that was her life, he was a safe harbor, light in the darkness. She moved even closer to Xian, as if she could bury her body in his warmth. Standing on her tiptoes, she placed her lips near his ear, then dipped her head and laid a soft kiss in the little hollow, playfully nipping at his earlobe.

Xian stopped breathing. After a moment, he let the air out of his chest. His body clenched in anticipation as he leaned down and kissed her, crushing her lips under his. Xian groaned. Her lips were warm, lush, and smooth. He thrust his tongue between her lips, exploring the soft recess of her mouth. His hands trailed down her body slowly, enjoying the velvet warmth of her skin.

Alex closed her eyes and sighed into his mouth. She felt her worries subside and fear disappear. His hands were touching her everywhere, leaving her in sweet torment. His fingers traced the pattern of her bra and cupped her aching breasts through the soft satin.

Alex unbuttoned Xian's shirt and watched it fall to the floor. The touch of his naked skin pressed against hers took her breath away.

"Alex, if…"

"Shh…" She gently rained kisses on his shoulder, his throat, his chest. Willing strength into her legs, she took three steps backwards towards the quilt-covered bed. Alex stood straight, shook her hair, looked at Xian, and spoke in a voice laced with need.

"Make love to me," she whispered, her voice low and sultry. She removed the straps of her slip and reached behind her, unclasping the hooks of her bra. It floated to the floor.

To Xian, it was a siren's song, seductive, addicting, desire brought to life; it was a summons he could never refuse. His eyes moved over her face, her upturned breasts, her stomach, her long legs. Her body was flawless and he was in awe: it was his.

Alex turned and pulled back the covers of the bed, her body shaking. She couldn't face him. His arm hooked around her like a vise, and she felt herself pulled backwards. She made a low sound, like a cat. He kissed her neck and she moaned.

She let him lower her onto the bed. His fingertips trailing over her sensitive skin inflamed her. His mouth found her lips and her neck; then his tongue stroked over her breasts, and her body of its own accord went hot and wet. His hands seemed to be everywhere at once. Alex could hear herself groan, the low sound almost a purring, loving the feel of his tongue, his breath, his kiss on her skin.

She felt his hands on her thighs and she opened for him. His fingers slid along her skin until they found her center. Alex curled her fingers in his hair and she brought her lips to his skin and began to lick the smooth hardness of his chest. His warm tongue ran over one breast, gently nipping the sensitive tip. Alex whimpered and her fingers gripped his shoulders.

Xian kissed her stomach and felt her fingers tighten on his shoulders as a shudder ripped through her body. His mouth marked a path across her stomach and traveled lower to the hidden treasure at the middle of her legs.

She shuddered, her fingers tangling in his hair. "Now Xian…" The sound of her moan almost snapped his already tenuous control. Then Alex was like a wild creature in his arms, matching his passion with a fierceness all her own. His fingers continued to explore. He caressed her stomach and the delicate outline of her hips before his fingers once more found her inner softness.

Alex cried out and opened her eyes to see Xian staring down at her. Heat seemed to flow through her body. Need burned her skin and flared throughout her innermost core. She looked into his eyes and saw something beautiful, something that undid her. She kissed him deep and arched her hips, wanting to take him inside. Needing him to cool the flames.

Xian felt his control slipping as he found her hot, moist and ready. He moved over her and Alex moved into him, welcoming him home, bringing him inside. He kissed her deeply as he slowly entered her warmth, wanting to be gentle, needing the pleasure to go on. Alex felt him fill her. She closed her eyes, giving in to the sensation and the sound of his whispered groan as he drew out and then returned, going deeper with each stroke.

He wanted to build a fire but found that it was he who was burning. He moved, nearly undone by the tightness of her desire wrapping around him, so hot and soft, bringing him to the edge of heaven.

Together they danced to a music older than time, moving together as if they were one body, one soul, one heart. A low moan rose from her throat, deep and soft. Xian heard her moan and kissed her long and deep. They moved together. Alex closed her eyes to hide the tears that threatened to spill.

It was incredible, the way he paid homage to her body as though she were beauty itself. A goddess to be worshiped, loved, adored. She held tight to him, holding him close as though afraid he would slip away. She felt her body tighten and her breath stilled. A wave of pleasure washed over her. She clenched around him, holding him close as the fire he fanned engulfed her.

When release came, they exploded together, blazing up like an inferno. She was floating, warmth flooding her body, and Xian was there with her. He was holding her tight, his breath hot against her skin, his moan low in her ear.

Xian shifted his weight and rolled to his side, taking Alex with him. He held her tightly, not wanting to let go while he waited for his breath to even out.

"Alex," he murmured against her throat. "Sweetheart, I didn't protect you." They could have made a child. Xian lowered his head to look at where their bodies still touched. For the first time since his wife's death, he felt truly alive, truly happy. He wanted this moment to last for all time. He wanted her in his arms, his life.

"Don't worry, there will be no child from this." In that moment, she was grateful for her years in the military. Twice a year she willingly received injections. A habit that she had yet to break.

"You can't be sure."

"Yes, I can…" Alex spoke in a low voice. She placed her finger over his lips only to pull it away as he sucked it into his mouth. "Now is not the time for talking, Xian. This is all a dream, my dream. Please don't make this more than what it is, Xian."

He pushed the hair from his face and looked into her eyes. He saw the shadows deep within her depths and wanted to take them away. He didn't completely understand the emotions she stirred up. All he knew was that he would not give her up.

Giving in to the sweet warmth heating her veins, Alex shifted and placed both hands on his shoulders, then straddled him.

"More…" She let herself fall back to bring him in deeper. Her eyes closed as her chest rose and fell in hard little breaths. Xian lifted himself and grasped her shoulders, his lips close to her ear, his breathing harsh and raspy. She moaned again as he ground his hips against hers, as she felt his erection inside her, the roughness of his chest rubbing against her sensitive breasts.

They remained that way for a moment, neither of them really moving, joined together as she sat straddling his lap. Then holding his head in her hands, her slender fingers sinking into his hair, she kissed him again, catching his bottom lip between her sharp little teeth and sucking it as she slowly began to move against him.

As he took over the rhythm of their coupling, Alex held back nothing and she cried and trembled violently. At the end, they rode into the sweet oblivion together.

Alex opened her eyes slowly and blinked. The sun had yet to rise, but she could see the beginnings of day come to the darkness. Her body felt loose, relaxed, and filled with a pleasurable ache. She closed her eyes briefly and drew in a deep breath, then looked down at the arm carelessly thrown around her waist and smiled. It felt so right. Alex laid her head back down on the pillow as last night's events rushed into her mind.

As she stared at Xian's sleeping face, her heart melted. Alex found herself wanting to kiss his lips and run her hand through his hair, just to make sure he wasn't a dream or a ghost. She wanted to stay in the bed, in the shelter of his arms. She wanted to memorize this moment.

A few minutes later, she forced herself to concentrate on the situation at hand. Alex carefully removed Xian's arm and slid out of bed. She stilled as he moved and released her breath only after he turned and settled back into sleep. She felt his loss even though he was still there. Quietly, she put on an old T-shirt and picked up her duffle bag. Slowly opening the bedroom door, she slipped into the hallway, turned towards the bathroom. As she stepped away from the door, Rafé appeared as if by magic.

She felt a warm blush creeping up her neck. Spying the look of disapproval on his face, Alex raised her chin as she looked at the man who was like a father to her.

"My choice, Rafé."

Alex watched as he nodded his head and turned to go downstairs. Feeling as if the weight of the world had returned to her shoulders, she entered the bathroom to take a shower.

Ten minutes later, Alex turned off the water when she heard the soft sound of the door opening and closing. Before she could pull back the curtain, a deep voice echoed off the tiles.

"You never could learn how to lock a door."

She smiled before stepping out onto the floor mat. Without breaking eye contact, she reached for the towel Khan held in his hand, only to have him step closer and wrap it around her.

Alex shivered when Khan whispered in her ear, "I read his file, Leila. He's not the one for you."

She moved only to feel Khan tighten his grip. Alex's breath quickened. She'd forgotten about his message. She thought of Xian asleep in the room.

"Khan…"

His grip loosened as she turned to face him.

"If I did not know you so well, he'd be dead."

She searched his face, making note of the shadows under his eyes and the presence of new stands of gray in his short wavy hair. His burnt copper skin was darker from the desert sun.

"Mahamood, did he die by your hand?" Alex asked before he could say more about Xian.

Alex had seen the bruises Khan's brother-in-law had left on Khan's sister. When he got word that she had suffered a broken arm, Alex had known he'd return to Egypt.

"No, his own evil made it unnecessary," said Khan. "Someone slit his throat before I had the chance."

"Serena is well then?"

"She asked that I give you a message."

Alex tucked the ends of the towel under.

Khan smiled. "My sister said, 'Tell Leila there are three matters which should not be deferred: the Prayer when it's due, the funeral as soon as it is needed, and a marriage when there is an unmarried woman and a suitable husband for her.'"

"Is that a hint?"

"She wants me to marry and return to raise my family in Egypt."

"And what did you say?" Alex joked.

"That you would be too much trouble as a wife."

The sound of her laughter was muted in the steam-filled bathroom. Alex took the second towel Khan held in his hand and wrapped it around her damp hair.

"You should have sent word that you were in trouble," he reprimanded.

"You were with family. I thought I could handle this on my own."

He raised an eyebrow and she watched as he stroked his short beard. "Tobias gave you my letter."

"All the more reason to keep you out of this."

"No, little pearl." He stood. "All the more reason to keep you from doing something you could regret."

"I can't do anything but wait," she bit out impatiently. "Wait to find out what they want, wait to find out who they are. I'm tired of waiting."

"Your haste will only lead to failure."

"They took one of mine," she countered. "Nothing comes after me or mine, Khan."

"And we will get him out safe. This isn't Africa, Leila," he said.

"Could you turn around so I can get dressed?"

"Why? I have seen you clothed only in Sudanese sand. Have you forgotten that we were married?"

She rolled her eyes and watched as he turned around. "That was a stupid idea."

"It kept you from being inducted into the tribe."

"No, it kept you from being dragged into the desert."

After putting on her clothes, she tapped Khan on the shoulder. As soon as he turned around, Alex found herself engulfed in a big hug. She relaxed, breathing in Khan's familiar scent of sandalwood. For a moment, she was tempted by the beckoning memories.

"I missed you," she grinned.

"You divorced me."

"How was I supposed to know putting your boots outside the tent was the equivalent of a divorce?"

"The same way you knew Yousef was going to try and kill me."

"I saved your life," she reminded him.

"And left me in the slums of Cairo while you played belly dancer with the young ambassador."

"We accomplished the mission."

"You took too many risks, Leila."

"And you forgot that we were partners," Alex pointed out. "Look, let's not go through this again. Can't I just be happy seeing you alive and well?"

Khan instantly replied, "Of course."

She pulled back in time to see the twinkle in his dark eyes. "So what'd you bring me?"

"Bring you?" he raised an eyebrow and stroked his little beard. Alex reached out and lightly punched his arm, then did her best to mimic his fluid accent. "If you come back from a journey, offer your family something, though it be only a stone."

"Ah, you mean your gift."

"No, I mean my request."

"Downstairs in the kitchen."

"Coffee?"

He shook his head and followed her out of the bathroom. "No, it is not fitting for you to drink so much of the stuff. I brought you mint tea."

Alex scrunched her nose. "Can you make me one of those drinks Abdul made the night the guide ran out of gas? The sweet one with green tea and mint leaves."

"You want a Moroccan whiskey?"

Alex nodded. "With extra sugar."

Glancing back at the half-closed bedroom door, she turned and continued down the stairs.

Xian woke alone in the bed and turned. He could smell the faint scent of Alex's perfume. He rubbed his eyes and smiled. He thought about Shay-Lin and for the first time since her death her image brought no pain. He threw the covers back, got up, pulled on his pants, and grabbed his shirt. Opening the door, he heard the faint sound of Alex's laughter coming from downstairs. Xian entered the guest room across the hall and picked up a pair of jeans, shirt, and belt that were lying on the bed.

Later after he had taken a shower and dressed, Xian studied himself in the mirror. He looked like some teenage hip-hop kid. *If only my colleagues could see me now*. He went downstairs to the kitchen, hoping to see Alex, but instead he found Rafé.

"Morning," he said.

Rafé poured another cup of coffee and handed it to him. He sat down at the table. "Where's Alex?" he asked.

"She went with Tobias. His wife wanted to see her."

Xian nodded, unsurprised by the guarded tone he heard in Rafé's voice.

"Alex is like a daughter to me. I won't see her hurt," Rafé warned.

Xian tensed and took a sip of coffee. "I won't hurt her," he responded, unruffled by the hint of threat that hung in the air.

"You might not but there are others who will not be, how can I say it, open-minded."

Xian shrugged. "That's not going to change the way I feel about her. As to the outside world, it will change."

"Will it?" Rafé challenged.

"It is changing. For now, I will get my son back and then we'll deal with it."

"What do you feel for my Niña?"

"That, my friend, is private. What I will tell you is that I'll do everything in my power to keep her safe."

Leaning back, Xian looked down into his rapidly cooling coffee. The truth was that he didn't know how to answer that question. The image of Alex standing next to the bed bathed in moonlight, her smile a mixture of seductive confidence and insecurity, filled his mind. Last night had only crystallized in his mind the fact that he wanted her with him. He wanted her to be a part of his life, his family.

"She's independent, my adopted daughter. She is also different."

"What do you mean?" Xian asked. He wanted to know everything about her.

"She was born on an island that resented her very presence. Only a child of eight, Alex watched as her mother's ashes were scattered into the sea and she fought back. She is one of the best soldiers the Special Ops ever trained and she almost got herself killed being the son her father never had. My Niña has seen death and come back from impossible missions with complete success. She fights her own battles, my friend."

"I wouldn't want her any other way. I just want to care for her."

Xian watched as Rafé let out a chuckle. "She'll fight you."

He grimaced at the memory of Alex flipping him onto the mat. "I'm a patient man." He stood up and placed his coffee cup in the sink. "I think she's worth waiting for."

"This time your luck may have run out."

Xian stared into his cold black eyes and shrugged, "Know this, *amigo*. I always get what I want."

NINETEEN

Alex stood in the middle of the room watching the computer images on the wall screen. She turned to see Rafé at her shoulder. She smiled at her foster father as she accepted the steaming cup of coffee. Seeing Rosanna stuff herself silly with crumbly Mexican sweets as she grumbled about her swollen ankles and ballooning stomach had been comic relief. She took a sip and followed him to the table set up in the right corner of the room.

"Take off your shirt so I can tape this on," Rafé ordered.

"Can't," she replied.

"Don't be stubborn, Leila."

"Butt out, Khan." She elbowed him as he stepped up beside her.

"We've done this before. If something goes bad, the only thing between you and a bullet is us," said Rafé.

Alex rolled her eyes. "These guys are professionals. They checked both Xian and me at the first meeting."

"Hand?"

"No, scanner. Looked like one of the new models. It'll pick up a transmitter no matter where we put it."

Alex watched as he put the tiny microphone down on the table.

"I don't like the idea of you going in blind."

"I don't either," she ruefully admitted, looking at Khan.

"Catch."

Alex's hands automatically lifted to catch the flying object. She looked down at an electronic watch.

"Receiver only," Rafé explained.

Alex took off her silver watch and replaced it with the digital one.

"Okay, guys. It's up," announced Tobias.

Alex turned and moved closer to the screen. She watched as he magnified a section of the image.

"What am I seeing?" she asked, moving even closer to the digital image.

"This is the meeting spot."

"It looks familiar," she added, trying to place the location. Alex didn't acknowledge the arm Khan placed around her waist. Instead, she watched Rafé take charge.

"It should. He picked the abandoned army barracks down by the Presidio. Good choice, not too many ways to enter without being spotted."

"Okay here's the plan," Rafé began. "This is the building where you'll be meeting our Mr. Banovic. Khan and Tobias, along with Xian, will stake out Banovic's compound. Miguel and I will head out to the barracks early and try to stack the deck in your favor, Alex. As soon as Banovic arrives at the meeting and we confirm that the kid isn't with him, Khan's team will go in for the boy. Khan will contact me once the kid is safe and then I'm going to signal you, Alex."

Alex looked down at the watch on her wrist.

"When that watch goes off, you get out of there. Try to make your way over to this bush. I'll leave your weapon there. Khan and I'll be covering you from this wooded area."

Alex looked carefully at the small bush Rafé pointed to. She absorbed all the information and nodded her head. The plan was a good one, but they had a snowball's chance in hell of getting away with it.

"What about Banovic?" she asked as she bent over to check the knife hidden in the heel of her boot.

If he weren't taken out, she'd spend the rest of her days looking over her shoulder. She wanted Chou home and safe, but the need to put Banovic away was strong.

Rafé smiled and Alex felt a small shiver run down her spine. "Don't worry about him. I know a couple of agents that have been itching to get their hands on him. Now let's get ready. We're wasting time."

Alex went over and picked up the gun, taking a moment to withdraw the clip. "Rafé, what's this?"

She'd expected standard small 9mm bullets, but what she saw brought her up short.

"I changed them," Khan volunteered.

Alex turned to look at him as he joined her at the table.

"They're soft point bullets." He reached around to pick up an extra clip.

Alex stared down at the one she held in her hand. 'Soft point bullets,' a.k.a. hollow or flat tips, had been outlawed by the Geneva Convention unless DELTA troops were participating in a hostage situation.

"You know what they can do?" Tobias asked.

Alex nodded her head. She not only knew, she'd seen the damage they could inflict. The hollow point caused the soft lead slug to expand into a mushroom shaped projectile upon entering the body. Maximum penetration, double the diameter of impact.

"Just aim and shoot, Niña," Rafé added.

Xian took that exact moment to enter the room. Alex looked up at him. She wanted to smile. With baggy jeans and a large basketball jersey, he looked like one of her former inner city karate students. Just as quickly, her smile slid off her face as she felt Khan's fingers tighten.

Alex looked down at the gun in her hand and without thought her hand tensed and the magazine clip locked into place. She double-checked the safety before putting it in the black duffle bag lying on the table.

"What's going on?" Xian asked.

Alex firmly removed the thick band of Khan's arm from around her waist and watched Xian's face as Rafé filled him in on their plans.

"Leila, why don't you introduce us?" Khan asked.

"Leila?" Xian repeated. His expression gave nothing away but she could see mounting anger in his eyes.

"He doesn't recognize your proper name?"

"Khan…" Alex warned.

He continued to bait Xian. "You haven't told him about us?"

Alex turned, glaring daggers at Khan. "Get that smirk off your face. I know what you're trying to do and this is neither the time nor the place."

Xian took a step toward Khan. "I disagree," he stated.

She heard the undercurrent of menace in his voice.

"Xian, this is Khan…"

"Her husband."

"Ex-husband," she said automatically and then aimed a glare at the solider.

"It's a joke, Xian," Alex explained. "We were on a mission and couldn't blow our cover; the ceremony wasn't legal."

"In the eyes of Allah…"

"You are about to get killed," she hissed.

Alex allowed Xian to draw her away from Khan.

"It's good that I am not a jealous man," Xian smiled. His eyes changed from fire to ice.

"Go away, Khan. You've done more than enough damage this round."

After the man went upstairs, Xian drew Alex away from the others. A hot stab of jealousy had rushed through him at the sight of Khan and Alex standing so close together. "So, is there anyone else you'd like to tell me about?"

"No."

"Do you mean no, there is no one else or no, you don't want to tell me?" he bit out.

"My past is a story best left for another day. We have more important things to discuss."

He lifted an eyebrow. "So you're going to tell me why you have that gun?"

"I'm meeting Banovic at the Presidio."

"With your friend Khan, I assume?"

Alex nodded. "No. Khan is the only one I trust to get Chou back unharmed."

"There has to be another way," Xian replied calmly. Last night he'd been filled with passion, anger, fear. That morning, fear for Chou's safety sat like lead in his stomach. He wanted his son back and he wanted Banovic to pay dearly for taking him away. But he also didn't want Alex getting herself killed.

Alex stepped forward. "There is no other way. We've run out of time and options, Xian."

"I won't let you risk your life. We'll just have to call in the authorities."

Alex turned and looked at Rafé. Her uncle nodded, reading the look she sent him.

"Alex, we'll be upstairs. We leave in twenty minutes," he ordered.

Alex nodded her head, grateful for his under-standing of the situation. Lord, she hated herself at this moment. She took a step towards Xian and reached up to run her fingers over his cheek. "Xian, everything is going to be fine."

Alex drew a startled breath as he grabbed her wrist, holding it tightly. She fought her first instinct to pull away. This was a man she trusted; the memories of the night in his arms held her still. She looked into his eyes and for the first time could put a name to the emotion she saw buried in their depths: fear. She watched as he took her hand and placed a gentle kiss on the inside of her wrist. Alex felt it to the tips of her toes.

"Shay-Lin said those exact words to me as she lay dying in a hospital room." His voice was low, brought down by the ghosts of remembrance.

Alex wrapped her arms around Xian's neck and hugged him close, inhaling the scent of his hair. She whispered comforting words into his ear while damming herself for the lies she would tell.

"Hey, I'm not going anywhere. I've got school in another week. Remember?" she teased.

She drew back to see a glimmer of a smile cross his face. She continued. "I've done this before, Xian. This will be a walk in the park for me." That much was true, but this mission would be different because she was emotionally involved. No matter what happened to her, Chou would live. This wasn't a tactics operation where she could close off her heart and follow orders. This was personal.

"I don't want you going in there alone. These men are killers."

So am I. Alex shook her head. "I need you to do a more important job. You just make sure that you concentrate on getting Chou out safe and sound."

"Was it true what Banovic said?" Xian questioned.

"What?"

"You're known for getting out of tight situations with low body count?"

Alex's stomach dropped and dread curled around her heart. Brian had never fully accepted her role in the military. It didn't fit that the woman he desired to be the mother of his children had been a trained solider. Instead, he'd chosen to forget and focus on what was going to be their perfect new life.

"Yes." She looked into his dark eyes. There was no pride in her voice or shame. She had done what her country demanded of her. She had paid her debt a thousand times over.

"Do whatever it takes to get out of there without getting hurt, Alex. If it comes down to you or them, don't hesitate to pull the trigger." Xian's eyes bore down into hers.

She nodded slowly and felt the muscles of her jaw unclench. He understood.

"Promise me, Alex."

"What?" she asked, leaning her head to the side.

"When this is over, we'll talk about last night."

Alex tensed and his arm tightened around her like a vise.

"Promise me you won't run."

"Why would I run?"

"Don't play games. I know you."

"Maybe you don't know me all that well, Xian." That wasn't true, he was right. Alex planned on running as fast and as far away from him as possible. She looked up into his eyes and her heart turned over. She both wanted and feared the emotion that she saw there. She nodded her head. "I promise."

She placed a soft lingering kiss on his lips before grabbing her bag and rushing up the stairs.

Rafé drove slowly towards the Presidio. The old army base had been transformed into a national park a few years back. Alex stared out the window at the passing scenery and the departing tourist busses. She sat quietly as Rafé parked the car and got out. He seemed to blend into the small crowd effortlessly. She watched as he put on his brown hat and began picking up litter, looking for all the world like an average park service worker.

Her father had loved this place. After years of active duty, he had come here to teach the younger generation of students about the sacrifices of African-American soldiers who had fought in the war against Mexico. Alex had watched as he spent numerous hours writing letters to the Presidio Trust, hoping he could motivate them to renovate the old Presidio barracks for African-American troops.

Alex shook her head to clear her thoughts. She pulled out her binoculars and followed Rafé's movements towards the designated meeting point. She watched closely as he bent down to pick up an imaginary piece of litter. His movements were quick and if she hadn't been watching for the drop, she would have missed it. Rafé had placed her gun and extra ammo underneath the designated bush. Alex was busy scanning the area when he returned to the car.

His question broke the silence. "What are you going to do? He won't walk away and let you go." She wondered if Rafé was referring to Khan or Xian.

"I will." She shrugged. "He won't have a choice. I'm not ready to have anyone in my life right now." Alex turned to face Rafé. His face was half covered with the green hat.

"He's not Brian, Alex. He accepts what you were, what you are."

"What's that supposed to mean?" she asked, surprised.

"You need someone in your life. You are too alone."

Alex protested, "No, I'm not. I have you, Karen, the team, the kids, Sensei…"

He shook his head. "It's not the same."

"You're alone," she pointed out.

"Niña, last week I saw Death lean over and gesture for me to follow. For the first time since my parents hid me in the forest when the rebels came to our village, I was afraid. I had so many regrets. I have decided to leave DELTA. I'm going to settle down with one woman."

Alex regarded Rafé closely. He was serious. "Who?"

"When I say, you will be the first to know."

She watched as he lifted the binoculars. "Get ready," he ordered.

Her heart jumped as she turned to look at the road leading to the recreation area. She saw the three dark Mercedes Benzes slowly drive past the adjacent parking lot. Then she turned her attention back to Rafé, who was on the cell phone.

"Khan, Banovic just arrived without the boy."

Alex took a deep breath and looked at her watch; the electronic dial read 7:45 P.M.

"Fifteen minutes," she announced.

"Alex, are you sure you can do this?" She heard the concern in his voice.

"Yes." Alex didn't elaborate. He would just have to trust her. She wanted it to be over. The waiting. She hated the waiting.

"Let's go."

Rafé started the car and drove along the winding road towards the Golden Gate Bridge. Alex saw her car waiting at the exact location Miguel had indicated. As she pulled the handle on the car door, she felt a light touch on her arm.

"At the first sign of trouble I want you out of there."

Alex felt her mouth go dry and words seemed to stick in her throat. She nodded her head and jumped out of the truck. A minute later, Alex put the car in reverse and pulled out.

Alex drove as close to Infantry Row as she could and parked. Taking the key out of the ignition, she picked up her small purse and got out of the car. She stepped into the cool California night, her eyes searching for hidden figures. As she walked forward, she automatically scanned the area, marking the location of her hidden gun. As she advanced slowly towards the waiting men, she counted three guards.

The whole area was illuminated by the moon and the overhead lights. As she moved closer, the guards came towards her with powerful looking semi-automatic guns aimed in her direction. She was about fifteen feet away from the building before they stopped her.

"Hold your hands up, slowly," the one closest to her instructed.

Alex did as ordered. The greeting was designed to intimidate. Alex had spent most of her life performing the art of keeping a serene and unreadable expression on her face no matter what. About five feet away, the Russian who'd accosted her at Club Envy leveled the barrel of a submachine gun at her chest.

Her mind automatically identified the weapon: suppressed Heckler and Koch 9mm. She knew that if she looked down an infrared beam would be on her heart. The weapon was designed to be accurate, highly lethal, and uncannily silent. The sight of what it could do in a close-quarter's battle environment, all the carnage, remained etched in her memory. The guard looked much too happy to see her. She matched his big smile with her own small, cold smile, as cold as the certainty that if given the chance, she wouldn't hesitate to pull the trigger.

He searched her from top to bottom. She gritted her teeth as he slowly ran his fingers over her breasts, between her legs, and tried her best to remain still. Glancing at the other guards, she saw both were scanning the area.

When he finished, Alex watched as the one of the other men came forward and ran a wand over her body and then her purse. When it didn't beep, he turned it off and reached to pick up her purse. Alex watched as he dumped everything out. The Russian immediately picked up the disk and put it into his pocket. Satisfied, the brown-haired man motioned for her to pick up her stuff and follow him into the building.

Alex was careful to keep relief from showing on her face. If he had paid closer attention to her boots, he would have found her knife. As she started walking, the taller, bald Russian stood at her back, so close she could feel his breath on the back of her neck.

The building was a colonial revival style barracks that had been constructed in the late 1890s and looked as though it had undergone restoration some time in the past. The leaded windows and peeling paint gave the front a haunted look. Stone steps led up to a heavy wooden door. The wooden porch creaked loudly in the quiet darkness.

Alex took a closer look at her guards. One had an extra clip in a belt around his waist, along with a .9-

millimeter automatic. The guards were soldiers, professionals. One turned to the tall Russian standing behind her.

"From the way Jarik described her, I expected much more."

Alex shrugged. "Sorry."

"You let this tiny woman disarm you?" His lip curled with scorn.

"Shut up, Serge."

Alex felt his hand push her towards the door. She took a step forward into the room. It took her eyes a few moments to adjust. What had once been a mess hall or a squad room had been turned into an administrative office after World War II. The room looked like the set of an old Alfred Hitchcock movie.

The rafters were covered with ropes of cobwebs. Old brown maps lined the walls and filing cabinets sat blanketed with dust. The room was lit by the dim glow of two swinging light bulbs.

Alex turned her head to the right. Banovic got up from behind a desk. In the dim light, his features took on a demonic look.

"Right on time, Ms. Thompson." His voice was gentle, pleasant, as though they were meeting for afternoon tea.

"I try to be punctual," she replied.

His mouth transformed into some semblance of a smile. "I wish we could have met under different circumstances."

Alex watched as his eyes roamed over her body.

"I don't," she bit out.

His smile disappeared. "Do you have the disk?"

Alex's stomach took a nosedive and her pulse sped up. "Where's the boy?" she answered back.

"Safe, Ms. Thompson."

She arched her eyebrow. "He's not here."

Alex watched as the brown-haired guard stepped forward with the disk in his hand.

"I found this in her purse."

"Good. Give it to Anton."

Alex took a step forward and found her arm enclosed by the guard named Serge. "I want the boy, Banovic. Where is he?"

He gave her a scornful look and turned back towards a slender, dark-haired man with glasses who now sat at the desk staring at a laptop. Alex tensed as the man called Anton inserted the CD-ROM into the laptop. Twenty seconds later, the sound of Tupac blasted out of the laptop speakers.

Banovic went around the desk to stand beside Anton. "What is this?"

The man answered in a thick Russian accent. Alex knew instantly that he was the one that Brian had contacted.

"I guess you're not into rap music. He's real popular here on the West Coast," she added.

"What game are you playing, Ms. Thompson?"

"No game, Banovic. I want the boy. You want the disk."

"That is why we are here." His tone was angry. "This is not what I wanted, Ms. Thompson."

"Seems neither of us is getting what we want tonight. I know about your track record, Banovic. I want him back alive." Needing time, she stalled. "Is it money? Did you take Brian's life for money?"

His face reddened and his eyes narrowed, making his heavy brows connect. "Money? Is that what you think this is about, Ms. Thompson? That is all you Americans think about. I care nothing for money, only vengeance."

He took a step forward and seemed to collect himself. "One cold night in the gorges of the southern part of Chechnya, a man was forced to his knees. As he begged for his life, a Russian solider put a rifle to his head and fired. They threw his body into the woods. Left him to rot, provide food for scavengers."

Alex shifted from her left foot and watched as he curled and uncurled his fingers. His voice was singsong. Alex's heart sped up. She had seen this before, the rage, the hatred, the insanity brought on by death.

"Who was he?" she asked.

"My twin brother," he responded. He turned his attention back to her.

"You need not fear for your country. America's hypocrisy sickens me." He shrugged, "Yet I feel no ill will. Your capitalist nation cannot be expected to care for those who fight for freedom, for their homes, their very lives."

She pushed him. "What does this have to do with Brian's program, Banovic?"

"I see you still don't understand. Yeltsin called the Chechen soldiers criminals, Russian mafia," he spat. "My brother will be avenged. The lives lost will not go unpunished. I will cripple what is left of Mother Russia. I have waited five years for this opportunity. I will use their own networks to create a chaos they have never known. The world will watch helplessly as the former Soviet Union once again self-destructs. In the chaos, Chechnya will rise. And you, Ms. Thompson, will help me."

Alex nearly let out a startled gasp at the slight vibration on her wrist. She quickly glanced down at her watch; the readout was flashing. She almost sighed with the feeling of release which washed over her. It was time to go.

"It's a little warm in here. Mind if I take off my jacket?"

Alex took a small step away from the Russian after he released her wrist. As she slid the coat off, she quickly bent down to grab the blade from her right heel. Without taking the time to think, she threw the knife towards Banovic while ducking to avoid the Russian's outstretched arms.

As his hand closed around her arm, she stepped towards him instead of away and jerked out of his grasp. Then she grabbed his right hand, stopping him from reaching for his gun. Alex stepped back and kicked into the man's private parts. The big man went down, helpless, and she took off running, hit the back door, and leaped off the stairs.

The light of the moon offered no cover. She could hear rushing footsteps behind her. Alex ran towards the line of trees and ducked behind the bush. Quickly, she grabbed her gun and ticked off the safety.

Not taking the time to target, she shot over the top of the bushes. Pausing, she heard other gunfire but couldn't tell which direction the shots were coming from. Then she heard Banovic's voice. "Stop shooting. I need her alive, you idiots."

Saying a prayer that Rafé had her covered, Alex moved out from behind the bush and sprinted in the direction of the woods. She ducked behind a tree just as a bullet came whizzing by her side. Apparently, the men hadn't listened. Looking around the tree, she spotted two of the guards making their way towards her.

"Drop your gun and come out. We won't hurt you," an accented voice coaxed.

Damn it, where are they? Trying to keep her cool, Alex ejected the empty clip and inserted the fresh one. She moved from behind the tree and fired off two shots, hitting one of the men. She crouched down and began making her way to the left.

Then she heard the metallic click of a hammer. Turning quickly, she raised her gun but then froze in place facing the man. Jarik. She stared at the tall Russian who had tried to kidnap her at the school. They each had their gun trained on the other. Alex could see the vengeance in his eyes. One of them would die.

For the first time, Alex felt fear twist in her stomach. Nevertheless, she kept her eyes on his face, her finger pressed tight against the trigger.

"I knew that we would meet like this. Killing your boyfriend was a mistake for which I have paid a great deal. Banovic will never forgive me for a second mistake. I'll run and he will hunt me forever. But you, I will see the life drain out of your eyes as you beg me not to kill you," he promised.

"Drop your weapon," Alex ordered. She never took her eyes from the Russian's face. Her arms were beginning to tremble from holding the gun, but she kept it trained on him, steady, ready to pull the trigger.

"The police are on their way. I suggest you leave now," she bluffed. She heard Rafé's voice calling out her name and allowed herself the thought of getting out of this one alive. She looked away from her opponent for a second and when she glanced back she saw him squeeze the trigger.

It seemed as though time almost stopped. The hammer on his gun came down just as Alex fired. She felt a burning sensation on her left side. Through a haze of pain she saw the Russian sway and begin to collapse. It was the last thing she saw before the ground rushed to meet her and darkness chased the pain away.

TWENTY

Alex woke to the loud beating of her heart. She jerked up quickly and agony spread like wildfire up her left side. Lying back down, she took a deep breath. As the pain began to dissipate, Alex turned her head and saw an IV running into her arm. She closed her eyes and tried to relax.

The next time she woke to see shoes. She turned her neck and looked up into Xian's beaten face. She tried to speak, but couldn't. Xian took a glass and held the straw to her mouth. The cool water flowed down her parched throat and she sighed.

"What happened?" Her voice sounded husky.

"One of Banovic's mercenaries shot you."

Alex closed her eyes. "Oh."

"Are you in pain? I'll call the nurse." His voice was filled with concern. Xian would never forget the sight of Alex bleeding in Rafé's arms. If he hadn't known that he loved her before that moment, the sight of her unconscious would have brought the truth home to him.

Alex opened her eyes, "No, I'm fine. Just a little tired. How's Chou?" she asked after a brief pause.

"Worried about you. He wouldn't leave the hospital until the doctor assured him you would be okay."

"What happened?"

Xian shook his head. "We got lucky. We arrived at the hideout just as they were making preparations to move locations. Miguel disabled their vehicles and Khan took out the mercenaries while I went in through the back of the house. They had Chou locked in a room upstairs."

"Did they hurt him?"

He grinned. "Not a scratch."

"Thank God." Relief seemed to pour down her spine. When she attempted to sit up, a jab of pain stopped her. "How long have I been here?"

"Two days."

She started. "What about Banovic?"

Xian took a seat in the chair next to the hospital bed. "He's on his way to Geneva to be locked away for a long time."

"Good." Alex gazed up at Xian. Even with his black eye, she had never seen anyone more wonderful.

"Xian, what happened to your eye?"

"Let's just say Khan and I came to an understanding."

She narrowed her eyes and had just opened her mouth to ask another question when a woman came into the room. She was short with brown, gray-streaked curly hair and wire-rimmed glasses. "I'm Dr.

Wallace, Ms. Thompson. I'm glad you've decided to join us."

"I am too."

The doctor smiled as she walked over to the hospital bed. "We've really not had this much excitement here at the hospital in a long time."

"Excitement?" Alex echoed as the doctor began checking her over.

"Yes, your fiancé, along with what seemed like the entire FBI force, brought you in."

"Fiancé?" Alex asked.

She watched as the doctor smiled at Xian. "The agents had to hold him back from running into the OR. He's been by your side since you got out of surgery." The doctor finally noticed the confused look on Alex's face.

"We haven't been engaged long, Dr. Wallace. I think Alex is still getting used to it," Xian smoothly interjected.

Alex turned to stare at Xian, then returned her attention to the doctor. The woman clicked on a penlight and shined it into Alex's eyes.

"Just follow the light."

"Do I have a concussion?" she asked.

"A mild one," she replied. "Your uncle mentioned that your head hit a rock after you were shot."

Rafé. "Is my uncle here?" Alex asked. She wanted to make sure he was all right.

Xian answered, "He had to run to the airport. He'll be back soon."

"Take a deep breath for me." The doctor's voice was mater-of-fact. She placed the stethoscope to Alex's chest. When finished, she made some notes on her pad.

"Is everything okay, Doctor?"

"Everything's good. You are a very lucky woman, Ms. Thompson. The bullet missed major arteries and made a clean exit. However, because you suffered a head trauma, we're just going to keep you another couple of days for observation. I'll come back to see you before I go off shift."

"Thank you."

Silence descended over the room as the door closed behind the doctor. Alex turned to look at Xian. His eyes were shadowed. She could tell that he hadn't slept much.

"You didn't ask," she commented after a moment, trying to lighten the mood.

"It was the only way they would let me in to see you," he replied.

Alex turned away, hoping that he didn't see the look of disappointment that had crossed her face. Maybe she had imagined the words.

I love you Alex. Don't die on me, damn it. You promised. You promised me.

Just as she turned back towards Xian, the door opened and two men wearing dark navy suits entered the room.

"Glad to see you're awake, Ms. Thompson. You've given us quite a scare," said the thin gentleman.

"Sorry," Alex responded sarcastically.

"You do know that that stunt at the hotel could have cost you your life. Why in the world would you run away from my agents?"

"I make it a practice not to get caught up in CIA/FBI political bullshit," she replied angrily.

His face reddened.

"That was a mistake on our part. The agents responsible are being reprimanded," he replied shakily.

Feeling the pain grow behind her skull, Alex got to the point. "What do you want, Agent Ramsey?"

He didn't look happy at her tone of voice. "We want *you*, Ms. Thompson. I looked at your records. I think you'd be a great addition to our team."

Alex stared at them incredulously. Just like that. Join the team; sign away your life.

"The FBI must be truly desperate to be recruiting a woman still in her hospital bed." Xian's tone was deliberately disparaging. It was all he could do not to get up and deck the bastard.

The man's face reddened again. Then the federal agent walked to Alex's hospital bed and placed his business card on the bedside table.

"Please give me a call after you've recovered. We'll talk."

Alex nodded her head. As soon as the door closed behind the agents, it swung open again. This time she saw the familiar faces of Rafé and her roommate Karen. Karen's arms were filled with flowers. Alex's eyes widened as she stared at Rafé's arm wrapped comfortably around her roommate's waist.

"Did I miss something while I was unconscious?" she questioned.

An answering smile appeared on his face. "No, Niña, we waited for you to wake up."

"Will someone please tell me what's going on here?" she asked, exasperated.

Karen answered, "Rafé and I are getting engaged, Alex."

All the pieces seemed to fall into place. She looked from one to the other and studied the glow on her roommate's face.

"I think she's in shock," Xian chuckled.

"This is the first time I've seen you speechless, Alex," replied Rafé.

Alex opened her mouth and closed it.

"Congratulations." Her words came out as a mere whisper. She tried to smile and found her eyes closing. She felt so tired. And for all her happiness at their love, she felt empty.

She opened her eyes as she felt a light kiss on her cheek.

"Get some sleep, girlfriend."

She nodded weakly and closed her eyes once more. The last thing she heard was Rafé's voice. "Take care of her."

She was sitting on the bed staring at the business card left behind by Agent Ramsey when Xian entered the room. They stared at one another in silence. Alex stood up and felt pain start on her side. Watching Xian stare pointedly at the card, she flushed and quickly put it in her pocket.

"Hi." She managed a weak smile.

"Dr. Wallace called to tell me that you insisted on checking yourself out tonight."

Alex frowned, "She shouldn't have called you."

"Where were you planning on going, Alex?"

"Home." She wanted to get out the hospital so bad it made her teeth ache. She'd had a stream of visitors every hour on the hour. The smell of flowers permeated the air. Even Brian's brother Tony had flown in from New York after learning about the shooting.

"How were you going to get there?"

She frowned, confused by his line of questioning. "I was going to take a cab."

Feeling weak, she sat down on the bed and stared up at Xian.

"You can't be alone, Alex."

"I won't be, Xian."

She watched as he took a step forward and then seemed to stop himself. "Karen is with Rafé in Argentina, Alex."

She shrugged. "I know. I'll have Shadow."

His lips curled. "The cat's at my house."

"I don't want a nursemaid, Xian," she snapped.

She heard his sigh of impatience and despite herself cringed at being its cause. Angrily she lashed out, "Look, I'm glad Chou is out of danger and I'll never be able to forgive myself for getting the both of you involved in this mess." She took a deep breath and tried to look at anything but his face. "Thank you for your concern, but it's time you got back to your life and I returned to mine."

She watched as he turned and left. For the first time she felt miserable and alone. She closed her eyes and willed herself to stand. *I can do this. Alex, old girl, you've been in worse situations.* But she had never been in a hospital. She hated hospitals. She had to get out of here. Memories of her father's death began creeping into her conscious.

She had just reached down to lift up her bag when the door swung open again. She looked up, expecting to see the doctor. Alex felt her breath catch as she saw Xian standing behind a wheelchair.

She frowned, "I am not getting in that chair."

"It's the only way you're getting out of here," he grinned.

"I don't need you," she protested.

"Yes, you do. Whether you like it or not. The only reason the hospital is willing to let you go is because you're coming home with me."

Alex recognized the tone of his voice. It matched his expression: determined. She wanted to tell him no deal, but he was her only ticket out. Instead, she shrugged her shoulders and sat down in the chair. She didn't speak as he wheeled her out of the hospital. Then he gathered her into his arms and gently placed her in the car. Alex closed her eyes to pretend sleep.

Alex woke as soon as the car pulled into the garage. Sitting up straight, she inhaled sharply as pain shot through her side. She blinked and turned, unexpectedly looking up into Xian's eyes. She wanted to smile but her mouth opened in a yawn. She let out a startled yelp as he picked her up, but her arms automatically wound themselves around his neck as he carried her towards the open door.

"Xian," she protested. "I can walk."

He didn't seem to listen. Alex found herself lying on the bed in the guest room she had occupied a week before. She began to sit up but his hand on her stomach prevented her from moving.

"Don't move, Alex."

She immediately bristled at the tone of his voice, but she felt a stab of pain from her wound. It must have shown in her face because Xian muttered a slight curse and left the room. Alex laid her head back and closed her eyes, trying to ignore the burning at her side.

"Take this," Xian's voice echoed in her head. She felt the bed move as he sat down. Alex turned her head and glanced down at the two white round pills in his hand. Codeine.

"No, thank you," she managed through gritted teeth.

Xian shook his head, frustrated. Would she fight him on everything? He had never met a more stubborn person.

"Alex," he said gently, "I know you're in pain. You need to rest so your body can regain its strength."

His voice was low and mesmerizing. Alex was reaching for the pills before she realized what she was doing.

"Xian." She hated admitting her weakness and couldn't get the words out of her throat, the words about her fears, the dreams, and the terror of being alone in the darkness.

Xian felt her struggle and he helped her sit up. He held her gaze. "I won't leave you."

Alex lowered her eyes, hiding the tears of relief that threatened to spill. She took the pills and slowly washed the acrid taste out of her mouth with the water he gave her. She let Xian lower her back down into the bed. She closed her eyes, trying to will the pain away. She needed something, anything to distract her.

"Tell me a story," she asked. Alex meant for her voice to come out strong, but instead it trembled.

She felt Xian settle onto the bed. When she felt the sensation of the rough wetness sliding over the back of her hand, she turned and saw Shadow curled by her side. She let her fingers glide through his soft fur and was rewarded by a low grumbling in his throat.

Then she saw Chou standing at the foot of the bed in his sleepers. His eyes showed fear he was bravely trying to hide. Alex felt her heart melt. Raising her hand, she motioned for him to come and join her on the bed. She saw his attention turn to his father, seeking permission.

She spoke before Xian could answer. "It's okay, Chou. Why don't you join me? Your father was just about to tell me a bedtime story."

Chou cautiously climbed into the bed and under the light quilt. Alex stared at Xian who had moved to sit in the chair positioned next to the bed.

Xian sat still, his mind seeking for a story. Then he settled upon an old Chinese legend.

A half an hour later, Xian ended his story and stood looking down on the three sleeping occupants on the bed. Shadow lay curled up at the foot of the bed. Xian found that he could not keep his eyes from watching the gentle rise and fall of Alex's chest. And then he looked at his son lying at her side. Chou had one arm curled around his teddy bear and the other hidden underneath the pillow. Xian bent over, placing a light kiss on Alex's brow before quietly leaving the room.

Alex's days seemed to settle into a pattern after arriving in the Liu household. Xian had gone back to her house and brought her clothes. She was never alone. Mrs. Lee had adopted her. Alex spent afternoons at the kitchen table learning how to play Mahjong and Go.

When Chou arrived home, he would drag her into the den to play games or help him with his homework. Then there were the nights. After Mrs. Lee left and Chou ran off to bed, she would sit at the table with Xian. They talked about everything and nothing. Not once had he tried to kiss her since bringing her home from the hospital. One night she was pulled out of her reverie by the sound of her name.

"Alex?"

"Hmm."

"Are you tired? Do you want me to help you upstairs?" Xian had noticed her staring blankly at her coffee

Alex turned her attention to Xian. "No, I was just thinking."

"About what?"

About the way your lips touch mine, the feel of your fingertips running over my body, the warmth of your smile. Alex shook her head to clear her mind of wayward thoughts.

"I was wondering about what I'm going to do with myself. I can't go back to teaching." She played with the spoon.

"You are not to blame for what occurred."

Alex curled her fingers around the cup of coffee and closed her eyes. She shook her head. "That doesn't matter. I endangered the lives of my students. No matter that the press thinks I'm some kind of hero. I almost got Chou killed. I can't take the risk of that ever happening again."

"You could take up teaching judo fulltime. With the money Brian left you, you could start your own school," he suggested.

She had tried not to think about the money. She still didn't know what to do with it. The day she had opened the envelope containing a cashier's check from Brian was something she still shied away from.

"Maybe. Maybe I'll go back in." Most of her former DELTA group had gone their own ways. Few officers stayed around for more than two or three tours with the Special Forces group. Those who did, like Rafé, were extremely dedicated to their units, and the idea that the worldwide terrorist threat and its network of supporters and killers should be met head-on and eliminated. Alex had been one of those people for a while. Saving the world, one kill at a time. She watched Xian's lips turn into a frown. "What do you mean?"

Alex laughed bitterly. "I'll go back to fighting, maybe join the CIA. I'll make the world safe for democracy." She uttered those words when everything in her wanted to stay in this place, in his life, cradled in this man's arms. She stood abruptly and began to walk away.

Xian watched her stand and eased his grip on the coffee cup. He had to get control. He had tried to be patient, gentle. He wanted to give Alex space but every moment he felt her pulling further and further away. He stood quickly and reached out to grab her arm. He turned her around and held her arms lightly, conscious of her wounded side.

He felt her push at his chest. "That's right, push me away," he baited. "Hide from your fears by running back to your old life of violence and war. You and I both know what's really bothering you."

"Really? And what's that?" she demanded.

"You can't take the thought of someone loving you. The idea of allowing people a place in your heart scares you to death. You can't face life. Well, I'm alive and I'm here. And I won't let you do this to yourself. I won't let you do this to my son or me. You are needed *here.*"

Alex twisted in his grasp. His every word cut like a knife. The truth of his accusations made her bleed. She jerked away from him and used anger to cover her pain. "You're wrong."

She turned to walk out of the kitchen, but Xian was faster. She found her path blocked. She tried to move past him but found herself pulled against his chest. Alex heard her breath come out in short gasps.

The intense feeling running through him shocked Xian. "No more running, Alex. This is real. You and me. No more ghosts. You might be able to hide from my words, but you cannot run from this."

He reached out with his left hand and gripped her hair and pulled. He placed his other hand on the small of her back and lowered his lips to hers. His kiss lacked any hint of tenderness; his lips demanded and took. He felt her body relax and sway towards his own. He fought to control his triumph as her body betrayed her by naturally responding to his.

The magic started in her stomach. Heat began to spiral throughout the lower part of her body. She opened her mouth to Xian's onslaught and began kissing him back, challenging his tongue for dominance. Her fingers found their way under his shirt. She loved the smooth hardness of his chest.

Xian pulled back and taking her hand in his, guided Alex upstairs. She went willingly into Xian's bedroom. She had never been in his room before and smelled the faint scent of incense and musk. She shivered and her nipples hardened underneath his gaze. Her breath caught in her throat as she watched him slowly take off his shirt.

The rain was pouring outside and Alex could hear it pounding against the roof. It matched the storm that was brewing in her heart. Alex let go of Xian's hands and slipped off her sandals.

Xian reached out and hesitated before embracing her. "I don't want to hurt you."

Alex found her arms trapped against his chest. She smiled and felt a wave of tenderness wash over her at the concern she saw in his eyes. "You won't."

She stood still by the bed and leaned into Xian's arms. As his hands curled around her waist, she pressed her body against his, feeling the evidence of his desire against her jeans.

"I'm in love with you." He said the words so quietly she barely heard them over the beating of her heart. Pretending not to hear, Alex began placing gentle kisses along his chest and felt shudders pass through him.

She shed her clothes, all the while looking into Xian's eyes, enjoying the heated desire she saw there. Then she stepped forward and her hands found him. As he kissed her, she ran her fingers over his maleness, enjoying the way her touch affected him. She lifted her head and found her mouth imprisoned by his lips. His tongue was hot, demanding, and hungry. Slowly unbuttoning his pants, she pushed them towards the floor.

Pulling her head back, she eyed Xian mischievously, then moved into his body and swept her foot under his left leg, sending them both tumbling into the bed. She felt a slight twinge of pain from her wound, but she pushed it away and positioned herself over him.

She looked down into Xian's face and found herself captured by its handsomeness. Alex stared at his high cheekbones, strong chin, and midnight eyes. Her lips curled into a soft smile as she studied him. When she bent down, her hair shielded them from the outside world. Then she kissed him, putting all

her need and passion into the kiss. When she released
him, they both gasped for air.

Her lips began to make their way across his chest.
The sound of his shallow breathing filled her with a
heady sense of power. She licked his nipple and then
blew out a soft cooling breath. She was rewarded with
a soft moan. She had made up her mind. If this were
to be her last night in paradise, she would give Xian
some measure of the happiness he had given to her.

Bending forward, Alex pressed against Xian's
arousal and slowly licked and kissed her way downward. She could feel his hands, his fingers in her hair,
clenching, releasing. She found his maleness and
marveled at its warm and hard softness. Giving into
temptation, she tasted him. Pushed by her own
growing need and the sound of his moans, she took
him slowly, gently, into her mouth.

Xian's world exploded in a myriad of colors. Her
warm lips caressing him softly, lovingly, were sending
him to the brink. Just when he could take no more,
he felt her take him into her mouth. The sensation
was almost too much. As wave after wave of pleasure
washed over him, he reached down and pulled her up
for a kiss. He knew he was about to lose control. As
he felt her shift to take him into her, Xian rolled,
placing Alex under him.

Before she knew what was happening, she found
herself pinned under Xian's body. Alex felt her body
scream with unfulfilled need. She opened her mouth
to protest only to find her lips captured by his.

Unable to control herself, Alex's nails scratched at his back. She seemed lost in a whirlpool of passion and heat.

She arched her hips, moaning his name, urging him to slide inside her heat. But he would not enter. Instead, Alex felt his hands and lips everywhere, driving her wild. She burned when he pushed into her tight wetness, almost crying at the sensation of completeness.

She met him measure for measure as he moved in and out of her body, caught his rhythm and matched it, driving him deeper and increasing the tempo. When her body clenched around him tight, warm, wet, he let go. He gave himself up to the feeling and sank himself fully inside her warm tightness once more before letting go.

When the end came, it crashed over them both in a wave of pure pleasure. Alex felt the wetness of tears escape her eyes and Xian's lips follow their trail.

"Are you all right, sweetheart?"

Alex opened her eyes and smiled up into his concerned face. She kissed him gently. "I've never felt so right in my life," she whispered.

Xian held her tightly as he rolled over on his side, still buried inside her warmth. Holding her tenderly, he watched as her shallow breathing slowed and as her heavy eyes closed in sleep.

He gently swept her hair from her face and placed a kiss on her brow. Lying there, with Alex curled in his arms, his body joined with hers, he experienced a deep sense of peacefulness that he'd never thought he'd have again.

"She won't stay with you." Khan's boast echoed in his mind. Gently caressing the contours of Alex's hip, Xian drifted to sleep, wondering how he would find the strength to let her go.

Alex woke just before dawn still locked in Xian's embrace. She didn't want to leave him. In the predawn darkness, tears clogged in her throat as she studied the relaxed face of the man's whose arms lay curled around her.

She let her mind explore the way he made her feel. Not like a solider, teacher, child. He made her feel like a woman who had found the most precious treasure of all: a soul mate with gentleness, patience, and strength. She felt her body tingle with memory of the way he'd made love to her the night before. She felt again his lips on her breasts, his gentle fingers caressing her skin, his tongue in her mouth and his hardness in her body.

Alex slowly moved out of Xian's arms. She stilled when she heard his sigh and stood at the foot of the bed looking down at Xian, feeling tears pool at the back of her eyes. God, she was so tired of having to say good-bye to those she loved. The ghosts of those who'd left her flashed before her eyes. Uncurling her fingers, Alex quietly gathered her scattered clothing before turning to leave.

She paused in the doorway. "I love you," she whispered, her voice low with regret. "I will always love you. I just don't know how to live with it." With clothes in hand, she walked out of the room.

Xian woke to an empty space next to his pillow. He inhaled deeply and the still lingering scent of jasmine let him know that last night had been no dream. The silence of the house confirmed his first thought. She had left him again. He sat up and swung his legs over the edge of the bed and closed his eyes. Soon his son would wake up and he would have to explain Alex's absence. Anger stirred in the depths of his heart. She left'd them both without bothering to say good-bye.

He wanted to find her and wring her neck, but the memory of the guilt he'd seen in her eyes the previous night stayed him.

"Dad, Ms. Thompson's gone."

His heart stopped at Chou's raised voice. Xian stood and barely managed to pull on his boxers before his son entered the bedroom. "Calm down."

"No, Dad. The bad men might have gotten her."

"It's okay. Alex went home."

"She didn't say good-bye."

"She didn't want to wake you."

"Oh." Chou plopped down on the bed. "Will she be back?" he asked hopefully.

Xian shook his head. "I don't know."

"I want her to come back, Dad. I thought you liked her."

"I do," he admitted. Alex had somehow captured his heart.

"Then bring her back."

He looked down into his son's eyes and hesitated before answering, knowing that Chou wanted Alex back as much as he did.

"I'll bring her home," Xian promised as determination began to gain a foothold in his heart. He knew the happiness Alex could bring to their lives and he wanted it back again. No matter what happened, he would try and somehow, some way, Alex would be in his arms again.

TWENTY-ONE

Alex jumped out of the car and ran through the pouring rain into the dojo. She glanced at the note on the door. Sensei would be late to their session. She sighed and entered the building. The smell of incense greeted her. Taking off her shoes, she walked into the dressing room and took her time changing into her gi. As she moved to close the jacket, she stopped, fascinated by her only visible scar.

She turned away and quickly walked into the studio, forgetting to tie back her hair. In the center of the mat, Alex closed her eyes and started to stretch, stopped when the pain of the wound pulsed up her side, then began again.

When she closed her eyes, memories of Xian crept into her thoughts. Alex tried to concentrate on the sound of the rain as it hit the windows, but it reminded her of the rainy night she'd spent in Xian's arms. No matter how hard she tried, the image of his hands entwined in hers as they made love would not leave her. She could even smell his scent. Her chest contracted as her heart shuddered with pain. Cringing at the memory of slipping away like a coward as he slept, Alex moved into a fighting stance, unaware of the tears slipping down her cheek.

Xian stood silent, aching to reach out and wipe the pain from Alex's face. His eyes traced the path of a tear as it slipped down her face. He had thought about her all week and it took everything he had not to walk over and hug her to him. It struck him as ironic that he should again find someone to love only to watch as she pulled away. Her swift and hasty departure had sapped the joy from his life. It had been one of the longest weeks of his life. He missed the sound of her laugh and her warm presence. His son had already begun to regress. Chou's teachers were concerned and so was he.

Xian moved to stand in front of Alex. He watched as she came to a standstill and opened her eyes. Expressions of shock, recognition, and resignation flitted quickly across her face.

She looked him over. "Nice uniform," she commented.

Xian smiled slightly and touched the jacket folds. "Found it in the back of my closet."

He looked into her eyes and saw the barely concealed sadness.

"How did you know I was here?" she asked.

"A little bird told me."

"Karen?" she guessed. Although her roommate was busy taking care of a new husband, she managed to keep an eye on her.

"I never reveal my sources," he answered back.

He watched as she walked towards the window. "Alex?" he called, his voice echoing slightly in the empty room.

"Yes?"

"I love you."

"You shouldn't," Alex replied simply. Everyone she loved died.

Xian moved forward quickly, stopping a few feet from Alex.

"I can't promise you forever," he said. "I would like to give my word, but I would be lying."

He watched as she shook her bowed head. Her hair covered her face like a veil.

"You cannot hide from life, Alex. You cannot go on running. Life is meant to be shared with people you love. You call yourself a fighter, but in your heart you are a coward."

Alex's head jerked up and Xian saw anger burning in her dark eyes. He stood still, waiting, as she took two steps towards him.

"I am not a coward."

"Then stay and fight. Stay and live. If you go back into the military another piece of your soul will die, Alex. The violence and death will kill you slowly."

Xian saw her shaking shoulders and couldn't hold back any longer. He gathered her into his arms and they both sank to the padded floor.

"No," Alex muttered against his chest.

Xian pulled back and looked down. "What?"

"I'm not going back. I've had enough of the political games. I want no more blood on my hands. I've decided to try something a little more challenging."

Xian relaxed at the teasing light he saw in her eyes.

"What would that be?" he asked.

"Kids."

Now that sounded good. Xian smiled and his heart swelled at the thought of Alex pregnant with his child. A daughter. "Chou would love to have a younger brother or sister."

"Slow down there. I was talking about trying my hand at volunteer work."

"You'd make a wonderful mother, Alex."

"I want to be with you," she smiled. For the first time the thought of a family of her own did not terrify her. "I love you, Xian," Alex softly declared.

"I love you too, and don't you think that we should think about making this official?" He massaged her shoulders.

"But I'm not sure I can fit into your world. I've planned school lessons and reconnaissance missions, not dinner parties." Her voice wobbled a little. "Not to mention that I'm not sure I'm cut out to be in love."

In all of her life, she had never been so acutely aware of how deeply she could care for another person. In just a few weeks, Xian and Chou had shown her the true meaning of love and family.

"Sweetheart, you are an extraordinary woman. And ours will be no ordinary love." He leaned down and kissed her gently, hoping to impart some of his love to her. When he pulled away, he saw the sheen of tears in her eyes.

Alex smiled at his confidence. "What am I going to do with you?"

"Love me, stay with me. Chou and I can wait as long as you need. Just promise me one thing."

"Anything."

"Promise me one day you'll be my wife. I don't want Rafé coming after me."

Alex nodded, leaning back into Xian's arms. She closed her eyes and smiled. A feeling of peace and happiness seemed to fill her up and spill over into every part of her being.

"Don't worry," she laughed, stroking his cheek. "I'll protect you."

"And love me?" He leaned over and nipped her lovely neck.

Her arms wound around his neck and pulled him down on the exercise mat. "Oh, yeah," she answered in a sultry voice. "Leaving you was the hardest thing I've ever had to do in my life. And being with you now, I know that nothing is more important than loving you and Chou. Not my fears, not my past."

"I'm not letting you go again, Alex," he vowed.

"You won't have to." She held his face between her hands and looked into his eyes. It was time to let go of the past and start anew. "I've found what I've been looking for. Take me home, Xian."

2009 Reprint Mass Market Titles

January

I'm Gonna Make You Love Me
Gwyneth Bolton
ISBN-13: 978-1-58571-291-5
ISBN-10: 1-58571-291-4
$6.99

Shades of Desire
Monica White
ISBN-13: 978-1-58571-292-2
ISBN-10: 1-58571-292-2
$6.99

February

A Love of Her Own
Cheris Hodges
ISBN-13: 978-1-58571-293-9
ISBN-10: 1-58571-293-0
$6.99

Color of Trouble
Dyanne Davis
ISBN-13: 978-1-58571-294-6
ISBN-10: 1-58571-9
$6.99

March

Twist of Fate
Beverly Clark
ISBN-13: 978-1-58571-295-3
ISBN-10: 1-58571-295-7
$6.99

Chances
Pamela Leigh Starr
ISBN-13: 978-1-58571-296-0
ISBN-10: 1-58571-296-5
$6.99

April

Sinful Intentions
Crystal Rhodes
ISBN-13: 978-1-585712-297-7
ISBN-10: 1-58571-297-3
$6.99

Rock Star
Roslyn Hardy Holcomb
ISBN-13: 978-1-58571-298-4
$6.99

May

Paths of Fire
T.T. Henderson
ISBN-13: 978-1-58571-343-1
ISBN-10: 1-58571-343-0
$6.99

Caught Up in the Rapture
Lisa Riley
ISBN-13: 978-1-58571-344-8
ISBN-10: 1-58571-344-9
$6.99

June

Reckless Surrender
Rochelle Alers
ISBN-13: 978-1-58571-345-5
ISBN-10: 1-58571-345-7
$6.99

No Ordinary Love
Angela Weaver
ISBN-13: 978-1-58571-346-2
ISBN-10: 1-58571-346-5
$6.99

2009 Reprint Mass Market Titles (continued)

July

Intentional Mistakes
Michele Sudler
ISBN-13: 978-1-58571-347-9
ISBN-10: 1-58571-347-3
$6.99

It's In His Kiss
Reon Carter
ISBN-13: 978-1-58571-348-6
ISBN-10: 1-58571-348-1
$6.99

August

Unfinished Love Affair
Barbara Keaton
ISBN-13: 978-1-58571-349-3
ISBN-10: 1-58571-349-X
$6.99

A Perfect Place to Pray
I.L Goodwin
ISBN-13: 978-1-58571-299-1
ISBN-10: 1-58571-299-X
$6.99

September

Love in High Gear
Charlotte Roy
ISBN-13: 978-1-58571-355-4
ISBN-10: 1-58571-355-4
$6.99

Ebony Eyes
Kei Swanson
ISBN-13: 978-1-58571-356-1
ISBN-10: 1-58571-356-2
$6.99

October

Midnight Clear, Part I
Leslie Esdale/Carmen Green
ISBN-13: 978-1-58571-357-8
ISBN-10: 1-58571-357-0
$6.99

Midnight Clear, Part II
Gwynne Forster/Monica
    Jackson
ISBN-13: 978-1-58571-358-5
ISBN-10: 1-58571-358-9
$6.99

November

Midnight Peril
Vicki Andrews
ISBN-13: 978-1-58571-359-2
ISBN-10: 1-58571-359-7
$6.99

One Day At A Time
Bella McFarland
ISBN-13: 978-1-58571-360-8
ISBN-10: 1-58571-360-0
$6.99

December

Just An Affair
Eugenia O'Neal
ISBN-13: 978-1-58571-361-5
ISBN-10: 1-58571-361-9
$6.99

Shades of Brown
Denise Becker
ISBN-13: 978-1-58571-362-2
ISBN-10: 1-58571-362-7
$6.99

2009 New Mass Market Titles

January

Singing A Song…
Crystal Rhodes
ISBN-13: 978-1-58571-283-0
$6.99

Look Both Ways
Joan Early
ISBN-13: 978-1-58571-284-7
$6.99

February

Six O'Clock
Katrina Spencer
ISBN-13: 978-1-58571-285-4
$6.99

Red Sky
Renee Alexis
ISBN-13: 978-1-58571-286-1
$6.99

March

Anything But Love
Celya Bowers
ISBN-13: 978-1-58571-287-8
$6.99

Tempting Faith
Crystal Hubbard
ISBN-13: 978-1-58571-288-5
$6.99

April

If I Were Your Woman
La Connie Taylor-Jones
ISBN-13: 978-1-58571-289-2
$6.99

Best Of Luck Elsewhere
Trisha Haddad
ISBN-13: 978-1-58571-290-8
$6.99

May

All I'll Ever Need
Mildred Riley
ISBN-13: 978-1-58571-335-6
$6.99

A Place Like Home
Alicia Wiggins
ISBN-13: 978-1-58571-336-3
$6.99

June

Best Foot Forward
Michele Sudler
ISBN-13: 978-1-58571-337-0
$6.99

It's In the Rhythm
Sammie Ward
ISBN-13: 978-1-58571-338-7
$6.99

2009 New Mass Market Titles (continued)

July

Checks and Balances
Elaine Sims
ISBN-13: 978-1-58571-339-4
$6.99

Save Me
Africa Fine
ISBN-13: 978-1-58571-340-0
$6.99

August

When Lightening Strikes
Michele Cameron
ISBN-13: 978-1-58571-369-1
$6.99

Blindsided
Tammy Williams
ISBN-13: 978-1-58571-342-4
$6.99

September

2 Good
Celya Bowers
ISBN-13: 978-1-58571-350-9
$6.99

Waiting for Mr. Darcy
Chamein Canton
ISBN-13: 978-1-58571-351-6
$6.99

October

Fireflies
Joan Early
ISBN-13: 978-1-58571-352-3
$6.99

Frost On My Window
Angela Weaver
ISBN-13: 978-1-58571-353-0
$6.99

November

Waiting in the Shadows
Michele Sudler
ISBN-13: 978-1-58571-364-6
$6.99

Fixin' Tyrone
Keith Walker
ISBN-13: 978-1-58571-365-3
$6.99

December

Dream Keeper
Gail McFarland
ISBN-13: 978-1-58571-366-0
$6.99

Another Memory
Pamela Ridley
ISBN-13: 978-1-58571-367-7
$6.99

Other Genesis Press, Inc. Titles

A Dangerous Deception	J.M. Jeffries	$8.95
A Dangerous Love	J.M. Jeffries	$8.95
A Dangerous Obsession	J.M. Jeffries	$8.95
A Drummer's Beat to Mend	Kei Swanson	$9.95
A Happy Life	Charlotte Harris	$9.95
A Heart's Awakening	Veronica Parker	$9.95
A Lark on the Wing	Phyliss Hamilton	$9.95
A Love of Her Own	Cheris F. Hodges	$9.95
A Love to Cherish	Beverly Clark	$8.95
A Risk of Rain	Dar Tomlinson	$8.95
A Taste of Temptation	Reneé Alexis	$9.95
A Twist of Fate	Beverly Clark	$8.95
A Voice Behind Thunder	Carrie Elizabeth Greene	$6.99
A Will to Love	Angie Daniels	$9.95
Acquisitions	Kimberley White	$8.95
Across	Carol Payne	$12.95
After the Vows	Leslie Esdaile	$10.95
(Summer Anthology)	T.T. Henderson	
	Jacqueline Thomas	
Again My Love	Kayla Perrin	$10.95
Against the Wind	Gwynne Forster	$8.95
All I Ask	Barbara Keaton	$8.95
Always You	Crystal Hubbard	$6.99
Ambrosia	T.T. Henderson	$8.95
An Unfinished Love Affair	Barbara Keaton	$8.95
And Then Came You	Dorothy Elizabeth Love	$8.95
Angel's Paradise	Janice Angelique	$9.95
At Last	Lisa G. Riley	$8.95
Best of Friends	Natalie Dunbar	$8.95
Beyond the Rapture	Beverly Clark	$9.95
Blame It On Paradise	Crystal Hubbard	$6.99
Blaze	Barbara Keaton	$9.95
Bliss, Inc.	Chamein Canton	$6.99
Blood Lust	J. M. Jeffries	$9.95
Blood Seduction	J.M. Jeffries	$9.95
Bodyguard	Andrea Jackson	$9.95
Boss of Me	Diana Nyad	$8.95
Bound by Love	Beverly Clark	$8.95
Breeze	Robin Hampton Allen	$10.95

Other Genesis Press, Inc. Titles (continued)

Broken	Dar Tomlinson	$24.95
By Design	Barbara Keaton	$8.95
Cajun Heat	Charlene Berry	$8.95
Careless Whispers	Rochelle Alers	$8.95
Cats & Other Tales	Marilyn Wagner	$8.95
Caught in a Trap	Andre Michelle	$8.95
Caught Up In the Rapture	Lisa G. Riley	$9.95
Cautious Heart	Cheris F Hodges	$8.95
Chances	Pamela Leigh Starr	$8.95
Cherish the Flame	Beverly Clark	$8.95
Choices	Tammy Williams	$6.99
Class Reunion	Irma Jenkins/ John Brown	$12.95
Code Name: Diva	J.M. Jeffries	$9.95
Conquering Dr. Wexler's Heart	Kimberley White	$9.95
Corporate Seduction	A.C. Arthur	$9.95
Crossing Paths, Tempting Memories	Dorothy Elizabeth Love	$9.95
Crush	Crystal Hubbard	$9.95
Cypress Whisperings	Phyllis Hamilton	$8.95
Dark Embrace	Crystal Wilson Harris	$8.95
Dark Storm Rising	Chinelu Moore	$10.95
Daughter of the Wind	Joan Xian	$8.95
Dawn's Harbor	Kymberly Hunt	$6.99
Deadly Sacrifice	Jack Kean	$22.95
Designer Passion	Dar Tomlinson Diana Richeaux	$8.95
Do Over	Celya Bowers	$9.95
Dream Runner	Gail McFarland	$6.99
Dreamtective	Liz Swados	$5.95
Ebony Angel	Deatri King-Bey	$9.95
Ebony Butterfly II	Delilah Dawson	$14.95
Echoes of Yesterday	Beverly Clark	$9.95
Eden's Garden	Elizabeth Rose	$8.95
Eve's Prescription	Edwina Martin Arnold	$8.95
Everlastin' Love	Gay G. Gunn	$8.95
Everlasting Moments	Dorothy Elizabeth Love	$8.95
Everything and More	Sinclair Lebeau	$8.95

Other Genesis Press, Inc. Titles (continued)

Everything but Love	Natalie Dunbar	$8.95
Falling	Natalie Dunbar	$9.95
Fate	Pamela Leigh Starr	$8.95
Finding Isabella	A.J. Garrotto	$8.95
Forbidden Quest	Dar Tomlinson	$10.95
Forever Love	Wanda Y. Thomas	$8.95
From the Ashes	Kathleen Suzanne	$8.95
	Jeanne Sumerix	
Gentle Yearning	Rochelle Alers	$10.95
Glory of Love	Sinclair LeBeau	$10.95
Go Gentle into that	Malcom Boyd	$12.95
Good Night		
Goldengroove	Mary Beth Craft	$16.95
Groove, Bang, and Jive	Steve Cannon	$8.99
Hand in Glove	Andrea Jackson	$9.95
Hard to Love	Kimberley White	$9.95
Hart & Soul	Angie Daniels	$8.95
Heart of the Phoenix	A.C. Arthur	$9.95
Heartbeat	Stephanie Bedwell-Grime	$8.95
Hearts Remember	M. Loui Quezada	$8.95
Hidden Memories	Robin Allen	$10.95
Higher Ground	Leah Latimer	$19.95
Hitler, the War, and the Pope	Ronald Rychiak	$26.95
How to Write a Romance	Kathryn Falk	$18.95
I Married a Reclining Chair	Lisa M. Fuhs	$8.95
I'll Be Your Shelter	Giselle Carmichael	$8.95
I'll Paint a Sun	A.J. Garrotto	$9.95
Icie	Pamela Leigh Starr	$8.95
Illusions	Pamela Leigh Starr	$8.95
Indigo After Dark Vol. I	Nia Dixon/Angelique	$10.95
Indigo After Dark Vol. II	Dolores Bundy/	$10.95
	Cole Riley	
Indigo After Dark Vol. III	Montana Blue/	$10.95
	Coco Morena	
Indigo After Dark Vol. IV	Cassandra Colt/	$14.95
Indigo After Dark Vol. V	Delilah Dawson	$14.95
Indiscretions	Donna Hill	$8.95
Intentional Mistakes	Michele Sudler	$9.95
Interlude	Donna Hill	$8.95

Other Genesis Press, Inc. Titles (continued)

Intimate Intentions	Angie Daniels	$8.95
It's Not Over Yet	J.J. Michael	$9.95
Jolie's Surrender	Edwina Martin-Arnold	$8.95
Kiss or Keep	Debra Phillips	$8.95
Lace	Giselle Carmichael	$9.95
Lady Preacher	K.T. Richey	$6.99
Last Train to Memphis	Elsa Cook	$12.95
Lasting Valor	Ken Olsen	$24.95
Let Us Prey	Hunter Lundy	$25.95
Lies Too Long	Pamela Ridley	$13.95
Life Is Never As It Seems	J.J. Michael	$12.95
Lighter Shade of Brown	Vicki Andrews	$8.95
Looking for Lily	Africa Fine	$6.99
Love Always	Mildred E. Riley	$10.95
Love Doesn't Come Easy	Charlyne Dickerson	$8.95
Love Unveiled	Gloria Greene	$10.95
Love's Deception	Charlene Berry	$10.95
Love's Destiny	M. Loui Quezada	$8.95
Love's Secrets	Yolanda McVey	$6.99
Mae's Promise	Melody Walcott	$8.95
Magnolia Sunset	Giselle Carmichael	$8.95
Many Shades of Gray	Dyanne Davis	$6.99
Matters of Life and Death	Lesego Malepe, Ph.D.	$15.95
Meant to Be	Jeanne Sumerix	$8.95
Midnight Clear (Anthology)	Leslie Esdaile	$10.95
	Gwynne Forster	
	Carmen Green	
	Monica Jackson	
Midnight Magic	Gwynne Forster	$8.95
Midnight Peril	Vicki Andrews	$10.95
Misconceptions	Pamela Leigh Starr	$9.95
Moments of Clarity	Michele Cameron	$6.99
Montgomery's Children	Richard Perry	$14.95
Mr Fix-It	Crystal Hubbard	$6.99
My Buffalo Soldier	Barbara B. K. Reeves	$8.95
Naked Soul	Gwynne Forster	$8.95
Never Say Never	Michele Cameron	$6.99
Next to Last Chance	Louisa Dixon	$24.95
No Apologies	Seressia Glass	$8.95

Other Genesis Press, Inc. Titles (continued)

No Commitment Required	Seressia Glass	$8.95
No Regrets	Mildred E. Riley	$8.95
Not His Type	Chamein Canton	$6.99
Nowhere to Run	Gay G. Gunn	$10.95
O Bed! O Breakfast!	Rob Kuehnle	$14.95
Object of His Desire	A. C. Arthur	$8.95
Office Policy	A. C. Arthur	$9.95
Once in a Blue Moon	Dorianne Cole	$9.95
One Day at a Time	Bella McFarland	$8.95
One of These Days	Michele Sudler	$9.95
Outside Chance	Louisa Dixon	$24.95
Passion	T.T. Henderson	$10.95
Passion's Blood	Cherif Fortin	$22.95
Passion's Furies	AlTonya Washington	$6.99
Passion's Journey	Wanda Y. Thomas	$8.95
Past Promises	Jahmel West	$8.95
Path of Fire	T.T. Henderson	$8.95
Path of Thorns	Annetta P. Lee	$9.95
Peace Be Still	Colette Haywood	$12.95
Picture Perfect	Reon Carter	$8.95
Playing for Keeps	Stephanie Salinas	$8.95
Pride & Joi	Gay G. Gunn	$8.95
Promises Made	Bernice Layton	$6.99
Promises to Keep	Alicia Wiggins	$8.95
Quiet Storm	Donna Hill	$10.95
Reckless Surrender	Rochelle Alers	$6.95
Red Polka Dot in a World of Plaid	Varian Johnson	$12.95
Reluctant Captive	Joyce Jackson	$8.95
Rendezvous with Fate	Jeanne Sumerix	$8.95
Revelations	Cheris F. Hodges	$8.95
Rivers of the Soul	Leslie Esdaile	$8.95
Rocky Mountain Romance	Kathleen Suzanne	$8.95
Rooms of the Heart	Donna Hill	$8.95
Rough on Rats and Tough on Cats	Chris Parker	$12.95
Secret Library Vol. 1	Nina Sheridan	$18.95
Secret Library Vol. 2	Cassandra Colt	$8.95
Secret Thunder	Annetta P. Lee	$9.95

Other Genesis Press, Inc. Titles (continued)

Shades of Brown	Denise Becker	$8.95
Shades of Desire	Monica White	$8.95
Shadows in the Moonlight	Jeanne Sumerix	$8.95
Sin	Crystal Rhodes	$8.95
Small Whispers	Annetta P. Lee	$6.99
So Amazing	Sinclair LeBeau	$8.95
Somebody's Someone	Sinclair LeBeau	$8.95
Someone to Love	Alicia Wiggins	$8.95
Song in the Park	Martin Brant	$15.95
Soul Eyes	Wayne L. Wilson	$12.95
Soul to Soul	Donna Hill	$8.95
Southern Comfort	J.M. Jeffries	$8.95
Southern Fried Standards	S.R. Maddox	$6.99
Still the Storm	Sharon Robinson	$8.95
Still Waters Run Deep	Leslie Esdaile	$8.95
Stolen Memories	Michele Sudler	$6.99
Stories to Excite You	Anna Forrest/Divine	$14.95
Storm	Pamela Leigh Starr	$6.99
Subtle Secrets	Wanda Y. Thomas	$8.95
Suddenly You	Crystal Hubbard	$9.95
Sweet Repercussions	Kimberley White	$9.95
Sweet Sensations	Gwyneth Bolton	$9.95
Sweet Tomorrows	Kimberly White	$8.95
Taken by You	Dorothy Elizabeth Love	$9.95
Tattooed Tears	T. T. Henderson	$8.95
The Color Line	Lizzette Grayson Carter	$9.95
The Color of Trouble	Dyanne Davis	$8.95
The Disappearance of Allison Jones	Kayla Perrin	$5.95
The Fires Within	Beverly Clark	$9.95
The Foursome	Celya Bowers	$6.99
The Honey Dipper's Legacy	Pannell-Allen	$14.95
The Joker's Love Tune	Sidney Rickman	$15.95
The Little Pretender	Barbara Cartland	$10.95
The Love We Had	Natalie Dunbar	$8.95
The Man Who Could Fly	Bob & Milana Beamon	$18.95
The Missing Link	Charlyne Dickerson	$8.95
The Mission	Pamela Leigh Starr	$6.99
The More Things Change	Chamein Canton	$6.99

Other Genesis Press, Inc. Titles (continued)

The Perfect Frame	Beverly Clark	$9.95
The Price of Love	Sinclair LeBeau	$8.95
The Smoking Life	Ilene Barth	$29.95
The Words of the Pitcher	Kei Swanson	$8.95
Things Forbidden	Maryam Diaab	$6.99
This Life Isn't Perfect Holla	Sandra Foy	$6.99
Three Doors Down	Michele Sudler	$6.99
Three Wishes	Seressia Glass	$8.95
Ties That Bind	Kathleen Suzanne	$8.95
Tiger Woods	Libby Hughes	$5.95
Time is of the Essence	Angie Daniels	$9.95
Timeless Devotion	Bella McFarland	$9.95
Tomorrow's Promise	Leslie Esdaile	$8.95
Truly Inseparable	Wanda Y. Thomas	$8.95
Two Sides to Every Story	Dyanne Davis	$9.95
Unbreak My Heart	Dar Tomlinson	$8.95
Uncommon Prayer	Kenneth Swanson	$9.95
Unconditional Love	Alicia Wiggins	$8.95
Unconditional	A.C. Arthur	$9.95
Undying Love	Renee Alexis	$6.99
Until Death Do Us Part	Susan Paul	$8.95
Vows of Passion	Bella McFarland	$9.95
Wedding Gown	Dyanne Davis	$8.95
What's Under Benjamin's Bed	Sandra Schaffer	$8.95
When A Man Loves A Woman	La Connie Taylor-Jones	$6.99
When Dreams Float	Dorothy Elizabeth Love	$8.95
When I'm With You	LaConnie Taylor-Jones	$6.99
Where I Want To Be	Maryam Diaab	$6.99
Whispers in the Night	Dorothy Elizabeth Love	$8.95
Whispers in the Sand	LaFlorya Gauthier	$10.95
Who's That Lady?	Andrea Jackson	$9.95
Wild Ravens	Altonya Washington	$9.95
Yesterday Is Gone	Beverly Clark	$10.95
Yesterday's Dreams, Tomorrow's Promises	Reon Laudat	$8.95
Your Precious Love	Sinclair LeBeau	$8.95

Order Form

Mail to: Genesis Press, Inc.
P.O. Box 101
Columbus, MS 39703

Name _____
Address _____
City/State _____ Zip _____
Telephone _____

Ship to (if different from above)
Name _____
Address _____
City/State _____ Zip _____
Telephone _____

Credit Card Information
Credit Card # _____ ☐ Visa   ☐ Mastercard
Expiration Date (mm/yy) _____ ☐ AmEx ☐ Discover

Qty.	Author	Title	Price	Total

Use this order form, or call **1-888-INDIGO-1**	Total for books _____
	Shipping and handling:
	  $5 first two books,
	  $1 each additional book _____
	Total S & H _____
	Total amount enclosed _____
	Mississippi residents add 7% sales tax

Visit www.genesis-press.com for latest releases and excerpts.